CW00406201

All rights reserved. No part of this publication may be reproduced, stored or transmitted in any form or by any means, electronic, mechanical, photocopying, recording, scanning, or otherwise without written permission from the publisher.

This novel is a work of fiction. Any resemblance to actual persons, living or dead, events or localities is entirely coincidental.

The characters described in this book are purposefully problematic and should not be idolized.

This book contains violence, swearing, character death, mention of drug abuse and mental health problems.

The Outworlder

Natalie J.Holden

Table of Contents

Every word I make up is pronounced exactly how it is spelled. A always sounds like in alphabet. E like in elephant. I like in inconvenient. Y like in yellow. U like in flute. Sh like in shame. Ch like in choice. H as in house. X as ks. R can be hard in Dahlsi-é words, akin to the one in German language or soft, smilar to English one in Tarvissi-é words. Double letters denote long sounds, but otherwise don't change the pronunciation. Diacritic marks are used to denote accent.

Every letter should be pronounced separately, regardless of the adjacent ones, i.e. Ma-urir, Alde-a-ith, X-z-sim.

A glossary is provided at the end of the book.

Prologue

DYAH LA'S EYEBALLS itched.

She popped another antihistamine pill and washed it down with a gulp of tonic. The pollen-heavy air took an opportunity to sneak under her mask and bite at her face with full force. She cursed and pulled up her veil, then recast the spells necessary for it to work.

Farming colonies were the worst. Dyah La's Dahlsian ancestors spent so much time in the airtight city that her body was simply not capable of dealing with the constant barrage of sunlight and allergens. In worlds like Maurir, with the merges surrounded by fields, orchards, gardens, and pastures, her allergies flared up. Her body itched in places she shouldn't have the necessary nerves to even feel.

And there was not a damn thing she could do except to pop pill after pill and hope for the best.

Dyah La sighed, then pushed away from the cart, stretching her stiff limbs. They were in the middle of the main yard of the Montak Mansion, the largest construction in Maurir. A few paces away, shadowed by suspended walkways, Talelouhani chattered with locals—a group of burly men and women of Tarvissian origin, so tall they made Dyah La feel like a child. It might have seemed like a friendly chat, but she knew it was calculated to discretely investigate the condition of the colony. Not that there was a need; there was never any trouble in Maurir.

Tax collectors, like Talelouhani, arrived twice a cycle to collect one-twelfth of the produce—or whatever locals said was one-twelfth. A token more than anything; Maurir produced nothing Dahlsi cared for. The food collected as tribute was either sold or distributed to other colonies. Still, Dahlsian officials came in regularly to assert their presence and check if the colonists needed any help. Mespanians, like Dyah La, were there to protect them.

Seeing Talelouhani's chat was not coming to an end, she decided to go for a walk. The yard was rather large, surrounded by tall, whitewashed walls with only two gates, one leading outside and the other to a second yard. Wooden galleries ran along the walls above their heads, and in their shadow rested large, reptilian daereleigs, the primary livestock of local people. Flower wreaths and moss-green ribbons decorated the wide windows.

"To celebrate the end of Edira," one of the locals had explained earlier. "The twenty-seventh month, the last of a cycle."

It was only the middle of a cycle for Dahlsi, despite the fact that both nations counted time starting from the same event. Dyah La found Tarvissian traditions charming, even if they made her itch.

Shouting came from the second yard. It was built around the exact spot where Maurir merged with Kooine, allowing free passage between the two worlds. But Dyah La wasn't aware of any scheduled visitors to Maurir—and frankly, she didn't think there were ever any visitors, other than tax collectors.

She walked back around the cart, just in time to see a group of men entering the main yard. They could almost pass for locals—tall, burly, and bearded. Even their clothing was similar, except their jackets were an identical green color. And they had weapons.

Dyah La's hand automatically fell to her wand. There were at least two dozen intruders—with more coming—and her heart sank. She was not a sorceress to fend them off, and so far, her role had been mostly for show. Oh, she was trained to fight, and Mespana armed her with the most advanced equipment known to man. But she had never actually had to use her skills. Certainly not against an armed mob.

One thing she could do, though, was sense the danger. And the men flooding the yard radiated it.

"People of Maurir!" exclaimed a young man she'd barely noticed against the group of warriors. He was short for a Tarvissi, with unruly hair, more brown than black but no beard. "Rejoice, for we come to liberate you from the oppression of the Dahlsian Empire."

Dyah La's eyebrow arched up. Oppression? Dahlsian rule was the exact opposite. Although, her perspective might have been skewed by her provenance.

"We come to restore the natural order of things," the man lowered his voice, trailing his gaze over the crowd, visibly thrown off by the quiet welcome from the locals. "Restore the way of Tarviss!"

A cold shiver ran down Dyah La's spine. So far, the colonists in Maurir seemed more than happy to leave their old ways behind. They had no reason to join his cause, but...

They were just farmers. The men like the speaker—especially surrounded by guards—must have been daunting. Could he bully them to stand against her country?

The invaders were filling the yard now, pushing locals aside. Even more stood on the walkways above with crossbows at the ready. There were at least a dozen yards in the mansion—were they all similarly filled?

"There must be some misunderstanding." Talelouhani stepped out, and Dyah La's heart clenched. He stopped right in front of the Tarvissian leader. He was taller but slender, with a delicate, almost feminine face. A pacifist, like all Varpulians, whose faith in humanity was stronger than any Dahlsi's.

Dyah La wanted to scream at him to shut up and walk back, run, hide, flee; but her throat was tight, and she could not make a sound.

"The Dahlsian Empire has never imposed any oppression," he continued with his soft, soothing voice. "People are free to live how they want. If you wish to follow the Tarvissian ways, no one will stop you."

"We'd rather pay our dues to the Dahlsi than parasites like you, lordling," came a voice from the crowd. The young leader's eyes darted to the side, searching for the one who had spoken, his lips twisting into an ugly snarl.

Dyah La expected him to say something, to snap at the bold farmer, but almost too fast for her to register, he pulled out a knife and thrust it into Talelouhani's chest.
A scream tore from her throat, but a heavy hand clasped her mouth. The wand was wrestled from her hand and tossed aside like a twig.

Chapter 1

LESS THAN AN hour passed after my return to Sfal when the unmistakable tingling of a telepathic message at the back of my head summoned me to the vessár's office.

The door slid open as soon as I approached, enchanted, like everything else here. I entered the office—a small, white, and sterile room with most of the furniture neatly folded into the walls. Over a large desk, Laik Var eyed me unsympathetically.

"Vessár," I said, straightening up and clasping my hands behind my back.

"Aldait Han." He motioned me in.

I tapped my foot on a darker spot on the floor, making a chair unfold. It was tight and uncomfortable, made for someone half my size, but after two cycles of living among Dahlsi, I was used to it. I looked at my commander expectantly. He was short and wiry, with a balding head and grass-blue eyes deeply seated in a web of crow's feet. They reminded me of two guards flanking the throne that was his enormous nose. The picture would be more dignified, though, if the eyes weren't always reddened and the nose always runny. Allergies.

Like me, he wore a black single-piece uniform with the logo of Mespana: a sword and a wand crossed over a diamond, along with the number of our cohort stitched on the right arm. The only sign of his office was a silver sash running from left shoulder to right hip.

"What the fuck is this?" he asked, throwing a thin scroll box onto the desk.

I looked at him in confusion.

"A letter for my family, Vessár," I replied. I had written it during the last mission and threw it into the box on my way here. It was the only thing I'd managed to do after submitting my report.

The mission had been a nightmare. We were in Sorox, a strange, colorless world, and the pervasive grays were getting to me. I almost forgot how my skin looked under normal light. Not to mention trudging through steep, rocky mountains with barely any life, being confined to our six-member group, locked in a tight, uncomfortable tent, and forced to survive on Dahlsian food rations after my own stock ran out. Now, I felt like my uniform was glued to my skin, and no amount of magic would make me clean. I needed to peel it off and take an honest bath: water, soap, and a good scrub. Then put on something comfortable that would let me breathe again, and go out, feel the sun on my face. See real colors, eat food that didn't come from a fucking tube and had a smell, taste and texture, that satisfied instead of just filling up. I was tired. I needed a break. I'd earned it, by Vhalfr!

But from across the desk, the vessár's eyes bore into me, and I knew my rest would have to wait.

"Fuck," he cursed quietly, leaning back in his chair. "Nobody told you yet?"

The city passed me in a blur. I was drenched in sweat, and my lungs worked like bellows in the hot, damp air. After days spent in chilly Sorox, I found the tropical heat of Sfal unbearable. Yet I ran as if chased by demons, and I didn't—couldn't—slow down.

Not until space opened around me and I knew I had reached my destination.

The market.

I had no time for a bath or even a decent meal. Mespana was mobilizing. In half an hour, we were to report in at the train depot, ready for departure to Maurir. But by Vhalfr, I was not going to spend another gods-damned day on food rations!

It was silly, I knew. Food was just sustenance, something to keep the body running. And the state provided all citizens of Dahls, even outworlders like me, with perfectly balanced rations. But I was no Dahlsi; I abhorred that sludge. I was a farmer's son; I needed real, fresh food: berries eaten from the bush, zeeäth eggs laid in the morning, arpa root thrown on the fire straight from the ground with green tendrils still wriggling, looking for dirt to dig in. Or at least some dry vye to make porridge.

So yes, I was determined to spend the last half-hour of my freedom shopping for groceries.

It was early evening, only one of the two triangular suns still open in the golden-pink sky. The market was almost empty; most of the stalls had closed, and the few remaining merchants were packing up. Only food vendors were still plentiful, serving the last dallying patrons, and filling the air with the scents of smoke, spices, and deep-fried habava fruit.

I was parched after the run, so I grabbed a bottle of palm sap from a besheq vendor. Their tentacles rippled more than usual, and I couldn't shake off the impression of being judged. I say "their" because I was never able to determine the sex of most of the nonhumans. Now, I wondered how much they could tell about me.

Human. Male.

... Tarvissi?

The vendor left without waiting for me to return the bottle, so I guess that was my answer. I used the spell to turn the flask into sand, and with creeping discomfort, I plunged into the market.

I always had a complicated relationship with that place. I was equal parts intimidated by its size and opulence, awed by the wealth of goods from all around the universe, overwhelmed by the crowds, and enraptured by the foods. Now the crowd was almost nonexistent, and the silk cloth hanging over the alley provided respite from the sun. Yet whatever semblance of good mood I could muster quickly soured when I noticed merchants stopping what they were doing to stare at me warily. None of them offered me their wares. Usually, it was hard to take a step without having someone throw their stuff at me, yelling encouragements and offers. Especially in the evening when there were more vendors than clients, and they had to fight for every sale. But now it was different. I—my position—was different. I pushed such thoughts to the back of my mind. I didn't have time for them. I stiffened my spine and pressed forward, looking around with my head down, focusing on the wares, not the merchants. Most sold luxury items: ornamental combs of ivory and tortoiseshell, dishes of natural glass shimmering in all colors, golden jewelry, and gloves made for nonhuman hands. A familiar scent reached my nose, and half-consciously, I followed it to where a vhariar stirred floatfruit soup in a big bronze cauldron.

It was my favorite dish after Chaarite red stew. Sweet and thick, almost like a mash, pairing perfectly with spicy and sour pickles. My mouth filled with saliva, my ears with a sweet song of a wooden spoon on the sides of the cauldron. For a moment, the whole world ceased to exist…

And then I realized I didn't have time for this. The portions were usually generous and steaming hot; eating one properly would take at least fifteen minutes, and by then I should already be on my way back. Gnashing my teeth, I resorted to buying a jar of pickled cabbage lotus. Maybe if I got some milkseed and cooked it to a pulp, I would get a similar experience.

But at least I found myself in the right part of the market. Firstly, I bought some freshly steamed milkseed buns for supper and a little roasted thing, a long fish or snake, I wasn't sure—one could find all sorts of things in the market. The meat was tender and doused in just the right amount of spices. I savored every bite as I gathered bare

11

necessities until the alarm spell I'd set told me it was time to go.

It seemed the entire depot had been seized by Mespana. Two ssothians, each twice my size and covered in bright orange fur, stood at the entrance and wouldn't let me through until they confirmed my identity. I cut my thumb on the obsidian blade provided and spilled my blood into the bowl of moonwater. The liquid swirled, blood dark against its bluish gleam, then calmed abruptly. The Dahlsian woman who held her hand submerged nodded at the guards to let me pass.

After crossing the threshold, I froze.

The hall was the biggest room I'd ever seen, but it was filled to the brim with a sea of black and white with occasional bursts of color from the outworlders and the nonhumans. There were three cohorts stationed in Sfal, around one-hundred-and-forty people each. Most of them were there.

And those closest to the entrance turned toward me.

My body tensed and my palms grew sweaty. All around me, dozens of eyes widened and mouths hung open. A Xzsim man curled his painted lips in a predatory smile. A miyangua's fleshy whiskers twitched nervously.

I ducked my head, clutching my bag tighter, like a shield. Dahlsi made up some ninety percent of Mespana, and their meager size allowed me to take up the entire room. But even without that, I knew there were no other Tarvissi in Mespana.

No other Tarvissi in Meon Cluster.

Two days ago, in retaliation for the rebellion on Maurir, the Directory ordered all citizens of Tarvissian origin be deported. I was the only one left.

It seemed surreal. There had been a couple dozen of us here in Sfal, but a few thousand lived in farming colonies like Maurir, Eben, and my homeworld, Nes Peridion. The thought that less than a thousand Mespanians rounded them all up and escorted them out in one-hundred-and-twenty hours—two Dahlsian days—was ludicrous.

But it was true.

My skin prickled. I felt exposed. Clutching my bag tighter, I scurried away, heading to the wall, trying to find a quiet, sheltered spot where I could pretend I didn't exist. The crowd parted before me, making my insides twist painfully. I dropped my head even lower and swore not to lift it… until I bumped into the only person in the whole depot too distracted to get out of my way.

"Sorry," I murmured, then froze. My gaze fell on a familiar broad face with green eyes, which, if possible, grew bigger than usual.

"It's all right," muttered Saral Tal. We worked together a couple of times in the past, including the last mission. And sure enough, when I lifted my head, I saw the rest of our team: Malyn Tol with one arm wrapped around Vareya La, and Argan Am, his cleft hand frozen in midair in some interrupted gesture. They all looked equally surprised.

I felt like the ground had opened beneath my feet. Up until then, I could push the dark thoughts away and pretend nothing had happened. I knew things went to shit, but I ignored that. I shopped, I moaned about the heat. People stared, but I was always getting weird looks, and even if not, my brain was pretty apt at conjuring reasons to be anxious. But now, facing people who knew me, who worked with me, and yet looked at me in shock and fear, I had no choice but to admit that things had changed; perhaps irrevocably. My life was no longer as it had been before.

Malyn Tol was the first to regain her footing, unwrapping herself from the other woman and rushing to grab my arms.

"Are you all right?" she asked, looking at my face with worry. Deep lines sprouted from the corners of her eyes and mouth, the kind formed from frequent smiling. Now, however, she was somber.

My throat tightened, and I realized I wasn't able to say a word. How could I be all right? My entire nation was gone, and we were heading toward the first major conflict in Dahlsian history.

"I'm so sorry." She wrapped her arms around me, but what would be a comforting gesture for any other person, only made me even more tense. Tarvissi weren't big on physical contact and most Dahlsi kept their respective distance, so I never got used to being hugged. At best, it felt awkward, at worst—like this moment—it became oppressive.

Luckily, she seemed to realize that, because she quickly released me.

"Where are you gonna go?" asked Argan Am.

He was an unusual sight for a Dahlsi, with a reddish-brown skin, dark eyes, and a completely bald head. I thought he must have a drop of alien blood in him—possibly Chaarite—but never got up the nerve to ask. He also had three fingers on his left hand and four on his right, all apart from thumbs fused together.

"To Maurir," I replied automatically, and only then realized the reason for his question.

"Of course he is," snapped Malyn Tol, glaring at Argan Am. He was a sorcerer and the unofficial leader of our team, but Malyn Tol had a way with people. She then turned back to me. "As soon as I heard what happened, I ran to Laik Var to tell him that if he wanted to deport you, he'd have to do it over my dead body. You're one of us, Aldait Han. We wouldn't let any harm come to you."

Nice sentiment, but I didn't believe it. Not standing here, taller and wider than any of the people around, with my tanned complexion starkly contrasting their chalky paleness. In the last two cycles I spent working for Mespana, I learned to shave my face and cut my hair short, wear a skin-tight uniform, and speak Dahlsi-é, but now I realized how ridiculous my attempts were.

I would never be one of them.

And yet hearing Malyn Tol's words, I felt a bit of my tension melting. I gave my best attempt at summoning a smile, hoping to let her know I appreciated her effort.

"Thank you," I said.

She nodded solemnly and stepped back.

"How are you holding up?" asked Saral Tal.

Out of everyone on our team, I knew him the best, and not only because we worked together more often than the rest. He was talkative when I was quiet, and that's how we got along. I never doubted, though, that after our missions ended, he was ready to return to his thousands of friends and forget about me until next time. But it was nice while it lasted.

I shook my head, not sure how to answer. "I'm trying not to think about it."

"Not thinking about problems doesn't make them go away," noted Vareya La. She was the youngest of us—ten cycles at most, barely an adult—with the last traces of teenage acne on her face. Sorox was her first mission, and I'd almost expected her to run by now.

"Could anything make my problems go away?" I retorted.

Vareya La looked down, and I felt like an asshole.

"It wasn't right what they did," Argan Am added quickly. "The Directory, I mean..."

"Yeah, it was definitely an overreaction," agreed Saral Tal. "Let's just hope it will blow over soon."

I nodded again, not sure how to answer. A part of me still hoped I would wake up, and it would all turn out to be a horrible dream. Or a practical joke. Or something. But I didn't count on it. And honestly, could the whole situation blow over? If we went to Maurir and quelled the rebellion— then what? Would the Directory suddenly change their minds and withdraw their deportation order? Reach out and invite back the people they just kicked out?

Would there be anyone to come back?

"Do you have any family?" asked Argan Am.

I flinched involuntarily. "No," I said quickly, for a moment feeling ridiculously immature. From what I overheard, Argan Am had two sons. Plus, a steady relationship and a sorcerer degree. He couldn't be much older than me, but he seemed so far ahead in life. "I mean...

I have a mother and sister. They live... lived in Nes Peridion."

I trailed off, not sure why I even brought that up. But doing so made my thoughts turn toward the next problem. Nobody told me where they'd gone, but it's not like there was much choice. The only way out of Meon Cluster led through Dahls, and the only ways out of Dahls were to Tarviss, Tayan, and Xzsin Nyeotl. The Tayani, despite their own internal conflicts, hated us with a passion born from thousands of cycles of feuds, and Xzsim were divided into innumerable tribes, only some of which allied with Dahls. Warriors could choose that path, but...

We were farmers, not warriors. So, the only possible way out was Tarviss.

And it wasn't hard to imagine how the Tarvissi ruling class had reacted upon seeing their runaways back. I knew I had nothing to look for there with my family history. My mom probably used a false name—I only hoped she'd be able to keep the deception. I wished I could follow them and take them... somewhere. But with Dahls and the entire Meon cluster out of the question, I had no idea where to go.

Malyn Tol squeezed my hand again. "I hope they're all right."

Before I answered, a loud bellow reverberated through the air. I looked up to see a small, bright red miyangua standing on top of the train, quickly emptying their vocal sacks. Three Dahlsi stood at their side, barely taller than them, with silver sashes running across their chests. Even at this distance, I recognized Laik Var's balding head and figured the other two were vessár-ai of Cohorts Eighth and Ninth.

"All right, people, listen up," spoke Laik Var. "Like most of you probably know, the rebels in Maurir blocked the merge. Luckily, our sorcerers managed to calculate an alternative route. We will take the train to Kooine, and from there to a newly discovered world, Espa Solia, where we'll join the rest of Mespana and proceed to the artificially opened merge with Maurir. Any questions?"

No one spoke. I wondered how we were going to reach Maurir. Here in Meon Cluster, most worlds only merged once, with one of the so-called junction worlds. By blocking this merge, the rebels had basically cut Maurir off. Most people could only stand aside and wait for the merge to open. Luckily, Dahlsi were masters of cosmography.

"Good. Now board up!"

The crowd rushed toward the train, in no discernible order. I guessed none of us really knew how to act in such a big group; we usually worked in twos, threes, or fours, rarely more than six. I lingered, not fond of pushing and pulling, and in the process managed to lose my team. In the end, I had to take the last available seat on the train, right next to a furry kas'sham with an expressionless face and big, murderous eyes, who didn't deign to speak with me.

The journey went without a hitch, but it was long and tedious, giving me more than enough time to ruminate. I tried to distract myself by reading or watching the news on my obsidian mirror, but all that everyone talked about was the rebellion on Maurir, so for most of the way I just stared out the window. The pink bushland of Sfal was easy to lose oneself in. The rocky desert of Kooine was slightly less so, but there we got to leave the train—since the tracks were only laid between junction worlds—and cover remaining distance by bikes, which allowed me a different kind of distraction.

I thought I was getting used to people's stares, but when we joined the rest of Mespana, my anxiety spiked again. Espa Solia was an ugly, swamp-covered world, refusing me even the small comfort of natural beauty. I was hoping we'd traverse it quickly, but after a few hours of trudging through the oily drizzle, we were told to set up camp. I hid in my tent and spent the evening chewing morosely on raw rock apples.

The next day we traveled farther, to the spot where a group of sorcerers drew a diagram of gold-and-black lines. The air above them rippled as if above fire. I've seen such an effect enough times to know what it was: a merge.

The path to Maurir stood open.

Chapter 2

I COULDN'T STAY in the camp. A shadow of guilt hung over me, as if the whole rebellion was somehow my fault. No one gave me a reason to feel this way; I guess it's just that no one gave me a reason to feel different, either. Malyn Tol tried, but she was alone, and, since she bestowed her motherly attention on everyone who seemed to need it, I found it hard to take her seriously.

So, I wandered across the hills surrounding the camp and tried to reconcile what I saw with what I knew about Maurir. It wasn't a big world; if I sat on my bike and stuck to the sky-dome, circling it would take about twenty hours. It was also rather flat, so I could probably scout it from edge to edge with a spyglass. Even now, I noticed the glimmer of the three seas and the pale belt of desert snaking across the world. Aviga, the closest thing to a mountain, stuck out near the geographical center, no bigger than my thumb. The most interesting feature, though, was the sky, with a sun shaped like an arch running from one edge to the other. Despite its size, the land beneath was quite comfortable:

warmer than Kooine, but still cooler than Sfal. Permeability, as I've been told. The size of the sun didn't matter as much as the amount of Vhalfrlight it let through.

It's only a shame that as far as I saw, the land beneath it was burned to the ground, with charred skeletons of farms and trees jutting out now and then. Only Montak Mansion, the biggest structure and the one taken over by the rebels, still stood, its walls darkened with soot, and checkered black-and-white banners with green tridents hung from the windows.

Last time I was here, Maurir was covered with a mosaic of blue bushland and fields of imported Tarvissian greens divided with irrigation channels and dotted with picturesque villages. It had been colonized by Tarvissian farmers, sometime after the rebellion on Nes Peridion liberated them from their old lords. People quickly cleared large areas of rubbery growth and planted their own crops. The world had rich animal life, full of small, slippery creatures with no bones but many tentacles. They were useless for keeping Tarvissian plants alive, though, so colonists had to bring over pollinators and worms to keep the ground aerated. I know because my father told me how in Nes Peridion they'd had to do the same.

It used to be a beautiful world, is what I'm saying. Now, the oppressive grays made me think of Sorox.

My eyes drifted toward the nearest burned farm, and I couldn't help wondering what our house looked like. Was it burned down to prevent return? Were our zeeäths roaming free? Or still locked in their coop, left to die? Was the garden overgrown with weeds? No, it was too early. Still, I thought about all the effort I'd put into weeding it and fixing roofs after the last storm—all for naught.

A crunching sound snapped me to the present. I turned around to see Laik Var coming toward me with purpose, and I immediately looked away.

"How are you holding up?" he asked, stopping next to me. His eyes were redder than usual, and a veil of magic covered the lower part of his face.

"I'm fine," I said mechanically.

His eyes fell on the farm below and a frown formed on his forehead. "It's not too late," he said quietly. "If you want to return to Sfal, the path is still open."

I peered off to the side, imagining I could see the air rippling, though, at this distance, it was impossible.

"We had that conversation," I replied, rubbing my forehead warily.

"I know. But it must be different... seeing with your own eyes."

He had a point. Back in Sfal, I was ready to do whatever it took to restore the peace, but now that I was here, my resolution was melting. What could I do about such destruction? Even if we were to defeat the rebels, what difference would it make if the entire colony was destroyed?

"It seems I have nowhere to go," I replied, waving my hand toward the horizon. I think he wanted to say something else—it was hard to tell with his mouth covered—but I didn't want to listen, didn't want to ponder the alternatives. If there even were alternatives. So I changed the subject. "Do we know anything about the rebels?"

He shook his head. "No, not yet. The minister of immigration is going through the paperwork from the last couple of cycles. Before he comes back to us, your guess is as good as mine." His speech slowed with each word, and at the end, he was almost reciting, quietly, uncertainly. "Maybe even better."

My body tensed. I should have expected it, though. I should have been surprised it took him so long.

Still, hoping it was not what it seemed, I swallowed heavily and asked, "What do you mean?"

"I mean…"

From the corner of my eye, I saw him fidgeting. He was a decent guy. Very careful to never insult anybody. He was almost like a father to me, though of course, I would never admit that. But now the situation has changed.

He breathed out through clenched teeth. "You *are* Tarvissi."

A pit opened in my chest. It took me a moment to collect myself enough to form a reply. "I was born and raised in colonies. I'm as much Dahlsi as I'm Tarvissi."

I'd also received the Dahlsian education, meager as it was, and joined Mespana as soon as I was able to. The only thing connecting me to the rebels was the blood in my veins, but there was no helping that. So, why was I being punished for it? Why were any of us punished for it? I was not assertive, but at that point, the stress of the last few days had become too much. Before I could stop myself, I asked caustically, "Unless my citizenship has been revoked?"

"It hasn't," he assured me. "What I mean is your ancestors came from Tarviss. Perhaps you've… heard something."

"Laik Var." I spun on my heel to face the man. Though relatively muscular, he was smaller than me and the size difference was never so obvious. "I'm a member of Mespana. For cycles, I've been spending most of my time among Dahlsi."

"But you do keep in touch with your people."

Your people. It shouldn't have stung as much as it did.

"I write letters to my mother and sister, and I assure you neither of them had anything to do with this."

And yet they were punished, deported, kicked out like mere criminals—for nothing but being the wrong nationality!

"All right, I believe you!" he cut in, lifting his hand in a placating gesture. "Look, I had to ask. Surely, you understand."

I huffed, still angry. But as much as I hated to admit it, I did understand. However it hurt, however unfair it seemed, those assholes put us all in a bad light. Not so long ago, they were no different from me or my family, just ordinary people trying to get by. Now they'd fucked up, and we had to pay the price.

My eyes drifted toward the burned farm. Compared to some, I got off easy.

"It's a difficult time," said Laik Var. "For everyone. But I trust you, Aldait Han. I wish things could be different. For your family, your entire nation. I just hope this mess will be over as soon as possible, and we can all start healing."

I had no answer to give.

Laik Var sighed again and turned away. "I'm not here to chat," he admitted after a brief pause. "The kar-vessár wants to see you."

My stomach dropped. Another thing I should have expected, though under normal circumstances there would be no reason for the highest commander of Mespana to even acknowledge my existence.

"What could he want from me?" I asked, hating how hoarse my voice sounded.

"I don't know, but it would be rude to keep him waiting." He gestured toward the camp. "Shall we?"

The vessár-ai tent was the biggest in the camp. It was made of pristine, white plastic and decorated with alternating banners: one with entwined lines of dull red and cobalt blue—colors of Dahls—and the other black, embroidered with silver-green threads forming the logo of Mespana.

When I entered, the tingle of a decontaminating spell washed over me. It was like stepping through the merge, and what I saw inside only exacerbated that impression. Spacious, bright, and clean, it clashed with the tent's outer shell, and the air reverberated with a subtle hum of ventilation and smell of disinfectants. A piece of Dahls in this faraway land.

I'd never seen Myar Mal-Maomik, kar-vessár of Mespana, before, but I had no problem recognizing him. He was probably the first thing anyone noticed when entering a room he occupied, his sheer presence filled it to the brim. He sat sprawled like an emperor from an old legend—right elbow propped on an armrest and left hand outstretched, fingers drumming on the table in a way verging on impatience, making me instantly ashamed of making him wait.

What surprised me the most was he wasn't much older

than me. Short, like all Dahlsi, but perfectly proportional, with neatly combed dark hair and eyes a color I couldn't determine: a particular shade of gray that could appear green, blue or even purple, depending on the lighting. His gaze was incredibly sharp and piercing, and I felt it drilling straight into my soul. He had a narrow face with a tall forehead and an aquiline nose, suggesting some percentage of foreign blood, but so distant it was impossible to discern its source. His skin had a healthy sheen, and I thought he must've been born in the colonies. Still, he looked like what every young Dahlsi man aspired to look like. They should have put his portrait on recruiting posters.

There were other people, too, almost invisible in Myar Mal's dominating presence, despite wearing silver sashes of vessár-ai.

One thing was plain, though. Small and pale, they were all native Dahlsi.

Now their eyes were on me, and I felt all will and purpose draining from me. I became an empty shell, existing only to be scrutinized. And there was a lot to scrutinize—my peasant's tan, my large, heavy body, perfectly exposed by the skintight uniform, my bulging stomach, even my height.

I was a stranger here. An intruder.

I let out a long, painful breath. It was all right, I told myself. I was summoned here. I had the right… I *should* be here.

I straightened my back in a vain attempt to regain my footing and clasped my hands behind me, hoping no one noticed how much they shook.

"Kar-vessár," I greeted him, looking the man in the eye

and trying to ignore the other twelve people present. Watching. Judging. "I heard you wanted to speak to me."

"Aldait Han-Tirsan," he drawled, surveying me with a razor-sharp gaze.

I shuddered. Dahlsi rarely applied titles when addressing someone—two names were usually considered respectful enough—and they almost never used surnames. It couldn't mean anything good. The worry about my citizenship resurfaced, but the kar-vessár's face was unreadable.

"I've heard a lot about you," he continued.

I nodded and let out a sigh of relief. It didn't have to mean anything though, I scolded myself. "Thank you, Myar Mal."

He wore a ring with a dallite gem as big as a human eye on his middle finger. I wondered what feat of heroism he performed to earn it. In any case, looking at it was easier than meeting his gaze.

"Laik Var seems to have complete confidence in you, however... I want to hear myself where your loyalties lie." His voice suddenly turned as sharp as his gaze, and my body tensed again.

It was a simple question. One of those I never thought about, instinctively knowing the answer, but never putting it into words. So, when it was actually asked, I was stumped. Moments passed and I stood, paralyzed no less than as if I had fallen victim to a spell.

"Well?"

The impatience in the kar-vessár's voice finally broke through my stupor. Though I still had very little idea what assurance I could offer, I needed to say *something*.

"I was born and raised in a colony," I started uncertainly, but he cut me short.

"So were they."

He didn't have to specify who "they" were. I took a deep breath, trying to loosen the tightness in my chest. It's all right, I told myself. Just relax. Breathe.

"My ancestors were low-class citizens," I picked up. "In Tarviss, we would be forced to work in the fields days and nights with no hope for change. Here, in the colonies, I could become who I wanted. I would never get such chance in Tarviss. And… I'd like for everyone to have that chance. That's why I joined Mespana, and from what I know, I never gave you a reason to doubt my loyalty."

I lowered my eyes, but I felt his gaze on me, making my skin crawl and my heart thunder. For a moment, he remained silent, and I wondered if my speech had made the proper impression. I was not a speaker, but I meant every word I said.

All right, maybe it was too much. Ridiculously idealistic. Would he think I was bullshitting? I wasn't. I meant every word I said. I wondered if I should add something, fix it somehow, but before I came up with anything he leaned back in his chair and asked, "Do you have any idea why they would oppose Dahls?"

"No, Myar Mal."

"Suspicion, then?"

"It's hard to say without knowing who they are."

Before I finished speaking, I already knew what he had in mind. He must have realized that, because as soon as the last word left my mouth, he requested, "I want you to find out."

Although I fully expected such a request, actually hearing it made my insides twist into a tight ball. I clenched my fists so tight it hurt, hoping the pain would keep me grounded. It worked only partially.

My jaw felt like it was welded shut, and I couldn't utter a word, even if I had known what to say. Somehow, I forced myself to let out a long breath that somewhere along the way turned into a cough.

"Is that an order, Kar-vessár?" I stammered.

I mustered the courage to look up, not at *him*, but Laik Var, in a silent plea for help. He kept his face down, eyes fixed on the table.

"A request."

He said this word like he didn't fully understand what it meant, like it was an order in everything but name. I started to suspect he must have gotten his position by barging into the Directory chambers and demanding the promotion. It's not likely they would have been able to refuse him.

"I know the risk too well," he added, almost softly. "But we want to give them another chance to resolve things... peacefully."

I'd heard what happened to the Dahlsi officials who were there at the time of the rebellion. The man was instantly killed while the woman was maimed and sent to Kooine with a list of demands. Believe it or not, their lot wasn't my biggest worry.

"I'm not a diplomat," I protested.

"I don't want you to negotiate with them. The Directory has made its decision. You are only to deliver the message. In a way they will hopefully understand."

"But I'm not a good speaker."

That was a massive understatement. I always scrambled for words and had the tendency to say all the worst things at the worst times. The crippling anxiety that paralyzed my tongue and froze my brain every time I had to interact with more than two people didn't exactly help. And I knew what people thought about me, they made it pretty clear on multiple occasions. That's why it was just easier for me to keep my mouth shut.

But even my panic-stricken mind knew that trying to explain that to my superiors was not a great idea.

"The little speech you gave us a moment ago seemed good enough for me." The kar-vessár's voice, while still adamant, lost its bite. I got an impression he must've noticed my distress and was trying to reassure me, but that only made me feel worse. Pitiful.

I didn't need pity. I needed a wand or a sword and an enemy to kill. Or a world to explore. I was perfectly fine doing ninety-nine percent of our job.

There was only one thing I struggled with, and now I had to do exactly that.

"Besides, you are Tarvissi—in blood and upbringing," he continued. I dropped my head again to avoid his gaze. "You share the language, culture, and mannerisms. Hopefully they'll be more eager to listen to one of their own."

"And if they won't?"

A snort sounded from the other side of the tent. I snapped my head up, only now realizing there was another man with us.

"That's in the job description, kid."

He was leaning on the wall, arms crossed and lips

31

twisted into a sardonic smirk. Something else drew my attention, though, making it impossible to tear my gaze from his face. Four puckered, parallel scars ran across it, deep and red against his chalky white skin.

He caught the horror in my eyes, and his smile widened and turned ugly.

I shuddered involuntarily. I bet they all noticed.

"Even if you only manage to talk to them, you will help us gather important intel," explained Myar Mal, completely ignoring the other man. "We will provide you with all the protection we can, the strongest spells at our disposal. There's also a small ritual which will allow us, all vessár-ai, to see with your eyes and hear with your ears, so that we know everything that happens to you. All we need is your agreement."

I guess he meant it as a reassurance, but I couldn't shake off the feeling that they were preparing themselves in case I never made it back. I didn't blame them. At the same time, a strange suspicion squirmed in the back of my head. The speech about my supposed kinship with the rebels was charming, but the truth was I was expendable. More than any true Dahlsi, anyway.

Then again, refusing a direct order–or "request"– probably wouldn't reflect well on my blindly declared loyalty.

I did this to myself, didn't I?

"All right then," I nodded. "When do we start?"

Myar Mal stood up abruptly. "As soon as you're ready."

Somehow, he was ahead of me, his scarred face looking even more horrible in the light of day. I tried to recall the moment he left the vessár-ai tent, but in vain. It seemed like he was there until the end, and yet now he was waiting for me.

"Here," he said, extending his hand. I looked down; he was holding a wand. A brand new one judging from the look: sleek and elegant, the shaft covered in black plastic with a rubber grip. I wasn't an expert, but even I could tell it wasn't the crap we were usually issued.

I raised my gaze to meet his. Beneath the heavy lids, his eyes were strikingly bright with almost mirror-like irises and pinkish whites. Close up he looked even more unhealthy than most Dahlsi; his cheeks were sunken and his skin waxy. The fact that he hadn't seemed to have used a razor since at least yesterday didn't exactly improve his image. And yet, he stood straight; his movements were energetic, if somehow erratic, and his eyes gave such an immense impression of focus I could almost feel them boring into my skull.

"What's that?" I asked stupidly.

He only grinned, stretching his scars grotesquely. "The newest model, courtesy of Kanven Sandeyron," he said with a strange mockery in his voice. "Three cores of tertium, nubithium, and khabun. Double lenses of pure dallite. Eighty-one saved spells. I think you'll have more use for it than me." Still, I hesitated, so he waved it at me. "Come on, take it."

I did. New spells flooded my mind, and it took me a while to regain enough control to push them back. I'd have to go through them later, provided I'd get the chance.

I looked into his eyes again. "Thanks. But... why?"

He waved his hand, with the palm up, in a Dahlsian gesture that meant something like "don't know, don't care." I liked to compare it to the Tarvissian shrug. "I have no use for it."

"Are you a sorcerer?" I asked, and immediately cursed myself. Very few people had enough potential and focus to use magic to any significant degree without the aid of wands. They were all sorcerers.

His smile faltered, but when he answered, his voice lost nothing of its mocking tone. "Unfortunately, yes."

That was surprising. I'd met many people who would have done anything to be sorcerers, but lacked the disposition, and none who could be one but didn't want to.

I wondered if I knew this guy. He made no effort to introduce himself and acted with familiarity, as if we were already acquainted. He definitely knew me, from the meeting if nowhere else. And though my memory was exceedingly poor when it came to faces, I was pretty sure I would remember scars like his. Also, his uniform bore no insignia, no cohort number, not even the logo of Mespana. Still, at this point, I thought asking for his name would be awkward, so I didn't.

Instead, I waved my new wand and tried to steer the conversation to lighter topics. "Are you not worried it may fall into the enemy's hands?"

He laughed, a short, mocking jeer. "Those idiots wouldn't know what to do with it. Besides, you're coming back. Myar Mal doesn't like losing people."

I snorted. "Yeah, I'll let them know."

Provided I manage to say a full sentence when I'm there.

And by Vhalfr, with that damned spell, all the vessár-ai would witness my ineptitude. *Why did I agree to this?*

"Courage doesn't always mean a lack of fear," he said, suddenly serious. "More often it's just acting despite it."

"That's what they say," I replied too sharply. I'd gotten similar advice for as long as I could remember. It wasn't worth shit.

And who was this guy to give me advice, anyway? My anxiety was probably obvious to everyone with working eyes, but it was my problem. His opinion, well-meaning or not, was nothing but an intrusion.

I was going to say something about it when his lips curled in lopsided smile that didn't reach his eyes, and he bowed slightly.

"Good luck on your mission then," he said simply, and left me alone with my anger.

I exhaled heavily, glaring after him until he disappeared behind a tent. Then I remembered the wand he gave me, and my gaze drifted to it. Sleek and shiny, like a tail of a scorpion, ready to attack. I drew my fingers over the hilt and sensed it humming with energy. Eighty-one spells, huh?

With a slight pang of guilt, I looked up to the spot where he'd disappeared. He probably had the best intentions, and I was overreacting, as usual. Good thing I hadn't managed to say any of the things I had been thinking of.

"You should stay away from him."

I jerked in surprise. Laik Var was standing behind me, lips pursed and eyes fixed on the spot where the man had gone. I sensed an opportunity.

"Who was he?" I prodded.

"Tayrel Kan-Trever," he said as if it was supposed to explain everything. When the only thing I could offer was silence, he elaborated. "One of the Kanven Sandeyron pupils." That didn't help either. "Kanven used to adopt unwanted children and experiment on them. Among them was Tayrel Kan. The company tried to increase the magical potential in humans, and, at least in his case, they succeeded. But..." He hesitated for a moment. "They messed him up pretty badly in the process."

I shuddered. "Those scars..." I said before I could think.

But Laik Var shook his head. "That's a later development. I meant psychologically. He's... not exactly stable. Only his substance dependence makes him, well, not easy, but possible to control."

I remembered the whites of Tayrel Kan's eyes. Initially, I thought they were reddened because of the allergies—after all, most Dahlsi suffered from them, and neither medicine nor magic seemed to relieve the symptoms. Now I wondered if it was because of drugs. From what I'd heard, the heavy stuff—ytanga, as they called it—painted one's whites pink. Such things were legal in Dahls, a sad necessity when the entire population was perpetually sick and miserable. Still, it was frowned upon in Mespana.

"Why do you even keep him?" I asked. "In Mespana, I mean. If he's unstable."

He huffed, making his veil flutter. "It's Myar Mal's decision. The official version is that we can keep an eye on him and make sure he doesn't do too much damage. And he is powerful, although not eager to share his powers. Anyway, he likes men and I know you Tarvissi are not... fond of such sentiments. We don't need any quarrels now, so, for your own good, I'd prefer it if you tried to avoid him."

I felt my skin crawl. I didn't care about others' personal lives—and I thought the universe would be a better place if more people shared my attitude—but I had no interest in men. And, frankly, I wasn't sure what I'd do if one ever became interested in me.

Unwittingly, my gaze drifted toward the wand.

"Should I give it back?" I asked, feeling uneasy.

Laik Var hesitated, looking at the weapon, but finally he gave me a wave-shrug. "If you want. But it's a good wand. It may save your life one day."

He didn't sound convinced, and anyway that wasn't exactly what bothered me. It was my turn to hesitate, wondering how best to explain it. It seemed so obvious to a Tarvissi, but things were different among the Dahlsi.

"Isn't it, like…" I stammered. "A courting gift?"

For a moment, Laik Var looked at me wordlessly, then he scoffed. "If he was interested in you, he'd tell you. No, this is innocent. I think Kanven tries to mollify him, so they send him a lot of free gear. He throws away most of it. You'll get more use out of it."

I wasn't entirely convinced, but giving it back would require me to meet Tayrel Kan again, and I wasn't looking forward to that. I reached for my old wand and submitted it to Laik Var. The new one was smaller, and I was wondering how it would fit in my holster, but the container shrunk around it. Enchanted.

Without another word, Laik Var gestured toward the medical tent. He walked with me—to prevent any other accidental encounters? I didn't ask.

I was so lost in my thoughts I only noticed the sorceress

waiting for us when we were a couple of steps away. She was an inconspicuous woman with shoulder-length hair and a face obscured by oversized glasses and a fringe. A yellow coat of a healer covered her Mespanian uniform.

"Amma," said Laik Var, stopping abruptly. I paused as well, confused. It was considered rude among the Dahlsi to use only one name unless it was done by a close friend or relative. However, there was nothing familiar in the look she sent him.

"Laik Var," she replied coldly, before turning to me. "You must be Aldait Han. I'm Amma La-Vaikra, allar of magic."

Allar was a title given to anyone who finished the Academy with any degree, whether in magic or science. But it was generally used by the latter—allars of magic were usually just called sorcerers.

"I'm supposed to lead you through the process. If you please." She moved aside, gesturing me toward the entrance.

I sent a questioning look to Laik Var, but he only nodded and walked off with a stiff, unnatural gait I'd never seen him walk with.

I went inside. The tent was large, but Amma La led me to a tiny section separated by folding screens. There were two cots, the one on the right already occupied and covered with a heavy throw.

"Who is that?" I asked, not able to hide my curiosity.

"Don't concern yourself with them," replied Amma La, making me flinch. There was nothing admonishing in her voice, but I thought I was being unreasonably nosy. So I clenched my teeth, determined not to ask any further questions.

38

Following the sorceress's orders, I unzipped my suit and removed the upper half—with another pang of self-consciousness about the dark hair on my chest—then laid on my stomach. I couldn't see what she was doing, but after a while, something cold and wet touched my skin, rippling with magic.

Amma La drew spells on my back. Her movements were slow but practiced, and I realized they must've come up with this plan some time ago. What would they have done if I refused? I guess they could have forced me through magic or hypnosis. Maybe that's why Tayrel Kan was there? Or they could send someone else. Although, Myar Mal seemed adamant that they needed me specifically—"my language, culture, and mannerisms," as he put it. What good they'd do me remained to be seen.

The stress of the day must've taken its toll, because at some point, I fell asleep. I woke up when the sorceress urged me to roll onto my back. The bowl and brush rested on a table next to my cot, and the woman was now holding a glass bottle with a dropper.

"It will allow the vessár-ai to see what you see," she explained, forcing my eye open and letting a few drops fall into it. It was unpleasant, and not only in the physical sense. The sharp burn of magic seemed to reach much deeper than the liquid itself, following the nerves and burrowing into my brain. Amma La repeated the procedure with the other eye and then switched liquids and poured some into my ears. In the end, my head felt like it was filled with swarms of insects ready to start crawling out of my mouth, my nose, my eyes.

Strangely though, I detected no trace of magic on my

back.

"Are you sure those protective spells are working?" I asked. "I don't feel anything."

"They're good spells," she reassured me. "You will be dizzy for a while, but the sooner you get up, the sooner you'll get better."

I didn't exactly believe her, but I complied. Nausea hit me as soon as I shifted, but Amma La was right—it passed. She walked out of the chamber, gesturing for me to follow. I couldn't help but steal a last curious glance at the motionless mass on the left cot. For a moment I got a strange feeling that things were not as they should be, but then I was struck by a wave of dizziness so strong I had to brace myself up on the cot.

"Are you coming?" asked the sorceress, sounding impatient.

Hurriedly, I pulled my suit back on and rushed to join her.

Chapter 3

"YOU KNOW, HE'S not exactly my type."

Laik Var's mental defenses sprung up so fast Tayrel Kan nearly winced. Nevertheless, the vessár didn't even bother turning around.

"I thought your type is anyone willing to buy you a fix," he said instead.

Tayrel Kan smacked his lips in dismay. "You wound me, Vessár. I have standards, believe it or not."

The only answer he got was a snort. Laik Var lifted his foot to resume his walk, but the sorcerer wasn't finished.

"You don't have to worry about the virtue of your golden boy."

To that, Laik Var turned instantly, as if struck by a spell. "I meant every word I said," he barked. "You stay away from him, too."

The sorcerer's smirk widened. "You're not curious about what I found?" he mocked. Now he could clearly see the commander's larynx moving as he swallowed the curse.

"Who sent you?" he asked instead.

Tayrel Kan spread his arms, his smile wide and dripping with insincerity. "A concern for my homeland."

This time Laik Var actually cursed and stepped away, but Tayrel Kan stopped him yet again.

"He's loyal." He paused, awaiting an answer, but the vessár refused to give him satisfaction. "You're welcome."

"Why are you doing this?"

"Why, can't I just want to do my part in defending Dahls?"

The vessár barked out a short, mocking laugh. "You're not that kind of guy."

"Oh, now you're gonna tell me what kind of guy I am? I can't wait."

Laik Var turned around and looked the sorcerer in the eyes. "Don't pretend you're suddenly overwhelmed with patriotic feelings. You don't give a shit if any of us live or die. I'm actually surprised you even bothered coming, instead of rotting in some filthy hole, covered in sperm and vomit, so high you don't care."

For a moment Tayrel Kan was at a loss, his smirk all but disappearing.

"Wow, Vessár. That was... brutal," he said finally, crossing his arms again. His smile returned, but it was an ugly, predatory grin that stretched his scars. "And strangely accurate. Almost makes me wonder if you ever went to such places yourself. You should come say hi one of these days; we could get to know each other better."

Laik Var frowned in disgust, and the sorcerer barely stopped himself from laughing.

"You're a degenerate. You should get your head checked."

Tayrel Kan scoffed. "I think I've had enough therapy for a lifetime. Maybe if it wasn't for them, I wouldn't be who I am now."

"You're the maker of your misery, Tayrel. If you want to drown it in ytanga, that's your business, I don't give a shit, but don't use it to justify everything you did. And if Myar Mal wants to use you, against me or Aldait Han or whoever, then make sure you're fucking useful, because he's the only one willing to put up with you."

The sorcerer's eyes widened and after a split second so did his smile.

"Oh, so that's what bothers you," he purred, "my association with him. You should be grateful, really."

Laik Var's face turned red, and his lip curled up in an angry snarl. Tayrel Kan didn't even have to read his mind to know he was right.

But then the vessár realized what many people had before him: he couldn't win this fight. So, he waved his hand, as if trying to drive off a particularly annoying fly, and growled, "I had enough of you, pest. Get out of my sight!"

This time Tayrel Kan let him go, but made sure to follow him with his most evil cackle.

Chapter 4

DEFENSIVE CIRCLES surrounded the Mansion. Through Vuilsumnaar goggles, I could trace their outlines. First, the red lines of simple alarms, but near the Mansion they intertwined with yellow and turquoise defensive spells. I knew their general function, but predicting their real-world effects would require knowledge I didn't have.

Sorcery in Tarviss was different than in Dahls. Though the energies it controlled were the same, the methods differed greatly. I wasn't sure about the details; I was no sorcerer. I wondered how deep Dahlsian understanding was of Tarvissian magic—and specifically if it was deep enough to counter their spells.

More specifically, if the protection they promised would be enough to keep me alive.

A few soldiers escorted me as far as they dared, but they stayed behind while I paused at the very edge of the protected area. For the first time, I took a good look at the rebels base.

It wasn't a real noble house, merely an imitation. Previously, it most likely served as the community center with offices, granaries, and a big yard used as a marketplace. It was short but sprawling, with whitewashed walls—now darkened by soot—and a gently sloped roof covered in red tiles. A few banners hung from the walls: a checkered, black-and-white background with a green trident, the central prong much thicker than those on the sides. The coat of Tarviss. I realized I'd never seen it displayed before today.

The outer windows were narrow—a relic of older times when such mansions were often used for defense. And it worked. With thick walls and double gates, the building was almost impenetrable. Thanks to a few wells and full storage, the rebels could stay inside for cycles.

Provided they didn't decide to send their troops back to Kooine. With most members of Mespana gathered here, they wouldn't have much trouble seizing other worlds.

Or maybe not. Despite harsh conditions in Kooine, there were large colonies of nonhumans living there, mining for rare metals, tertium salts, and natural glass. I didn't think they'd give their homes to the Tarvissi without a fight.

And yet, I hesitated. It's not that I didn't trust the Dahlsi…

Okay, maybe a little. But I couldn't just turn back. Not now, not after everything.

I sucked in air. It tasted of smoke.

Well, now or never, I thought.

I moved my left foot over the spell.

46

The red line rippled, and the magic current ran up my leg. But apart from that, nothing. No trace of resistance. I waited for a few seconds, but nothing else happened. My right foot joined my left on the other side. Still nothing.

I exhaled.

Just an alarm, I chided myself. They probably knew I was coming. The real test of Dahlsian protection was yet to come.

I moved forward, walking carefully but steadily, my eyes fixed on the mansion, looking out for danger. It was no use, though. They wouldn't come out for me, and the windows were too narrow for me to peek inside. Still, I watched, thinking that if they decided to shoot me down, at least I might glimpse the incoming arrow. Or spell. Something. Maybe I would spot movement behind one of the windows; catch a gleam in hateful eyes.

I saw nothing. Beneath my feet, spell after spell faltered before snapping back into place. They were all red. All harmless. Soon, though, I stood before a different line. A yellow one.

What would that one do? Turn me into stone upon crossing? Set me on fire? A real sorcerer could probably identify it, determine if my protections were strong enough to counteract it, but I was not a sorcerer. I was just a guy with a handful of devices, the inner workings of which I would never understand.

I took the next step.

That time, I felt something—the faintest hint of resistance; a numbness crawling up my leg and overwhelming my whole body for a heartbeat.

Then it vanished. The yellow line disappeared. I let out a long, shaky breath.

So, the Dahlsian spells were working after all.

I picked up my trek, but my steps became slower, more calculated. I felt a slight tingling at the back of my neck, and I knew I was being watched. I braced myself for an attack, but none came.

Sooner than I would have liked, I found myself standing before the gate. Twice as tall as me, flanked by the white, black, and green banners of Tarviss.

It opened.

Did the rebels want to talk to me? Or turn me into an example?

It was dark inside. There was light in the distance, in the main courtyard. I whispered a spell, and my goggles changed mode: the blackness melted into shades of gray. Ahead of me ran a wide corridor with doors on both sides. I was struck by the realization that if I walked in, I might never come out. But, I guess, despite all logical evidence, my brain rejected that idea, because I felt nothing. No fear, no anxiety. Not yet. Just cold, silent numbness.

I stepped in.

The gate closed slowly behind me. I walked straight into the courtyard. When I emerged from the darkness and took my goggles off, I realized it was crowded, with only a small opening left for me. All around stood burly, bearded men in traditional Tarvissian outfits: black trousers, loose white shirts, and jyats—knee-length, sleeveless coats—in the same shade of green.

My insides coiled in anxiety.

Then, following my brain's tendency to focus on the weirdest thing, I realized something. Being surrounded at all times by people who could fit under my armpit, it was easy to forget, but the Tarvissi were tall. And I wasn't, by any means, the tallest. In fact, I was closer to the lower end of average.

And why hadn't I brought my Tarvissian garb? It hadn't even occurred to me in Sfal, and now all I had was my Dahlsian uniform, suddenly too tight, too exposing. And why did I shave this morning? No chance I could grow anything to compete with what these guys were sporting, but now I felt like a kid.

In fact, I felt no less alien here than I had in the vessár-ai tent.

"Tearshan."

Hearing my name spoken properly for the first time in ages came as a shock. My body tensed. I feared it wouldn't listen to me, but somehow, I managed to turn around, trying to locate the speaker. It wasn't hard. He was standing one step ahead of everyone else, slightly to my left.

"Peridion," I countered, almost barking the name out.

I knew him, as much as I regretted it. We grew up together—sort of. Despite the fact that my parents let him live, he was never really part of our community. He remained outside, skulking at the edges of the colony, barely talking to anyone, thinking himself far above us solely because of his ancestry.

Because Karlan Peridion was a noble. The son of the lord who was in charge of my family before my father slit his throat to free himself from aristocratic oppression.

I was so fucked.

"Aldeaith Tearshan," he drawled languidly. His voice was naturally high pitched, and he always tried to make it sound lower. The result was grotesque at best. Everything about him was grotesque: strangely disproportionate body with long, frail limbs and a barrel-like chest, wide face with small, sharp features, adorned with thick, brown curls on top, but unable to grow a half-decent beard. Almost as if someone had taken random elements and connected them without an ounce of care about how they fit together.

"Look at him, thinking himself a real Dahlsi," he said, turning away from me. He had a knife he was waving around carelessly. I just waited for him to drop it.

I felt a kick to the back of my knee and I collapsed, more from surprise than pain. Someone twisted my hands behind my back. My thoughts scattered in panic, until I spotted something that grabbed my attention and allowed me to focus for long enough to collect myself. My wand. Some bastard was already handing it to Peridion, having apparently snatched it from my belt. That wand had been with me from the beginning, covered in scratches and slightly chipped at the end from the close call in Sorox. The sight of it made some half-forgotten thought scratch at the back of my mind, but I pushed it away. I had more pressing problems. Peridion didn't even seem interested in my weapons, putting them aside and studying me with pure, unadulterated hatred.

His lips twitched in a cruel smile when he addressed the crowd again, "Maybe we should cut his legs at the knees. He'd be just like them imps."

They laughed.

I wanted to say something, but my jaw was frozen and my mind blank. And no, it wasn't because of the looming death. My brain had already detected a much bigger threat.

He might talk to me.

Myar Mal, I thought. He didn't send me here to die.

I focused on the knife Karlan was wielding and tried to pretend it was just him and me. There was no crowd surrounding us, surrounding me, witnessing my ineptitude in all of its ingloriousness.

"I come as a representative of Dahls," I stammered. It sounded weak. Pathetic.

Karlan's face contorted in anger. He jumped forward and slapped me. For a moment, my universe shrank until nothing but the pain remained.

"I see your manners have slipped in Dahls," his sneer broke through. "But in Tarviss, those like you don't speak unless asked."

I was certainly glad I was not born in Tarviss.

My mind cleared, but I did my best to limit the amount of sensation I let through. I focused on the slap. I could have avoided Karlan's hand; I could have grabbed it and broken it. I was much stronger than him, after all. But that wouldn't be wise when I was in his domain, surrounded by people, who, judging by the reaction, were his subjects. So I let it slip. I dropped my head, like the meek, obedient peon I was supposed to be, and hoped he didn't notice that my hatred for him was as strong as his for me.

"But, since you're so eager, tell me if your masters have agreed to our terms," he said.

I had no masters, only higher-ups, but it wasn't time for discussing semantics. I just repeated what I was instructed to say, "As part of Meon Cluster, Maurir belongs to Dahls, and is and will always be, subject to Dahlsian rule." I barely finished the first sentence before the crowd started booing. I waited for them to calm down before picking up. "If the people living here decide to live according to Tarvissian laws, they're free to do so. If they want to obey the Tarvissian Council, they can. If they want to pay taxes to Tarviss, they can. But only after paying their due to Dahls."

"See, that's the problem," said Peridion, waving his knife in circles. "Dahlsian rule means the people's rule, and if we let the people decide, sooner or later the decision will fall to those like you. And we can't have that."

I ignored him and continued with my message, "If you surrender now, none of you will get hurt. You will be deported and barred from reentering, but the Directory will consider allowing other people of Tarvissian descent to enter the colonies in the future."

Was it a laughable sentence? Yes, it was. Did it make my blood boil when I heard it? You bet it did. Those assholes were murderers and insurgents. They deserved to die.

But there were too many of them. Dahls had never faced such a big group and was not eager to try now, especially when there was a risk of angering its bigger neighbor. So, the Directory was willing to let them out, to restore the peace and pretend the whole thing never happened.

I understood that. I hated it, but I understood.

"Are you listening to me, or are you just repeating what they told you?" Peridion's eyes narrowed. "I shouldn't expect much; you were always dumb, even for a peon. Let me say it simply: Dahls has lost this colony. It's Tarviss's territory now. If your people come here, we'll kill them."

"You don't even have a connection to Tarviss," I said, letting my opinion slip for the first time.

They didn't think this uprising through. True, they could stay in the mansion for days, but certainly not forever. With the merge blocked, they had no means to bring in more people, weapons, or food. Mespana could step aside and wait for them to starve.

But, I guessed, we needed a show of strength to discourage other potential dissidents. Besides, making sure the rebels wouldn't try to expand their territory to Kooine would require a constant guard, something we couldn't afford. So maybe quelling this rebellion as soon as possible was our best option.

"That was one of our terms," said Peridion condescendingly.

Yes, and Tayrel Kan had fun responding to it.

"You assholes think it's enough to draw a magic circle, make fart noises, and you can bend the universe to your will," he'd mocked. "It's bullshit. The laws of physics are unbreakable. You can't merge the worlds that are not properly aligned in the first place. It's just physically impossible. Tell it to those morons."

"It can't be done," I said.

"Why not?"

"Maurir and Tarviss are not aligned," I explained, trying not to mimic Tayrel Kan's tone. "They can't be merged."

"Somehow all the worlds can be aligned if the Dahlsi want them to," he spat, and I realized he knew as much about magic as I did. That didn't stop him from making outrageous claims and demanding the universe to obey, like the spoiled brat he was.

"Not really," I said, trying to sound calm. "Look, I'm not a sorcerer. People smarter than me made calculations; they're in my pouch if you want to check."

"I'm not interested in calculations; I'm interested in results."

"And the results are physically impossible."

"Well, maybe we just didn't state our terms clear enough."

Before I could respond, someone grabbed my hair and pulled my head back.

"I think we should remind your friends in Dahls we're not playing games here," said Peridion, coming closer to me, waving his knife menacingly.

"Think about it," I rasped, trying to break the grasp, but those who held me—at least two—were stronger. "This is your last chance to back off. If you kill me, there will be no more talk; Dahlsi will kill you all!"

"It would do you better to stick to farming," he said, ignoring my words. "You wanted to play with real men? Now you're gonna pay for it."

"You know, I think I figured out why you cling so much to old customs," I spat, desperately trying to break the grip of the thugs holding me. "They give you a sense of privilege, no matter who you are as a person. Because stripped of them, you are nothing!"

"Well, I hope your personal qualities have earned you enough merit among those imps to grant you a decent funeral once we're done with you."

Someone's hand grabbed my face and forced my eye wide open. Peridion was standing right next to me now, his blade tracing lines over my cheek.

I was not a religious man, but at that moment, I prayed. If there was ever a god who listened to those like me, I prayed for salvation.

Lo-and-behold, just when the blade touched my lower eyelid, my vision blurred, and the grip of my fellow Tarvissi lightened. Peridion's eyes widened comically. He threw himself at me, and I instinctively jerked back—or tried to. Something hard was pressing against my back and a new set of arms, smaller and weaker, held me down. My instincts kicked in, and I struggled to break free, barely noticing what was happening around me.

"For Vhalfr's sake, Aldait Han, calm down!"

The voice was familiar, but my addled mind couldn't place it. Something soft and warm fell on my face, and I sensed a sweet, nauseating scent. Kalikka. I held my breath, but it was too late: the drug had dispersed into my system, and my panic faded into a strange numbness.

When I stopped moving, the person holding me removed the mask. My vision was filled by a bright disk with four angry red lines, and it took me a while to recognize it as a face.

"What have you done?" I rasped. I wasn't sure what had happened, only that something was not as it should be.

Tayrel Kan clicked his tongue in disapproval. "You really don't appreciate your leaders. You thought we were just going to send you to death?"

That was the plan. So I'd been told.

"What have you done?" I repeated, feeling the drug leaving my system as fast as it had overcome it. I tried to get up, but Tayrel Kan's hand held me down.

"Calm down, I said, or I'll dope you again. It was a simple projection." My face must have been making my confusion, clear, because he started explaining: "We transferred your mind and soul into a golem, wrapped it in an illusion to make it all nice and pretty, then sent it forth. Your body was here the whole time, completely safe."

"When… did you do that?"

As soon as the words left my mouth, I knew. The moment I lost consciousness under Amma La's brush.

"Seriously, you should be more aware of what's happening to your body," murmured Tayrel Kan.

I glared at him, but his face split into a wide grin.

How the fuck could I have known? It's not like I understood the sigils they were drawing on my back. And no one had bothered to tell me.

"Look, it was the lady's idea." The mage spread his arms as if trying to say he had nothing to do with it.

The warning hiss came from the other side of the cot, and when I turned, I saw Laik Var glaring at Tayrel Kan with murder in his eyes.

Not that it left an impression, the sorcerer's amusement didn't slip for a moment. "Apparently, we needed you to act naturally" he continued. "They had to believe it was really you, or the whole ruse wouldn't have worked. And we weren't sure how good of an actor you are."

Bile rose in my throat. They let me believe I was going to die, that I was going to be tortured. And didn't even bother pulling me out until the last possible moment!

"Oh, I'll show you how good of an actor I am!" I growled, sitting up and reaching for the sorcerer, but he dissolved in a cloud of smoke, leaving only a toothy grin hanging in the air.

"Calm down!" I heard Laik Var say, and the cycles of conditioning kicked in; I obeyed.

Still, my eyes kept darting around, trying to locate the sorcerer. Only then did I realize we were in the medical tent, back where the initial spell was cast. The cot on the right side was empty, despite me clearly remembering getting up from it—and lying down on the one I was on now. How could I miss that? Was I really that dumb?

"Your mind was a bit addled," said Tayrel Kan, appearing out of nowhere.

Was this bastard reading my thoughts? I made sure to send him a few nasty words.

But there was another thing gnawing at me, not letting me just accept it and move on.

"That wasn't the only reason," I guessed. "You wanted to see what I'd do. Where my loyalties lie." I repeated Myar Mal's words, heavy and bitter with the new meaning. "If I decided to betray you and join the enemy… you would finish me before I spilled your secrets."

Laik Var pursed his lips but didn't say anything. He didn't expect me to figure that out, I realized, which added to my growing sense of betrayal.

Tayrel Kan, on the other hand, merely scoffed. "Well, of course we were covering our asses! We're at war with your buddies over there! But we covered yours, too, saving you from a slow and painful death. So, you know, you're welcome."

I didn't answer. He was right. I hoped those Tarvissian bastards had fun with the pile of mud they were left with. I only wished it was rigged to blow up, but I guess there are only so many spells you could place on one machine.

But still…

"Catch your breath," advised Laik Var, putting his hand on my shoulder. "We have a meeting in half an hour."

Chapter 5

I WAS BACK in the vessár-ai tent. This time, I got a chair—too small and so uncomfortable that I considered just sprawling on the floor. But I welcomed it. If I were forced to stand, I would probably collapse.

"How are you holding up?"

I glanced up, and my eyes met Myar Mal's. As it had before, his dominating presence made me forget about the thirteen other people—Tayrel Kan included—who were there with us. However, I wasn't sure anymore if it was a good thing.

"Sorry?" I asked, instantly hating how dumb I sounded. I came here for questioning, but that was the last question I expected.

"You were almost tortured and killed; how are you holding up?" His tone verged on impatience, and I flinched involuntarily.

"I'm fine," I mumbled, dropping my head again.

"Are you sure?"

I felt his inquisitive gaze on me. "Yes, Myar Mal."

"Your hands are shaking."

I looked down; he was right. I clenched my hand into a fist and wrapped the other one around it.

"It's... not that," I murmured, hoping he wouldn't press further.

"What then?"

The truth sounded stupid even for me, but no matter how long I tried to come up with a plausible explanation, my head remained empty. The silence was getting more awkward by the heartbeat.

"Nothing," I said lamely, hating myself a little more.

"You don't have to deal with everything on your own." His voice softened, once again making me feel pitiful.

"I'm used to it," I replied automatically.

"Maybe. But it's unhealthy. You're probably not comfortable asking for help. You outworlders seem to think it's shameful or some shit. But all things considered, I'd rather have you humiliated and alive over proud and dead. So, I strongly suggest you go to the medical team and talk to someone about your experiences. Understood?"

It wasn't pride, but I was so used to people misreading my feelings, I didn't even try to protest. "Yes, Kar-vessár."

I'd rather return to Montak Mansion.

"All right, then," said Myar Mal, leaning back in his chair and returning to his brisk, official tone. "Tell us what you found out."

My tension melted a bit. This was the type of conversation I was fine with—a cold, official report, nothing more. Nothing personal.

"I know the leader, Karlan Peridion," I started.

"Peridion?" asked one vessár I didn't recognize, an older man with steely hair and a repeatedly broken nose.

I realized that apart from Myar Mal and Laik Var—and Tayrel Kan—I couldn't name any of the people present. When I joined Mespana, I was probably introduced to all of our leaders, but it was so long ago. I knew I could ask anyone anytime, but that would be awkward, so I didn't. Besides, up until now, I only really needed to recognize Laik Var.

"Of Nes Peridion fame?" continued the old man.

I nodded. Nes Peridion was my homeworld—like Maurir, inhabited mostly by immigrants from Tarviss. It was named by the late Arlo, Karlan's father, and the Dahlsian officials wouldn't let anyone change it.

"From what I've heard," interjected Myar Mal, "your families share a history. Would you mind telling us more about it?"

His face showed nothing but polite curiosity. I wondered how much he knew. For denizens of Nes Peridion, it seemed like a defining moment. But there were thousands of colonies in Meon, millions of people, from all species and cultures. Perhaps what was so important for us, warranted nothing but a brief note for the Dahlsi.

"Twenty cycles ago, the Tarvissian noble Arlo Peridion decided to settle in one of the worlds in the Meon Cluster. He brought his whole court, a small army, and a couple thousand workers. Soon, though, the workers realized that without aid from Tarviss, there was no way for Peridion to enforce his rule. So, they rebelled."

"Your father was among the leaders of the rebellion, correct?"

I licked my lips, suddenly dry. "More than that. Haneaith Tearshan killed Arlo Peridion."

A heavy silence fell on the tent.

After a while, Myar Mal asked, "What happened then?"

I shrugged. "Our people created our own state and pledged fealty to Dahls."

"With no repercussions?" inquired a man with a slight tan on his forehead and pale cheeks and chin, giving an impression of a recently shaved beard.

"No," answered another vessár, a woman for a change. She was old, her hair completely white and her face marked with deep furrows. If appearance was anything to go by, she could have been around when it happened. "It was the very beginning of Mespana. We probably didn't have resources to challenge, as Aldait Han said, a couple of thousand people. Especially since they didn't want to fight us."

"And Tarviss didn't call for retribution?" asked the half-tanned guy.

"They were rebuffed," replied the elder man. "We couldn't extradite all the rebels, and we refused to let the Tarvissian army into our worlds."

"What about Karlan Peridion?" demanded Myar Mal, putting an end to the disruption.

"He is Arlo's son," I explained. "He was a child at the time of the revolution, so he was spared and adopted by one of the peon families."

"Did you know him personally?"

I shrugged, too late realizing this gesture probably meant nothing to the Dahlsi. "He was raised among us, but he was never one of us. He's faithful to the old Tarvissian class system."

"What does that mean?"

I snorted. "He's a noble, I'm a peon. He wouldn't speak to me unless to give me an order."

"I guess that didn't sit well with your... community."

I took a moment to consider the question. I couldn't say from experience—I was born after the rebellion, when he had already been "put into place" and never wondered what that meant. But when I was growing up, he was a sulky, moody youngster who always kept to himself. We often bumped into each other while trying to avoid everyone else. Only by speaking with older children did I learn that the first few times he had tried to boss others around, he was beaten to a pulp. So, he stopped commanding and, soon after, stopped talking to anyone other than his group of cronies.

But the Dahlsi didn't have to know that.

"He was free to leave at any point," I stated instead.

"Did he?"

"I don't know," I said, feeling a pang of annoyance. "I wasn't interested in his whereabouts when I was living in Nes Peridion—and certainly not after I joined Mespana."

Then I recalled the clothing he wore in Montak Mansion. Although of a familiar cut, it was of better quality than anything I'd ever seen: a shirt of blue silk and a green jyat embroidered with black and white beads. I thought he must've gotten it off world, perhaps even in Tarviss itself. But when I opened my mouth to say that, the next question was already being asked.

"What about the others? Did you recognize anyone else?"

I huffed, slightly annoyed at the interruption. "Arasha Meralith, Kiraes Auridion, Taneem Kiovar," I listed. While Peridion occupied most of my attention, I had managed to look around a bit. "They were children of the courtiers of old Peridion. Spared, like Karlan."

And following his lead like dogs.

"And, I guess, they were of a higher class and didn't mingle with you," said Innam Ar-Leig acridly.

I had no problem recognizing him: vessár of the First Cohort, responsible for training fresh recruits. It'd been a few cycles since I joined in, but the sheer sound of his voice still made my skin crawl.

"You guessed right," I replied, equally inimically.

My thoughts briefly turned to the surrounding area, burned to ashes. The rebels' provenance made it clear why it had been so easy for them to destroy the livelihoods of people who called Maurir home. They didn't give a shit about us.

There could be other reasons. They could seek revenge for old Peridion—and their own parents who had died by his side. Or wish to restore the old order—nowhere was it as broken as on farming worlds. The Tarvissi in cities also came from the lower classes, but they were free people: merchants and craftsmen, sometimes soldiers. Us, peons, on the other hand, belonged to the lords. Leaving wasn't an option. So, those of us who lived here, in Maurir or Nes Peridion or any other world in Meon, were either rebels or runaways. And nobles couldn't stand that.

"Do everyone in the Mansion come from Nes Peridion?" asked the elder guy who spoke earlier.

"I don't know, Vessár. Despite what you may think, I don't recognize all the Tarvissi in Meon." Belatedly, I thought I should probably keep my annoyance in check while speaking to my superiors.

"No one expects you to," reassured Myar Mal. He paused for a while, then said, "I apologize. For putting you through this. I wasn't... familiar with the conflicts within the Tarvissian community." He went silent, apparently awaiting an answer.

But what could I say? Everything I felt in the last couple of hours—anxiety, fear, betrayal, relief, and anxiety again—was still fresh in my mind, still raw, twisting and coiling and knotting into a big ball that seemed like sheer exhaustion.

And he didn't apologize for lying to me.

I shifted uncomfortably. "It's all right," I murmured.

For a moment, he remained silent, like he expected me to say something else. Nothing came to my mind.

Finally, he started talking, pausing frequently, and if it had been anyone else, I would have thought he was hesitating. "I do appreciate what you did for us today. I know it must have been hard for you. To face your kin like that."

The tip of the knife flashed before my eyes, and I snapped them shut. I didn't feel any particular kinship with those assholes. But truth be told, I never felt any particular kinship with anyone, save for my closest family.

"If you wish to back out now," continued the kar-vessár, "you can return to Sfal. No one will hold it against you."

Head spinning with anxiety, I raised my gaze to look at him. But his face was turned, and I couldn't catch his eyes.

What was he talking about? And why now? Why not before...?

Well, it was pretty obvious why not before, I thought, with a sudden surge of bitterness.

Under the table, I clenched my fists, digging nails into my palms. I took a deep breath.

"Is that an order, Myar Mal?" I forced my voice to sound calm. At least, I hoped I did.

"No. But neither is staying here. It's your choice. Perhaps the last one you're going to get."

I was tempted to ask if he meant I could die if I stayed or get kicked out if I left.

"Then I choose to stay," I said simply.

The faces of my mother and sister flashed through my mind, sending out ripples of guilt. I just got a chance to quit, go to Tarviss, and at least try to help them. Instead, I stayed to play soldier.

But if the situation in Dahls didn't change, I'd have nowhere to take them. So, in a way, staying there and trying to sort things out was helping them.

Myar Mal nodded across the table, then moved on to the next question so swiftly, I thought he forgot about me.

"Any estimates about the number of rebels?"

Another woman, this one with a square face and eyes so dark they were almost black, spoke. "We tried casting spying spells on the mansion, but they give us a different number each time. One time it's two great grosses, next time it's five great grosses."

Damn the Dahlsi and their dozenal system. A great gross was around seventeen-hundred, so the total number she proposed was between thirty-five and eighty-six hundred. Tight fit, given the size of the mansion, but not exactly impossible.

"Any thoughts?"

There was no immediate answer, and I raised my head only to find everyone looking at me. I shifted awkwardly and cleared my throat. "I'd say the numbers are on the lower end. The people of Maurir were mostly of low class, not many of them would follow nobles willingly."

And that meant more of them were killed. Slaughtered like animals and probably tossed outside, since I doubted the rebels would bother with a proper funeral.

"Does their background tell us anything about them other than numbers?"

I took another moment to think. "They were probably trained to fight from a very young age," I said without conviction. The nobles were different, even though my parents' uprising strove to erase those differences. Still, old traditions were strong, even if those upholding them were young.

The problem was, as a peon and the child of the revolution, I knew very little about tradition.

"I thought you killed their parents during your revolt?" asked another man I didn't recognize. I swore, after the meeting, I'd have to find a way to learn their names. Although I probably wasn't going to need them ever again.

"I think they started learning earlier and just continued practicing."

Kiraes Auridion was almost an adult when the nobles were killed. And I still remembered Karlan carrying a long stick in place of a sword and waving it every day as mock practice. I doubted any of them was a sword master, but at least they knew which end to hold.

"What about magic?"

The question came from Tayrel Kan. He stood in what I started to think of as his usual spot against the wall, and I wasn't sure if he had been invited to the meeting. Even if not, I doubted anyone could keep him out—he was just that kind of guy.

Come to think of it, I wasn't even sure if he'd been included in the spying spell they'd cast on me before my mission.

"A few of the rebels were wearing what looked like mirror armors," said the dark-eyed woman.

Indeed, now I recalled seeing small, oval mirrors some Tarvissi wore over their sternums.

"I saw something similar on the bandits from Csivelin," she continued. "They are enough to disperse a direct killing spell. Not so good against swords, though."

"Do all the rebels have them?" pried the elder guy.

"Out of those in the yard, I'd say around one-third," answered the woman. "But who knows how many there are."

"What about those crystal balls?" asked Tayrel Kan, his eyes fixed on me.

I had no idea what he was talking about until an image popped up before my eyes: a man with a few transparent spheres hanging from his belt like a bunch of grapes. I was pretty sure it was implanted.

"They are weapons, aren't they?" he pressed.

I shook my head. "Probably, but I don't know how they work."

"You don't seem to know very much about the military of your people," said the half-tan, and I felt my face heating up.

"Magic in Tarviss is reserved for the members of the highest class," I explained, doing my best to control myself. It wasn't easy. My heart was hammering, and I felt like instead of blood, it was trying to pump the words out before they turned into a scrambled mess. I caught myself before my speech became too fast and too loud. People have often mistaken it for anger, and I got into more trouble for it than I could count. "My people had no access to it, and even now, primarily associate it with oppression. My family won't let me cast cleaning spells when I'm home."

Only when I noticed gazes filled with shock and disgust, did I realize exactly what I had just said. "We use soap and water," I grunted, wishing I could melt under the floor.

"By higher class, do you mean nobles or sorcerers?" asked Tayrel Kan, mercifully closing the topic.

"Sorcerers, mostly. But," I added, suddenly remembering something I once read. "I think the spheres have spells trapped in them. They are released upon shattering."

"So, at least they're single-use items," remarked Tayrel Kan. "The next question is: do they have a sorcerer among them who prepares those spheres on-site, or did they get them earlier, from outside?"

"We had an answer from Veyn Ay," said the half-tanned guy. "There was no major transport of goods from Tarviss in the last cycle."

"They could move them in small batches," I suggested, and the half-tanned guy sent me a condescending smile.

Heat rose in my cheeks again. Of course, they had thought about it.

Trying to save face, I asked, "But wouldn't they need a sorcerer's help, anyway, to close the merge?"

There was no point in asking about the defensive spells; they were sold in every self-respecting magic shop, and they came in all flavors: Dahlsian, Tarvissian, Tayani, Csivelinian, Chaarite, and so on.

Tayrel Kan studied my face for a moment. "What do you know about merges?" he asked.

I shrugged. "Not much. Only that they let us move between the worlds."

He hummed, then raised his left hand—he was left-handed, like most sorcerers—and curled his fingers in a peculiar gesture, conjuring an image: a large, semitransparent sphere, peppered with lights, with a smaller and brighter ball in the center. A rough model of the universe.

"The Great Sphere spins around Vhalfr," he started as if trying to narrate a story, but still unable to shake off his usual mocking tone. "But on its surface, each of the Nine Circles, and even each of the worlds, moves at its own pace."

The outer sphere divided into nine rings moving individually.

"That's an exaggeration, by the way; the differences are minuscule. A few seconds here and there. Anyway, as the worlds move, they get closer to or farther away from each other. Sometimes parts of two worlds may occupy the same spot on the four-dimensional Sphere—that's where merges form. Now, some of them are pretty stable, remaining intact for centuries. But others change, shift locations, swap worlds. Some just close or fluctuate. And what do you know—the one on Maurir is fluctuating. It remains open most of the time, but twice a cycle, it closes altogether. When it happens, it's so weak that a slight push is enough to close it. Anyone with two working brain cells and some familiarity with cosmography could do it."

"But that doesn't make sense," I said. "With the merge fluctuating, they won't be able to keep it closed forever. And when it opens, we'll be able to send our troops right in the middle of their fortress."

"The merge can only accommodate one man at a time," replied the elder woman. "Two sentries would be enough to defend it."

Tayrel Kan shook his head. "I think they just wanted to show us they can do it. It doesn't seem like they planned ahead."

"Besides, if someone inside the mansion knew a thing or two about cosmography, shouldn't they know opening the merge between Maurir and Tarviss is impossible?"

Tayrel Kan's smile vanished as he sized me up, strangely thoughtful.

"That's a good question. Maybe they knew... but didn't bother telling anyone else."

A shiver ran down my spine. Could that mean the whole rebellion was a ruse? A vain attempt to draw our attention while...

What?

"Did you scan the mansion?" I asked and immediately chided myself; it was probably the first thing they did.

71

"See, here's the problem. I did... and didn't find anything. Sorcerers are usually easy to sense, even if they shield themselves. But here, there's nothing. So either the bastard is insanely powerful and can somehow protect himself from detection, or he's using some form of indirect magic we can't track."

"Did you try sifting through the minds of the rebels?" asked the half-tanned man.

Tayrel Kan sneered. "Yes, but it's like sifting through raw sewage. Even if there are pearls somewhere, pretty soon you start questioning your life choices."

"Nevertheless, I have to ask you to put aside your delicate feelings and keep doing it," ordered Myar Mal, fixing the sorcerer with a pointed gaze. "After all, you're no stranger to questionable life choices."

"We can't all be perfect, Kar-vessár," the sorcerer purred, putting his hand on the leader's arm.

Myar Mal huffed and shook it off.

The familiarity in this gesture made me uncomfortable. Who exactly was Tayrel Kan? What was his role in Mespana? And what was his relationship with Myar Mal?

Well, the last one was none of my business, I scolded myself.

I noticed Tayrel Kan giving me a quizzical look and felt heat rising to my face. If he was still reading my thoughts, he'd have a great laugh at my expense.

"There's one more issue we should address," suggested Laik Var. He'd remained silent until now, but at this point, everything about him—his posture, his tone, his turned gaze—screamed disapproval. I'm not sure whether of me,

Myar Mal, Tayrel Kan, or the situation. "The involvement of Tarviss."

"We haven't received any answer from them," said the half-tan almost immediately.

"Of course we haven't," scoffed Tayrel Kan. No one seemed eager to reply, though, so he continued, "What? Didn't we just agree the whole rebellion was a cover? And who would benefit from it more than Tarviss?"

"So, we shouldn't expect their answer?" asked the older guy.

"I think they're going to wait and see, then do whatever fits them best. If we yield, they're gonna come out with their demands. If we lose, they're gonna join the rebels and tear Meon apart. If we win, they're gonna blame us for killing their people and attack anyway. Whatever we do, we're fucked."

"Provided Tarviss has anything to do with that," observed Laik Var.

"Who else?"

"They may just be a bunch of kids with no idea of what they're doing," suggested the dark-eyed woman. "Maybe their plans sounded better on paper, and they've yet to realize they've made a mistake."

"They are a bunch of kids, but someone stands behind them, pulling their strings," insisted Tayrel Kan. "They wouldn't come up with this on their own; it doesn't make any sense! What outcome do they hope for? That we'll just give them our world, let them do as they please because they say so? That's dumb, even for some backward rubes with a superiority complex. No offense, Aldait Han."

"None taken," I assured him.

"That's a provocation," he continued, paying me no mind. "I wouldn't be surprised if the Tarvissi start gathering their armies next to the merge with Dahls right now."

"Should we move our forces there?" asked the older guy.

"No, we need all the people here to quell the rebellion," protested Myar Mal. His face was locked in a dark, determined expression, and once again I was struck by the intensity of his gaze. "But we should warn the Directory—advise them to prepare for evacuation."

"And we should contact Tayan," added Tayrel Kan.

Tayan was another big world merging with Dahls, and the tension between it and Tarviss was what kept Dahls safe for millennia; they were both too busy with themselves to pay any attention to their tiny neighbor.

"The Republic of Yth, the Nine Kingdoms, Muraan country—see what they have to say about Tarviss's supposed movement against us."

"Sanam Il," called the kar-vessár.

The half-tanned guy straightened his back, and I felt stupid joy at the fact I had just learned his name.

"Yes, Myar Mal?"

"Send couriers to Sfal; we need to prepare diplomatic missions to Tayan. And Xin Nyeotl."

"Yes, Myar Mal. What about the rebellion?"

"The plan remains the same," barked Myar Mal sharply. "When is the next sun opening?"

"In sixteen hours," replied Sanam Il.

"We attack in fourteen."

Chapter 6

"WHAT TROUBLES YOU?"

Taneem jerked, almost slipping from the windowsill he was sitting on. He glanced nervously toward Karlan before returning his attention to the outside.

"Nothing," he lied.

The weight of the young lord's hand settled on his shoulder, and he barely stopped himself from flinching.

"You don't have to lie to me, Taneem. I know you don't approve of our actions here."

As if any sane person could approve of them. The corpses of the peons had started rotting in the ditch they had been thrown into, belching noxious gases and feeding swarms of fat, black flies. No one had thought about moving them away or covering them with anything more than a few inches of dirt. And now it was too late. If the Dahlsi didn't kill them, miasma would.

The few who had agreed to serve them were locked up in the cellars, since they couldn't even be sent out to work on rebuilding what Karlan's thugs had burned down.

"It's just…" started Taneem finally. "Not what I expected."

Karlan sighed, then sat on the sill next to him, and this time Taneem wasn't able to hide his flinch.

"War can get messy sometimes," said the young lord with elation. "But you know this is no different than what befell our parents in Nes Peridion. We're doing what they did to us. Repaying our debt, restoring the natural order—"

"We're not in Nes Peridion," cut in Taneem, unable to listen to this crap anymore. "These were not the people who killed our parents."

And even if they were, Taneem couldn't find it in himself to justify the slaughter. He left Nes Peridion cycles ago, trying to build a new life away from violence, bloodshed, and class warfare. The only reason he agreed to follow Karlan was because Kiraes came and fed him some crap about claiming their legacy. He never said a word about murder and… whatever the fuck was happening outside.

Karlan watched him intently, and Taneem clenched his fists. He realized he was shaking.

"If there was any chance of keeping Nes Peridion from the hands of the tyrants, we would be there, you know it."

Excuses, Taneem thought. The sorcerer mumbled something about flickering merges, but the truth was, the people of Nes Peridion were tough—and wary—while those in Maurir spent their entire lives in peace and safety. They never expected the attack.

But he didn't say anything. He just swallowed the bitter taste that had been filling his mouth for days, and nodded. "Of course."

"Besides, old Haneaith is dead. We can only get to his idiot son. And we will."

His tone left no doubt that he regretted the fact. Taneem thought that if Haneaith were still alive, he would grab Karlan by the scruff of his neck and tan his backside before kicking him back to Tarviss. This whole moronic project would die before Dahls even got involved.

A shame his son didn't take after him.

"It will be over soon, my friend," continued Karlan, and Taneem felt something inside him break.

"Yes, as soon as his Dahlsian friends breach the gate and kill us all," he snapped. He realized what had happened, and for a moment his heart stopped, seized by panic. He glanced at Karlan, but the lord seemed too shocked to say anything. With nothing to lose, Taneem decided to press on. "You said it was going to be different. You said they were going to run as soon as they smelled blood." He pointed toward the Dahlsi camp, less than a league from the walls of the mansion. "Well, it doesn't seem to me like they're running."

Karlan composed himself and followed his gesture with a disinterested gaze. His lips flickered in disgust. "They will. If not now, then after the first battle."

A hysterical laughter escaped Taneem's lips. "First battle? Last time you said there wasn't going to be a battle! Make up your mind, Karlan!"

"Enough!" The lord sprung to his feet so suddenly, Taneem reeled in shock. "Even if we'll have to fight—so what? Are you afraid of them, Taneem? A bunch of fags and junkies? They may seem imposing, but I assure you, half of them will flee before dusk, and out of those who remain, half will be too high to pose any danger. We'll crush them, all of them if we have to, and restore the rightful rule in Maurir. After that, in Nes Peridion. Then we'll cut our way to Tarviss, and nothing will stop us!"

He looked manic, with cheeks flushed and teeth bared. But as soon as it flared, his wrath settled. His eyes rested on Taneem, and the young courtier felt smaller than ever before.

"You'll see," added Karlan after a while. "You may doubt me now, but in time you will witness the true glory of Tarviss and regret your lack of faith."

Taneem was clenching his fists so hard, it hurt. He tried to swallow, but his mouth was dry.

"I hope you're right," he croaked.

He wished he could believe it.

Chapter 7

I DIDN'T FOLLOW Myar Mal's suggestion. Instead, I headed straight to my tent. It was a sterile cocoon of silk and protective spells, small and cold, almost suffocating at times. Saral Tal once told me it reminded him of home, but I couldn't fathom why. I tried to adorn it with various trinkets to make it seem less empty. Sadly, my attempts at keeping a plant had been unsuccessful; the magical compression killed everything unfortunate enough to be inside the tent when it folded. A shame, it would be a great help, especially while exploring worlds with no native life.

When I was dismissed, the sun gate was halfway to closing. With Maurir's twenty-something-hour long days, I still had some time before nightfall. But there was not much to do. The bleak landscape discouraged any thought of wandering, and my mind was too troubled for reading. So I lay on my cot, chewing on dried meat, thinking about everything that had happened that day. Going through every conversation, turning around every sentence I'd uttered, smoothing them, finishing them, wondering if there was anything else I could have said to have changed how things turned out.

It was late into the night when I finally managed to fall asleep.

I was awakened by a tingling of magic. For a moment, I lay with my eyes wide open, trying to figure out what was happening.

A doorspell.

I sprang from my cot, twisted my fingers in a cleaning spell, then quickly put on my suit, and grabbed my weapons. When I pulled away the flap, I faced Saral Tal, with no trace of his usual smile.

"Myar Mal wants to see you," he said simply. The coldness of his tone woke me up.

I glanced up: the sun was barely a thread across the sky. But even in the half-light, it was clear no one else was up yet.

"What happened?" I asked.

Saral Tal only shook his head. "You should ask him yourself."

That smothered all the questions I had. Without a word, I followed him to the outskirts of the camp where a peculiar construction stood—half a sphere of white plastic. From what I saw yesterday, we used it to store our kites.

Many people, usually outworlders, believed the kites were the pinnacle of Dahlsian technomagic. In truth, they were flying garbage. Gravity put a limit on the weight that could be lifted, and it topped at about one Dahlsi. There was no way to equip the kites with any kind of useful machinery: motors, steer, weaponry—forget it. They could only glide using natural streams of ae, the magical energy.

Still, we kept them for aerial reconnaissance, and passing messages.

The kites were gone.

The chains we used to keep them down lay crumpled on the ground, while Myar Mal and other vessár-ai paced around, arguing and cursing. It didn't take much to figure out the kites had not been deployed.

A quick glance up revealed black triangles, barely visible against the dark blue sky. Luckily, the skydome in Maurir was pretty solid, otherwise they would have floated Out and disintegrated.

But whatever comfort I drew from this quickly died when I saw the expression on Myar Mal's face. His lips were pressed tight and brows furrowed, casting shadows over his dark, angry eyes.

A figure I hadn't noticed earlier sprang from the ground: a kas'sham. Almost humanlike but strangely proportioned, with a longer torso and shorter limbs and a large, expressionless face. Their uniform was puffed out by fur and cut around the joints, allowing greater range of movement. They strode toward me with the soft, dance-like steps of a natural-born predator. Their pink nose fluttered when they leaned forward and started sniffing.

"Ith not him," the kas'sham announced.

"Are you sure?" asked Myar Mal. His arms were crossed, his face pursed in discontent.

The kas'sham regarded him with disdain—although that seemed like their default look—and drawled, "If you don't trutht my ekthpertithe, why do you even athk?"

Confused, I turned to the kar-vessár. "What's happened?"

He clenched his jaw, but didn't answer. For a moment, no one spoke, and even I could feel the tension rising in the air.

"Someone released our kites at night," said Laik Var from somewhere on the side.

This much I had deduced, but before I spoke, it struck me.

They thought it was me.

At first, I felt nothing—just a vast, all-encompassing emptiness. I was a statue with no feelings or thoughts. All around me, there were real people, watching me, expecting… something.

But what could I give them?

"Aldait Han?" Laik Var's voice broke through my stupor.

"I was ready to die for you," I stammered.

"We wouldn't have let you die," protested the kar-vessár, and his tone commanded me to listen.

"But you didn't bother telling me," I snapped, the betrayal still raw in my memory. "And I did it anyway, and now you—"

"Who else could do it?" Myar Mal cut me off, looking me in the eye for the first time, and I felt like he had poured oil on my smoldering rage.

Yeah, I know! I wanted to scream. You're a perfectly normal, well-spoken man, while I struggle to form a simple sentence. Trust me, I know that better than anyone, dipshit; you don't have to rub it in.

But my jaw was frozen, and my thoughts jumbled. I barely registered the next thing he said.

82

"Give me one person in the entire camp who would have a reason to sabotage our efforts and aid Tarvissi rebels?"

"Why the fuck would I aid them? They were ready to kill me!"

"People do many things out of a misplaced sense of duty," remarked Innam Ar, but I didn't even look at him— my gaze locked with Myar Mal's in a battle I had no hope of winning but couldn't give up.

The kar-vessár's jaw was tight, and his eyes shone with iron resolution. In any other circumstance, the sheer strength of that stare would have paralyzed me. But the one thing capable of breaking through my anxiety was anger.

And I was angry. Angry at the situation, at Dahlsi, Tarvissi; at Myar Mal and his bloody self-assurednes.

"You know what I'd do if I really wanted to sabotage your efforts?" I reached to my pouch and scrabbled until my fingers closed on what I was after. I raised it for all to see.

The Dahlsi around me paled; someone took a step back. A slight tingling suggested that more than one protective spell was cast. Only Myar Mal stood immovable, never turning his eyes from me, cold and calculating as ever, and I hated him so much, it hurt. So, I opened my hand and let a red carai nut fall to the ground, where it got stuck in the damp ash, like a drop of blood.

"Put that in our water supply, and take out half of Mespana in one go."

No one said a word. They were all watching, and my anger started cracking, letting in the first pangs of anxiety. I wasn't going to wait for it to take over. I made a stiff nod, never for a moment turning my eyes from Myar Mal. "With all due respect, Vessár-ai, I'm leaving."

"You can't do that!" protested one of the vessár-ai; I didn't see—or care—who.

"You wanted to send me away yesterday." The bitterness crept into my voice. Bile rose in my throat, and I worried that if I were to stay here much longer, I would throw up. "Should've just kicked me out with all the others. Though I guess that your need for me was more important at the time."

Again, no one answered, so I turned and started walking, a jumble of thoughts and emotions boiling in my mind. I tried to push them all away and formulate a plan. I had to take my personal stuff and then, I don't know, find Tayrel Kan and ask him to open a merge with Espa Solia. Or with whatever. The one we—no, not we, not anymore—Mespana used to move our—their!—forces, was obviously closed.

Laik Var caught up with me. I didn't stop—if anything, I only started taking longer steps, relishing in the way he trotted to keep up. It was childish, and I regretted it later, but at that moment, I didn't care.

"Aldait Han, wait," he pleaded, and following the cycles of conditioning, I obeyed.

"What for?" I growled. They should all be fucking happy to be rid of me, anyway.

"We didn't mean it like that."

"I can't see what else you could mean, Laik Var," I shot back. He didn't deserve it; he was the only one who stood up for me from the beginning, and who bothered trying to stop me now. But he was also the only one here for me to lash out at.

"They're going to check everyone in the camp. And outside, if needed. You were just first in line."

"Because I'm Tarvissi."

A particularly loud huff of air escaped his lips—an attempt to sigh or combat the shortness of breath, I wasn't sure.

"Where are you gonna go anyway? To Tarviss? You think they'll be happy to see you?"

I stopped and turned to him angrily. "It didn't bother you when you sent my family there!"

He raised his hands in a placating gesture. "And for their sake, I ask you to stay."

That finally gave me pause. I crossed my arms and glared, waiting for him to go on.

"Look, we made a mistake," he started. "Deporting all Tarvissi was clearly an overreaction. We didn't know what to do! Didn't know who to trust. So, we decided to distrust everybody."

"A lot of innocent people had to pay for your overreaction."

"I know, Aldait Han. I'm sorry. But if the choice is between our people and others—"

I didn't let him finish. "The thing is, many of those people considered themselves Dahlsi up until the point you kicked them out."

"We were driven by fear, not malice. Look around you." He grabbed my arm pleadingly. "We're not an army. We have never waged a war. Fuck, we have never fought more than a dozen people at a time!"

He was right. Dahls always occupied the precious spot between two powerful worlds, Tarviss and Tayan, being too small to be worth conquering and at the same time too rich for any of their neighbors to allow the other to have them. The situation changed when advancement in magic and technology allowed the Dahlsi to open a merge to the new cluster—thousands of uninhabited worlds ripe for the taking.

But Dahls had yet to establish its own military force that others would have to reckon with. Mespana was created ten cycles ago—if it were a man, it would be just reaching adulthood—and it had less than two thousand people trained to work in duos or trios, in dozens at most. Even with the most advanced magic and technology at our disposal, both Tarviss and Tayan could crush us with sheer numbers.

Not to mention the complete lack of military experience on our side. Fuck, we weren't even real soldiers! Our primary job was documenting new worlds. We were only called when things got violent because, well, there was no one else.

Still, we were not an army.

"Tarviss cannot wage war against you without facing retribution from Tayan," I protested, inciting a bitter laugh from my commander.

"Unless Tarviss and Tayan band together and rip us to pieces. There are plenty of worlds for them to share," he answered mirthlessly.

"In that case, a few hundred Tarvissi living in colonies won't make any difference."

He sighed and rubbed his forehead. "We both know it. And perhaps other people know it too, but they're afraid. Can you blame them?"

No. For me, war was a thing from old legends. I fought almost every day, but it was all skirmishes, man against man. But the clash of two armies? Hundreds, thousands, of people standing against each other? That was something else. Something I read about but never imagined I would take part in. And it terrified me.

So no, I couldn't blame the Dahlsi for fearing it too, and doing anything in their power to avoid it.

I shook my head, resignation heavy in my chest. "What do I have to do with it?"

"You are here. I convinced some people you can be trusted. As a member of Mespana, as my subordinate. As a Dahlsi. If you can uphold this trust, maybe in time… people will see that Tarvissi doesn't have to mean a traitor. Maybe that will make them more amenable to letting your family and other Tarvissi back to Dahls."

"That's a lot of maybes, Laik Var."

"None of this will happen if you leave now."

"What can I do?"

"Stay. I know it's going to be hard, and I know it's not fair. But nothing worth fighting for ever is."

Chapter 8

SO I STAYED. In Mespana, I mean. I actually left the camp to wander the hills alone; I didn't feel like witnessing Myar Mal's attempts to find the culprit.

Mostly, I thought about Laik Var's words.

Dahlsian society differed from the Tarvissian. It was egalitarian, so all citizens, including those of foreign descent, held equal power; but since it was spread among so many, how much could be carried by one person?

Or not strictly power but influence? I knew myself; I wasn't charismatic. Even at the best of times, surrounded by people I was familiar—and comfortable—with, I was not cut out to be a leader. But now Laik Var wanted me to be more—an example. The walking representation of a perfect Dahlsi-Tarvissi. Could I be that?

Could anyone be that?

Our people were different, no doubt. But at the same time, I thought we had more in common than we wanted to admit. Our ancestors all came from old Karir, right after it was destroyed by dark elves ten thousand cycles ago. We both had the same straight black hair and bright, upturned eyes. The same wide faces with pronounced features. Even our languages were similar—as long as one ignored the pronunciation—with identical grammatical structures and comparable words. But while we grew tall and tanned under the sun, Dahlsi became pale and frail in their sheltered city. Still, we were much closer to each other than any of us were to the pale, ethereal Tayani or yellow-eyed Xzsim.

So, what made it so hard to live together?

Arbitrary bullshit, I concluded.

"You're right."

I jerked in surprise and turned to see Tayrel Kan. I was so lost in my contemplation that I hadn't even noticed him before.

"Were you reading my thoughts?" I asked.

He gave me his shrug-wave. "I wouldn't if you weren't screaming them around."

I started wondering if he was always doing it. It was considered rude, but he didn't seem like a person who'd care. I felt sorry for everything I'd thought about him when we first met.

He waved his hand dismissively. "Oh, don't worry, Aldait Han; I'm used to people thinking shit about me."

His words did nothing to diminish my embarrassment, but with him reading my mind, there was no point dragging out this conversation. I just put up the mental defenses I'd been taught when joining Mespana.

Tayrel Kan paused next to me. From somewhere, probably outside of the three-dimensional space, he procured two pieces of reed stuffed with dried herbs and handed me one. Tchalka, as they called it (or tsalka, if you're

Dahlsi). I rarely indulged in such things, but then, following some strange impulse, I took the reed and let the sorcerer light it with a flicker of his fingers. The smoke scratched unpleasantly at the back of my throat. I coughed, trying to clear it, and before I knew what was happening, I went into a fit, almost throwing up in the process.

"Careful there. It's strong stuff," he warned too late, with obvious amusement.

My fit soon passed, and I felt at ease; all worries melted away in a cloud of narcotic smoke.

"So, did my screamed thoughts get you out of your hole?" I asked. My head was spinning, and I was trying my hardest not to sway. He hadn't been kidding with his warning.

"I just wanted to show you something."

Holding the tchalka in his left hand, he rolled up his right sleeve and presented it to me. Inside, I noticed a curious mark: a triangle divided into four smaller ones, the one inside red and the others white; the whole things encircled by Dahlsian letters.

"Kanven Sandeyron," he said, not giving me the chance to read it. Sandeyron meant "company", but the name meant nothing to me, although I thought I'd heard it before. He was quick to elaborate, "The bastards that adopted me."

I felt like I'd been punched in the gut.

The companies weren't driven by compassion while adopting unwanted children. They needed to test their inventions somehow, and if things went wrong, well, there would be no one left to complain. I only had a very vague idea of what happened inside—I guessed only those who'd been there knew the truth—but that was enough to make my skin crawl at the very mention.

"What I was about to say," he picked up, face blank, almost like he wasn't talking about his own past—like it was someone else who had to go through this. "Is that sometimes it doesn't matter whose symbol you wear. Sometimes you don't fight for someone. You just happen to find yourself on the same side."

"And then you can ignore your associates?" I asked.

"As long as they don't stand in your way. I mean, look around."

I did as he said. We were some distance from the camp, but on the outskirts, a few people busied themselves preparing meals, repairing equipment, or socialising. Mostly non-Dahlsi and nonhumans, which made it painfully clear how few of us were there.

"You think any of them give a shit about Dahls? Most of them don't even speak Dahlsi-é. Shit, I'm sure you don't speak Dahlsi-é."

"I speak perfect Dahlsi-é," I responded proudly in his native tongue.

Dahlsi-é and Tarvissi-é were practically my mother tongues, but I actually spoke five languages. I enjoyed learning, and at some point, I focused on them, imagining they would help with my communicative difficulties. But in the end, nothing could help me if I had nothing to say.

"Yes, if one can overlook that terrible accent," he laughed.

That was the best irony of it all: I spoke Dahlsi-é with the melodic accent of Tarviss, never quite able to master the hard r the real Dahlsi use; just as I spoke Tarvissi-é with the hard accent of Dahls, sometimes skipping consonants or even switching sh to s.

Linguistic divagations aside, did he have a point?

Did I care about Dahls?

Definitely not for the almost mythical world that linked Meon Cluster with the rest of the universe. But Meon itself was my home, and it was inextricably connected with Dahls. At the same time, it was so much more—a mosaic of species and cultures coexisting in near-perfect harmony only possible thanks to the advanced status of Dahlsian society. No one else could organize it like that. Dahlsi knew their way of life was too specific to impose on other people, so they mostly left the colonists to our own devices. They were merely standing guard, checking out everyone who wanted to enter, shielding us all from crime, wars, exploitation, and other calamities that plagued other worlds.

So yes, I did care about Meon. And I knew whatever change would come, it would only be for the worse.

Pain flared in my fingers and I opened my hand, dropping the butt of my tchalka to the ground. Most of the smoke escaped, and Tayrel Kan was looking at me with reproach.

"You just wasted it," he scolded.

"Well, I'm surprised you even have that. I've heard you prefer stronger things," I retorted, realizing too late that he could take offense.

He only snorted. "Myar Mal insists I stay away from the strong stuff for a while. Which is rich coming from someone who pops vaka like candy. He must be hallucinating half the time with the amount of proper sleep he's getting. Anyway, that's the only thing I'm allowed now. The only thing that keeps me sane." He was already lighting another tchalka. "That reminds me," he let out a puff of smoke. "Did you even try my wand?"

Only then did I remember his gift. A brand new one, courtesy of Kanven Sandeyron. That's where I heard the name.

"I didn't have time," I murmured apologetically.

He arched an eyebrow. "You know, most Dahlsi would piss themselves in glee if they could put their hands on it."

I hummed, not sure what to say. It was an impressive feat of Dahlsian technomagic, no doubt, but so were kites, bikes, tents, and dozens of other things. If I got excited about every one of them, I wouldn't have time for anything else.

He shook his head slowly. "You are incredible."

Well, I was not Dahlsi. But now that he mentioned it, another thing occurred to me.

"Why did you even give it to me?"

He chuckled. "I just wanted to help you out a little." He paused to take another whiff before continuing. "I knew they weren't going to let you bring it into the mansion."

"I didn't notice," I murmured, embarrassed. How could I not notice? When the Tarvissi took my old wand, I was so preoccupied by their sheer presence, I didn't even think about how I gave it to Laik Var earlier.

"Yeah, I know." There was no judgment in his voice, only a small sardonic smirk dancing on his lips. I started suspecting his face was permanently contorted; it was his neutral expression.

Still, I was feeling stupid, and I scrambled for something to defend myself. "I think I had more pressing things on my mind. I was almost killed."

"It's all right," he assured me, looking at me seriously. For the first time, I think. "The spell was meant to keep you focused on the task. Not questioning anything."

If anyone asked, I'd say they didn't need a spell. I could focus pretty well, and when I did, the whole world might stop existing.

"Besides," he continued, "no offense, but you never struck me as perceptive."

I scoffed. "Thanks."

"I don't mean you're stupid. You just seem like more of a… reflective type."

He was probably right. Except—

"What do you even know about me?" I asked. We met less than a Dahlsian day ago. Was he watching me? Had they all been spying on me before that little mission, trying to figure out if I was the right man for the job? But it was only a few days since the revolution started, and I spent most of them in Sorox.

Did they have spies there?

Tayrel Kan looked at me and his smirk widened. "Apart from your thoughts I overhear?"

I bit back the curse. "I thought that's considered rude."

He spread his arms, and his smile took on an almost disarming look. "Let no one accuse me of being polite."

I didn't know what to say. My face was hot with embarrassment, but at the same time, I felt a growing annoyance. And then I realized my defenses had slipped again, and he was probably perfectly aware of everything I had been thinking.

His smile faltered a little, and he added, "But you know, that works both ways. You can be straight with me, and I won't hold it against you."

I paused to consider his proposal. There was one thing…

"Can I ask you an awkward question?"

His face almost split in half by the wideness of his grin. "You want the names of the vessár-ai?"

I grit my teeth, my face burning like a bonfire. "Is there any chance to convince you not to tell anyone?"

"I won't. But you know, I wasn't the only sorcerer in the room."

I cursed mentally, and he laughed.

"That may actually be to our advantage," he added thoughtfully after a while. "Stand still."

I wasn't planning on moving and wasn't even sure why I would, but then pain flashed inside my head, in a place I didn't realize could hurt. It blinded me for a heartbeat, but when it passed, my head was filled with new knowledge. I became familiar with every vessár in Mespana—their faces, names, specialties, even some saucy gossip I'd rather not have known. And it didn't seem like it was going to vanish anytime soon.

"Thanks," I murmured.

"You're welcome," he answered offhandedly.

He looked away and focused on his tchalka, giving me a moment to digest the newly-found knowledge. There were all kinds of facts, from the genuinely helpful—like Innam Ar-Leig, vessár of the First Cohort and the man responsible for training fresh recruits, having a degree in psychology and profiling us all before graduation—to useless but interesting trivia, like Sanam Il-Asa being a big Tarviss sympathizer and sporting a beard up until the rebellion started.

Curiously, there was nothing about Myar Mal. I was about to ask about it, when Tayrel Kan spoke.

"I forgot how boring Mespana is. It's all humanoids here. You won't even find a bloody besseq."

"Besheq are not fighting species," I replied, inadvertently accenting the correct name rather than bastardized Dahlsian version. The lithe, tentacled creatures I often encountered on the market, selling palm sap or baskets, rather gave an impression of being ready to collapse from a hard shove.

"Unless you get slashed with one of those tentacles. Hey, you wanna hear a funny thing?"

I murmured something noncommittal, not sure if I wanted to.

"Besseq are not naturally venomous. They absorb poison from some shit they eat in Van-Yian. The more they have, the more potent their venom is. But in lower doses," he sent me a sideways glance, smiling mischievously, "some people would describe their touch as arousing."

I coughed nervously. "I wouldn't know anything about it," I murmured.

Tayrel Kan chuckled. "I wouldn't expect you to."

The remark stung. Despite the deepest wish to end this line of conversation as soon as possible, I couldn't help but protest, "Not being attracted to nonhumans doesn't make me a speciesist. I'm just not interested."

"Oh. What are you interested in, then?" Now his voice was lascivious as he stared at me even more slyly.

Laik Var's warnings echoed in my head.

I shuddered and grit my teeth, with no idea in the worlds how to react.

"I'm… not…" I stammered finally.

His smile fell, and the look in his eyes shifted to more curious. "Not at all?"

"No," I said sharply, hoping he'd get the point and shut up.

"Men? Women?"

"Nope."

His smile returned. "Yourself?"

My face was so hot, I was afraid my skin may start to peel off. At the same time, I started feeling first pangs of annoyance. Sex was not something that was discussed in our culture, and I was still not comfortable with the casualness Dahlsi treated it with. "No."

Another hum. "So you never felt that particular itch in your wand?"

It took me a moment to realize that he hadn't suddenly switched to talking about magic.

He waved his hand and said lightly, "That was a euphemism, I meant your dick."

Oh. Talking about itch and sex in one sentence made me think of pubic lice.

Before I could say anything, Tayrel Kan choked on his smoke and twisted his fingers. A familiar tingle ran over my body. I winced, not sure whether out of embarrassment or anger.

I could cast cleaning spells myself. And I knew you didn't mean it that way. I'm not that stupid.

As if struck by a sudden thought, the sorcerer asked, "But you do know you can do it yourself?"

"Yes, Tayrel Kan, I got some education, imagine that," I said, now only annoyed.

"They taught masturbation in your school?"

"No! It's just..." Talking about education was easier than talking about my pitiful adventures and the realization I had absolutely no interest in bringing them to fruition. "Our teacher was very open, and she allowed us to ask anything we wanted. So, naturally, most kids asked about sex."

Especially since it wasn't something our parents talked about.

He hummed again, then went silent for a moment. My body was tense as I waited for him to speak. Finally, I couldn't take it anymore.

"Okay, just say what you have to say, and let's get this over with," I snapped.

He arched his eyebrow. "What do you expect me to say?"

What everyone else had said. "That I'm stunted."

I thought saying the words myself would make them sting less, but they only left a bitter taste in my mouth.

Tayrel Kan looked me in the eye. "You are not stunted."

I tensed, not sure how to react. I was so used to scrutiny, I never imagined someone might... not do it.

I cleared my throat, trying to push through the tightness. "Do you really think so?"

"Sex doesn't make anyone mature. Or smart. It's just a bit of fun to temporarily kill existential dread. Or pass it onto others, I guess. People experience it in different ways, and some choose not to experience it at all. There's nothing wrong with that."

My tension melted, and a strange warmth spread in my chest. So far, the kindest reactions were assurances I would learn to love my wife (from Tarvissi) or musings I hadn't met the right person (from everyone else). He was the first one ever who just accepted me for who I was.

Especially since he was, well…

"I have a lot of existential dread to kill," he said lightly. I wasn't sure if he was joking. Luckily, he quickly changed the subject. "But I have to say, your school sounds pretty cool."

"It wasn't a real school," I explained. "Just a woman, Girana Da-Vai, with a mission to make our lives better. She was a bit of everything: official, healer, sorcerer. And a teacher. She used to gather all the kids in the old Peridion mansion to teach us to read, write, count. She let us ask whatever we wanted."

"What did you ask her about?"

"The universe," I replied without hesitation. "I was always interested in what lies beyond. Dahls and other worlds, anything really."

"So, I guess you're pretty happy in Mespana."

Was I? I thought so. Even apart from visiting a different world every couple of days, it was nice to leave people behind with their problems and just be myself for a while.

But it was equally nice to return to the city, the warm apartment, and the fancy restaurants. And with Mespana's salary, I rarely had to worry about the prices.

"Sometimes I dream about traveling beyond," I said. "To some of the old worlds. See all the wonders I only read about. Ancient civilizations and all that."

"Why don't you?"

I smiled wistfully. "I can't. Since my dad died, there's no man in the house, so I have to help my mom and sister every once in a while. Do the heavy lifting."

Then I remembered there was no home for me to go back to, and I felt my heart clench. Before I succumbed to despair, though, the sorcerer came up with another question.

"Have you tried to consider this an opportunity?"

"What do you mean?"

"There's nothing holding you back now. You can go wherever you want, do whatever you want."

I wished it were that simple, but I still had a family to care for. I hoped, in time, they would be able to return, although I knew our lives would never be the same. We could start again somewhere, maybe even in Sfal. Although, I wasn't sure my mom would agree to live in the city. I wasn't keen on it either. Don't get me wrong, I liked the city sometimes. But I equally liked getting back to the country, the simple house built by my dad from scratch, and fields green with vye and gilded with maak. I needed balance, I guess. A little bit of the city, a little bit of the country, and a new world to explore every once in a while. If I could travel farther away, that would be a bonus, but I was fine.

Except now my comfortable existence was over. Our farm was deserted, and my family banished. And it seemed like I made an enemy out of the kar-vessár.

Now that my head had cooled down, I realized I acted like a total fool. My insides clenched and, not for the first time in my life, I wished I could run away, leaving everything and everyone behind.

Desperate for distraction, I looked to the plain before me and tried summoning the memories of it from before the rebellion. Before I knew it, I started talking, not sure if to myself or to the sorcerer. "Around this time, namia would flower. It has these big, purple flowers you can spot from the other side of the world. Maak and sabha would be fruiting together—tall, proud maak with green threads of sabha trailing between the stalks, heavy with berries. Coclaxi trees from Llodra would shed their petals, filling the air with their scent."

"I don't even know what that shit is," he laughed, sending a pang of anger through my chest. "I'm not the best person to talk about such things with. Last time I was here, I couldn't breathe from all the pollen. I think one good thing the whole rebellion brought was clearing the air."

"How can you live like this?" I sized up at his pale, lithe figure and thought, for all the similarities, we may as well be coming from different species. "You left your city, settled outside, and yet you keep to yourself, eat the synthetic shit. Most of you can't even breathe without those masks. And you do nothing about it!"

"Arbitrary bullshit," he replied smoothly. "I can't do anything about how I was raised. I still remember seeing an old guy walking outside for the first time and getting anaphylaxis from the pollen. He died before anyone knew what was happening. So sorry, but I'm not parting with my mask. And I can't help being disgusted when I see you eating gods-know-what."

"Have you ever tried natural food?"

"No, and I'm not going to. I hate this sludge as much as you do, but at least it's safe."

"Come on, you're a sorcerer!"

"It's hard to think of a proper spell when you're choking."

"There must be a way around this."

"They say it gets better once you survive your fifteenth shock," he joked, but then his smile faded, and he sighed deeply. "Look, maybe there is a way, but we don't know it, and doing research is rather tricky when every misstep can cost someone their life. So, I guess we're stuck with it." The corner of his lips curled up again, and he sent me a mischievous glance. "But you know, certain proteins get transferred into semen, so in a way, I can taste natural food."

I felt the heat rising to my face, and this time, he actually laughed before patting me on the shoulder.

"I'd love to stand here and chat with you all day, but I'm afraid my helpers have finished with the kites."

He looked pointedly at the sky. I followed his gaze and noticed that, indeed, there were no more stray triangles dotting it.

"I better go check on them before they get any silly ideas."

"Which cohort are you even in?" I asked, remembering his lack of insignia.

He wave-shrugged. "My own."

I arched my eyebrow, prompting him to elaborate.

"I've been to a few, but no one could put up with me, so now I answer directly to Myar Mal," he explained.

"You don't even have a partner?"

As soon as the words left my mouth, something in Tayrel Kan shifted. His smirk all but vanished, his eyes darkened, his whole posture became rigid. Had I imagined it, or had his scars become deeper, angrier?

"No." His voice was low, and strangely hollow and my insides clenched in anxiety. Have I misstepped? "I don't have a partner."

As quickly as the change came, it disappeared, and he reached for another tchalka. "But now I'm working on this super-secret project for Myar Mal. I'm not supposed to talk about it."

He fixed his eyes on me, and I got a feeling he was expecting something. But I didn't know what, and it's not like I was about to pry into Myar Mal's super-secret project. I smiled awkwardly and nodded.

He turned his head and continued. "Anyway, he gave me those Llodran vhariars to help. Sa'tuir, Sa'nuum, and Sa'taba. I don't even know what to call them; they only use single names. It's awkward."

"Now I feel discriminated against," I joked lamely. "I had to take a middle name when I applied to work for Mespana. I accidentally got it after my father because, at the time, no one in our colony understood the Dahlsian naming system."

To be fair, it was convoluted. People inherited surnames—which they almost never used—after the parent of their own sex and their middle names from the first syllable of the first name of the parent of the opposite sex. So, sons had the surnames of their fathers, and their middle names derived from their mothers' first names. I guess for a culture with no concept of marriage, that was the only way to denote both parents. It always seemed pointlessly complicated to me, and when I joined in, I was encouraging people to call me Aldait—I had no hope for Aldeaith—but no one did. So, I gave up.

"Why don't you change it?" he asked, sounding serious.

"I dunno. I just don't care enough."

"Names are important, Aldait Han," he stated with sudden gravity. "They tell us who we are and where we came from."

"Aldeaith," I smiled. "That's my name."

I only got a few minutes of peace before another voice reached me.

"You're making friends."

I turned around to see Malyn Tol standing a few paces behind me, her hands clasped in the same way mine were when I tried to stop myself from fidgeting. She must have been watching me talk with Tayrel Kan, and I wondered why she hadn't come out.

"Be careful with him," she said finally. I blinked, suddenly realizing I was gaping at her wordlessly for a few seconds. "He's not the best person to have around."

I dared a peek back, but the sorcerer had already disappeared. I recalled Laik Var giving me a similar warning the first time I had spoken with him. And Myar

Mal's contempt as he shook his hand off. But I also couldn't think of any time when Tayrel Kan said anything wrong or hurtful to me, which made him one of a few.

"Is it because of him, or because of what other people are saying?" I wondered, realizing too late how that might have sounded.

Luckily, Malyn Tol didn't seem offended. She shook her head. "I'm not sure myself. It seems like it's going on forever, and I never like prying into other people's lives. But I noticed you can be..." She waved her hand as if not sure what to say.

"Oblivious?" I suggested.

Her lips curled into a smile. "Innocent," she corrected. "I don't want him to take advantage of you."

"We were just talking. About our duties, lives, and so on."

"That's how it starts."

"How what starts?"

"Well... you know."

"Oh." I felt myself blushing again. "I'm not interested in such things."

I cursed mentally, once again regretting my words as soon as they left my mouth. Speaking with Tayrel Kan put me at ease. I forgot myself.

I turned away to face the horizon. "I mean, not with men," I explained. "Just... not at all."

She hummed, and I wasn't sure if she believed me or not.

"Look, I'll be careful," I promised, just to end this line of conversation.

She sighed. "No, Aldait Han, I'm sorry. Maybe you're right and I'm biased. And anyway, it's not my place to tell you what to do and who to talk with."

"I do appreciate your concern, though." I wasn't convinced if I did, but it seemed like the right thing to say.

Malyn Tol smiled awkwardly. "It's not why I'm here, anyway. I heard what happened." She paused and sucked in a deep breath. "I wanted to say that what you did was very, very stupid."

I cringed, flooded by the memories of my morning blunder. Tayrel Kan did a pretty good job of making me forget.

"How do you know?" I stammered.

She sent me an admonishing look. "Saral Tal has a wand for a tongue, shooting words wherever he goes. Prepare to soon have the entire camp buzzing."

Should I laugh or cry? I did neither, and after a moment, Malyn Tol picked up.

"If it makes you feel better, Argan Am says you were right, and that the prick deserved it. I think he has issues with our kar-vessár."

"What issues?"

"I don't know. You can ask him."

I hummed, disappointed, knowing full well I'd never do it.

She sighed again. "He doesn't bite. None of us do."

My cheeks burned and lowered my head, still not finding anything to say. Idiot.

"Also, I wanted to give you something."

She extended her hand toward me, holding a small, crocheted doll. It was rather plain—a black suit, white face, black top that could be either short hair or a cap, and pale green dots for eyes and the rank.

"When I was working at the Immigration Office, there was a Tarvissian woman; she was making dolls like these," explained Malyn Tol. "I asked her to teach me, and she did. It's very relaxing. I make so many, I have to give them away. Or, rather, throw them at everyone around me." She gave a small, slightly awkward laugh. "You're the only one who hasn't got any yet, so here you go."

She pushed the doll at me, leaving me no choice but to take it. I trailed my finger over the front, feeling the smoothness of the yarn. It was different from what I was used to, but the pattern was unmistakable.

My heart clenched, and before I knew it, the words spewed out of my mouth. "My sister made them, too. In old Tarviss, they were some form of worship, so obviously, our parents weren't fond of them. But Aeva thought they were cute. She asked our mother to teach her. Whenever there was spare yarn, she would make one. We would play with them for a while, and then our mother would undo them and use the yarn to fix our clothing or something."

Malyn Tol's hand settled on my elbow, sending shiver up my arm. Without lifting my gaze, I asked jokingly, "Was that supposed to be me?"

The doll didn't have any facial features, but the eyes were green like mine, and without others to compare the size to, who could tell?

Malyn Tol paused and cocked her head. "I don't actually know. I just wanted to make one of us. It might as well be you."

Her words startled me, but as I kept studying the doll... I felt she might have been right.

Chapter 9

MYAR MAL LOOKED up from the paper he was holding.

"Laik Var," he started, leaning back in his chair. "You do know that even if he hadn't decided to quit, the earlier incident would be enough to get him dismissed?"

"I convinced him to stay," said the elder man without blinking.

"You convinced him to stay," repeated the kar-vessár acridly. "Has it occurred to you to convince me to keep him? Or the Directory?"

"He's a good soldier. He had a lapse of reason, that's all."

"That lapse could have cost someone their life."

Laik Var scoffed. "He's not the only person in Mespana who eats nuts."

"He's the only one to wave them around."

Laik Var didn't answer, his eyes fixed on the leader with unshakable conviction, lips pressed into a tight line. But Myar Mal didn't let it shake him; he answered with a gaze just as hard, dropping it only for a moment as he leaned forward and rested his elbows on the desk.

"Look," he said finally, softer than before. "This boy has nothing to do with us. Don't drag him into this."

Laik Var's lips twitched. "Not everything is about you. Kar-vessár." He threw in the title after a moment's hesitation as if belatedly realizing he owed his superior a modicum of respect.

"Isn't it?" asked Myar Mal with a small, bitter smile. He wished he could believe it. He was never the one to beg for acceptance, but he wouldn't mind if his efforts were appreciated, just once. But Laik Var didn't even answer, and for a moment, the two men glared at each other in a silent battle.

Finally, the kar-vessár leaned back and sighed again.

"Very well, then."

If there was one thing he loathed, it was defeat.

Chapter 10

THERE WAS NO further announcement. It was maddening. I liked having my life ordered—even if that order meant I could die tomorrow. I think my brain didn't fully comprehend the idea; death was just an empty word, even when I faced danger every day. But the uncertainty filled me with dread.

Night had fallen with no further development, and with a heavy heart, I went to my place and tried to catch a couple of hours of rest.

But, once again, I was awakened. This time much less gently by Laik Var barging into my tent without warning.

"Put that on," he commanded, pushing something into my hands.

The artificial light was dim at this hour and sleep still muddled my brain, so it took me a while to realize what it was. A pale-blue sash. A sign of nami vessár, leader's right hand.

Laik Var was out before I could say anything, so I hurriedly put on my suit and the sash. It was long and I worried it might hang loose, but as soon as I hooked it up, it tightened and clung to my body. I followed my vessár, still trying to blink away the sleepiness. Laik Var already had a nami: an outworlder woman named Arda Nahs, but I haven't seen her recently; she must have stayed in Sfal. I wanted to ask about her, but Laik Var was ahead of me, so I shrugged it off. He probably needed someone to fill her role here.

Outside was bathed in darkness, the world's peculiar sun not even visible yet.

"What's happening?" I asked Laik Var after catching up with him.

"We're attacking," he answered in half-whisper.

But the camp was still, and it seemed most of our people were asleep. So, we weren't going to charge like in old legends. What then? Send a small group inside to eliminate the leaders? Blow the mansion up? Open the gates? I wanted to ask, but two shadows grew before me, barring my way. The white face-masks flashed in the darkness.

"I'm sorry, Aldait Han, but we were told to check your belongings," said one of the shadows, a man judging from the voice, but too tall to be a real Dahlsi. When he moved, I noticed a yellow armband—medical team.

The memory of my yesterday's stunt flooded my mind, and my guts twisted in shame.

"Is that necessary?" I asked, grinding my teeth. But I didn't hope for mercy.

"If you please."

I unbuckled my belt and handed it to him. It had a couple of pouches, used to carry everything from tools and weapons to medication and food. Usually, there was no problem with it—people around me were well adjusted to living with allergies, and ubiquitous decontamination spells reduced the risk to the minimum. However, given my recent behavior, I didn't blame them for caution.

Still, I watched wistfully as my stash of nuts and dried meats was thrown into the bag marked for incineration.

"After the battle, submit all potentially dangerous products to the medical team. Kar-vessár's order."

I twitched in surprise. Over my dead body, I thought. If all went well, after the battle we were bound to return to Sfal, and there was no way to prohibit possession of potentially dangerous products there. The whole world was one big allergen!

"Also, your adrenaline has expired," noticed the second man, this one Dahlsi-short, going through my set of medications.

I rolled my eyes. "It's not like I need it."

"Someone else might. After the battle, go to the field hospital and collect a fresh sample."

"All right," I said, knowing full well I would never do it. I was not allergic to anything, and if someone else was, they probably had their own stock. Having me carry it until it expired was a waste of resources. But I didn't like arguing, so I nodded.

The first man returned my belt and stepped aside, letting me through. Only then did I notice that all the vessár-ai and their nami-ai had gathered at the edge of the camp, and an uncomfortable number of them were staring at me. I caught hushed but angry whispers and turned to see someone arguing with Myar Mal, his silver sash blinking as he gestured wildly. But then kar-vessár said something, and the man snapped his mouth shut and glared at me. My guts knotted into a tight ball.

But my attention quickly shifted as something flashed in the darkness, round and brighter than the vessár-ai sashes. Eyes, I realized, big and bright like flashlights. Kas'shams.

There were a few of them in Mespana, although I never got to work with any. Despite my nation's legendary prejudice, I had nothing against them. But then and there, seeing their tight, lithe silhouettes, almost melting in with the darkness, I felt uneasy. Kas'shams were obligate carnivores, often employed as headhunters for their predation skills. And they were on our side. Logically, there was no reason for me to be afraid. And yet… they were predators, no doubt. Everything about them screamed it— their movements, their long, nimble limbs with sheathed claws, their big eyes, and mouths filled with sabre-like teeth. Yes, they were predators, and I felt like prey.

Absurd, I knew. Maybe Tayrel Kan had a point. Maybe, despite cycles spent in the colonies, I was a little bit speciesist.

"Aldait Han."

I turned around to face the kar-vessár. He held a pair of binoculars; he must have been watching the mansion.

"Myar Mal," I replied, nodding slightly.

"Congratulations on your promotion," he said. His voice seemed friendly enough and the message innocent, but it sent a chill down my spine.

"Thank you, kar-vessár." I nodded again, and instead of stopping, had to add, "Though I have to say, I'm surprised you allowed it."

"And why is that?" His lips quirked, but his eyes remained cold. "It's a perfect solution. Laik Var gets to show people how much he trusts you, I get to keep an eye on you. Everyone is happy. But let me tell you something." His smile disappeared, and his gaze turned even colder. "I have the lives of almost a great gross of Dahlsi in my hands. Anyone who wants to take them will have to go through me. Do you understand?"

I nodded, unable to speak. And then, despite my best efforts, I failed to stifle a yawn.

Myar Mal looked at me with disdain. "Do I bore you?"

"No, Myar Mal. I'm sorry; I wasn't prepared to be up so early."

"Well, some of us haven't slept in three days, but please, tell me more about your plight."

He turned back to watching the manor through the binoculars, but I could feel him rolling eyes at me. I swallowed a curse.

I sensed movement on my left and felt something pressed into my hand. I looked down to see a large, white pill in a transparent wrap.

"Vaka," explained Laik Var. "Keep it under your tongue until it melts."

I knew how to use it, but for once I kept my protests to myself. The pill filled my mouth with acrid foam, and almost immediately, I felt the surge of energy. My mind reached an almost painful clarity. The world around me became brighter, lines sharper, sounds louder. Even the darkness seemed less imposing, although that might have been an illusion. Vaka was a drug, after all.

Then it hit me. It was today. We were going to battle. And we were going to fight… my people.

Could I do it? I was one of them, after all. Tarvissi by blood, and, for the most part, upbringing. They were tall like me, and tan like me, they spoke my language, they pronounced my name properly, for gods' sake!

But on the other hand, I didn't know most of them, and those I knew were assholes. They were more than ready to kill me and send my mangled corpse back as a message. Logically, I had no reason to hesitate.

The funny thing was, I wouldn't even think about it if I hadn't been constantly questioned.

A few more shadows joined us. My vision adjusted so well that I could probably count them if I squinted. But before I did, Myar Mal ordered, using a particular shouting whisper only natural-born leaders can successfully pull off, "All right, you know what to do. Go."

The lantern eyes flickered and disappeared, leaving nothing but shadows behind. Soon, even those melted into the darkness.

Laik Var shoved a pair of binoculars into my hands, and I scrambled to put them to use. They were enchanted, of course, dissolving total darkness into shades of gray. Memories of Sorox flooded my mind, and I fought to return to the present. Then something jumped, seemingly with enough force to land in front of me, and I jerked instinctively. It was just Myar Mal adjusting his elbow. The movement was exaggerated by the binoculars; probably to make up for the lack of colors.

With a thumping heart, I turned toward the field between us and the mansion. Descending on all fours, the kas'shams half-ran, half-crept along the ground, with the tips of their tails curved upward. They crossed the alarm spells, doubtlessly alerting the rebels inside, though at least the darkness shielded them from the crossbowmen. I didn't think Tarvissi had access to magic-vision devices.

I briefly wondered how the kas'shams were going to scale the walls. From what I saw, they didn't carry ladders or any other tools. Before I mustered the courage to ask, the first of them had reached the mansion.

And leaped.

Huh. Apparently, fifteen feet meant nothing for kas'shams. They landed effortlessly on the roof and the rest soon followed: some made it on the first try, others clutched the lower windows and climbed, a few bounced back and fell gracefully to the ground before trying again. But eventually, all of them managed to get in.

Sounds of battle erupted, carried far by clear morning air. The clash of metal, the roar of spells, the high-pitched, inhuman cries. I tried to imagine what was happening inside. Wands were slower than swords, and kas'sham didn't carry any other weapons. But they did have natural tools—claws and teeth, speed and agility unmatched by any human being. Not to mention the element of surprise. Still, I doubted they could deal with all the rebels on their own.

"They don't have to deal with them. All they have to do is open the gate," I heard behind me. I turned around to face Tayrel Kan. He didn't bother with binoculars, but his eyes gleamed and I knew he cast his own spell.

"How are they doing there?" asked Myar Mal. Spying spell then? Like the one they had cast on me when they sent me inside?

"Not well, kar-vessár," replied the sorcerer. "I think they could use some help."

Myar Mal nodded and gestured to one of the vessár-ai. "Kiarn At, deploy kites."

"Yes, Myar Mal."

Immediately, dozens of kites took off behind us, probably awaiting telepathic order since the very beginning. They glided toward the mansion and stopped just above the outer walls. Now, even without the binoculars, I saw green and blue beams shooting down. And then the explosion.

On the wrong side.

"Fuck!" yelled Myar Mal.

I glanced aside to see his face twisted with anger, teeth bared, hands clenched on the binoculars so hard, his knuckles turned white. The explosion was small, but the shock-wave toppled over two machines other than the one it hit, and their riders fell. Most likely to their deaths.

"Tarvissian magical weapons in action," remarked Tayrel Kan with almost clinical interest.

"You said the only magical weapon they have are crystal balls." Kar-vessár glared at me with anger, and I flinched involuntarily.

"That's all I saw," I confirmed, confident in my report, yet still feeling a pang of guilt.

"Care to explain how the fuck they got them so high?" he screamed, waving his hand toward the mansion. Two more kites fell, and others scattered around like a flock of birds.

"I don't know, Myar Mal." A far-fetched idea came to my mind and before I could think better, I sputtered, "They may be using slings."

"What?"

His face showed no sign of comprehension. No wonder, I scolded myself, he probably spent his entire childhood inside the City.

"A piece of rope with a leather pouch used to throw small, round projectiles. Like magic crystals. Though it's not usually a nobles' weapon…"

"Whose weapon is it then?"

"Well… children, mostly. We used it for hunting raishook back in Nes Peridion."

He was still glaring at me, and even with my shitty emotion reading skills, I could tell he was not impressed. "And can it throw a projectile that high?"

"Well, once I shot a rock through the sky-dome. It was closer to the edge, though."

"I'm not interested in your bragging, Aldait Han, yes or no?"

"Yes, Myar Mal." I dropped my head. "Sorry."

"Fuck!"

In the meantime, the Dahlsi aerial forces were practically decimated. The last few riders tried to flee, but only a dozen or so made it to safety. And the gates still weren't open.

"Do you want me to go?" asked Tayrel Kan. His voice sounded nonchalant, but he was stiff, with no trace of his usual ease, head high and eyes carefully fixed on the mansion as if to avoid looking at anyone.

Myar Mal gritted his teeth. His gaze had also been focused on the battle scene, but he didn't answer straight away. *What kind of spell made kar-vessár hesitate so much when we were all but defeated?*

"Yeah," said Myar Mal finally over his shoulder. "Go."

Tayrel Kan nodded sharply, his face impenetrable—except now I was sure, the scars were deeper and redder than just a moment ago—and he scurried away. The last kites returned to the camp and were ushered to the ground. The clangor was still coming from the mansion, but it was dying down. I wondered how many of our people were still alive.

For a long moment, nothing else happened. I looked around discretely, trying to locate Tayrel Kan. The camp was awake now and buzzing with activity. Members of ten Cohorts lined up on their bikes, ready to charge. We, from Seventh, were to stay and defend the camp in case something went wrong. I wasn't sure when that information appeared in my mind.

A rumble tore through the air and I saw a flare of light shoot from one of the tents. I looked up. The sun-gate was open now, not wider than a human's arm, but all around it, the sky darkened, with strange shapes swirling outside.

Outside. They were going to pull matter from the Outside. The sudden revelation sent a shiver down my spine; I was not sure if from fear or awe. I knew Dahlsi were powerful—that Tayrel Kan was powerful—but this... this was affecting the sheer structure of the world. It was more than I thought possible.

A small rock fell at my feet. I stared at it, my mouth agape, as if it was the most amazing thing I'd ever seen.

"We better take cover," said Myar Mal.

I noticed a slight glittering of a magic shield. Just in time; seconds later we were hit by a downpour of rocks. But it was nothing, merely gravel. Bigger pieces, round, amorphous, and spear-like, were concentrated at the manor. I saw the red-tiled roof caving in and the mast with Tarvisian flag being knocked down. Finally, a wagon-sized boulder struck the gate and pushed it in.

A moment later, a stone javelin fell a few steps from us.

"Fuck!"

I snapped to the present. It wasn't gravel hitting us now, but proper projectiles, some as big as my fist. The shield flickered under the assault.

"They're diverting the spell." A female's voice came from behind Myar Mal. I recognized the woman who transferred my consciousness into the golem. I couldn't remember her name. She stood shoulder to shoulder with Myar Mal, closer than I thought was appropriate, and if her crossed arms, slumped shoulders, and wide eyes were anything to go by, it was the last place she wanted to be.

"Back up, everyone," ordered kar-vessár. "To the tents and put up the shields."

The next projectile brushed his arm.

Vessár-ai were scrambling to retreat, with rocks big enough to kill raining at our heads. But I stood, petrified, my heart hammering, adrenaline burning in my veins. I couldn't say I was surprised. Tarvissian magic wasn't as ubiquitous as Dahlsian, but it was powerful. If there really was a sorcerer in the mansion, sooner or later he was bound to find a way to protect himself.

"You," Kar-vessár yanked my arm, snapping me to attention. "Go to Tayrel Kan, tell him to stop. Now!"

I remained motionless, unable to tear my eyes from the object I saw over his shoulder, knowing there was nothing I could do…

"Amma!"

Faster than a striking spell, Laik Var leaped and shoved the sorceress out of the way. A disgusting crunch tore through the air as the stone javelin broke through his chest.

"Papa?" Amma La looked at him, her face and clothes splattered with blood, grass-blue eyes wide with shock.

"Go!" Myar Mal pushed me, breaking through my shock.

I turned to run, not looking, guided by the memory of the pillar of light. It was a miracle I found the right tent. I stumbled inside, almost tripping on a brazier. Tayrel Kan stood in the center, surrounded by three vhariars, all drowned in a cold, magical luminescence making their skin blue and the scars black.

"Tayrel Kan," I yelled.

He didn't seem to notice. His hands were outstretched toward the sky and his eyes burned like little moons.

"Tarvissi are diverting the spell. You need to stop it now!"

A rocky spear tore through the tent and hit the ground inches from my foot.

"Damn it!" I cursed, jumping aside. "Wake up, you damn imp!"

No reaction. I reached out, hoping to shake him out of this trance, but a surge of energy ran up my arm, burning it to the shoulder. I yelped in pain. Desperate, I looked around, searching for something—anything—to aid me. My eyes fell on the brazier.

"I'm sorry," I said, then lifted the thing and threw it at the sorcerer.

Chapter 11

"HOW THE FUCK did that happen?"

Myar Mal's screams must've been perfectly audible all over the camp. Tayrel Kan leaned back in the chair and lit his tchalka. His head pounded, but the magic helped heal the bruises and burns from being hit with the brazier. Sadly, abusing it caused its own set of problems.

"You tell me, you designed the spell," he replied, not even bothering to look up. He sucked in the lungful of smoke and a cold numbness flooded him, dulling the pain and cushioning the tangible anger radiating from kar-vessár, even through his shields.

"Tayrel," Myar Mar growled with a clear warning in his voice.

The sorcerer let the smoke out. "You told us to focus on the strength, so we did," he explained. "Directing the spell wasn't our priority, so we left it to chance. They simply took advantage of that."

"Oh, so it's just an oversight." Kar-vessár straightened, his tone so caustic it could corrode his sword if he wore it.

"An oversight that got people killed, including one of my best vessár-ai—"

"I thought you'd be grateful," Tayrel Kan cut him short, lifting his eyelids for the first time and looking Myar Mal in the eye. The commander's face was reddened and lips pressed so tightly they turned white. He looked beautiful when he was angry—though the sorcerer had enough survival instinct not to say it out loud. "He was a pain in the ass."

"That's beyond the point." Myar Mal's lips twitched in disgust. "Although I do see how you, of all people, aren't bothered by friendly fire."

Tayrel Kan felt as if someone drew an icy dagger through his heart. His smile fell. "Perhaps you spend so much time in the city, you forgot," he said with deceptive calmness. "But people die. It's in the job description."

"No." Myar Mal pushed away from the table and shook his head. "Not like that."

Tayrel Kan only leaned forward, following him, gaze fixed on the man's face. "Things happen, Myar. No matter what you do, you can't save everybody."

"Enough." Kar-vessár raised his hand in protest, then, as if having second thoughts, clenched it before finally pointing at the sorcerer. "You're going to Sfal."

Tayrel Kan scoffed and leaned back, crossing his arms. "Fuck you."

"As commanding officer—"

"Command your dick! Look, now we know they have a magic-wielder, and he's one powerful son of a bitch. As long as he's out there, I'm the best chance you have to win this fight. When I get my hands on him, I'm gonna grab him by the balls and drag him all the way to Sfal, so you can tell him exactly where he hurt you. Until then, I'm not moving an inch."

For a moment, they stood motionless, sizing each other up. Until this point, Tayrel Kan kept up his facade, but now, under the commander's gaze, he couldn't help parting his lips slightly, as in invitation. The argument was a farce. They both knew he would do anything, if only Myar Mal said a word.

But he said nothing, and Tayrel Kan stormed out.

Chapter 12

AMMA LA SAT motionless in front of the healing tent. Blood stained her coat and hands, strikingly bright against white skin. She did everything she could to save her father, fix his heart, his lungs, his spine. But the damage was too much…

Myar Mal stood a few steps behind her. He reached out, wishing he could touch her, console her; but his hand froze mid-way. A few seconds later, it dropped uselessly at his side.

There was a time when he would walk to her and hold her. When he would whisper in her ear and tell her everything would be all right. And she would lean back onto his chest and believe him, if only for a moment.

But now the only thing he could bring himself to do was ask, "Do you want me to come with you?"

She didn't answer. Her head was turned slightly, revealing her pale, sunken face and red-rimmed eyes, magnified by glasses. But she never looked at him.

After what felt like an eternity, her lips twitched and she asked with a dry, dead voice, "Don't you have work to do?"

"I can take a moment for you."

"You never do." She paused. "Don't bother now."

Chapter 13

RIDDEN WITH GUILT, I took Tayrel Kan to the field hospital. The frailness of his body terrified me. He always seemed emaciated, but he weighed almost nothing in my arms; his ribs were prominent even through his suit, his stomach not flat but sunken in, his hipbones sharp and protruding. I feared I might crush him if I squeezed too tight.

But it was when I dropped him in the field hospital, that a real dread descended on me. There were so many people here...

I saw Malyn Tol with blood dripping down her temple, her eyes hazy. Argan Am, his face covered in burns, a hand with conjoined fingers the only defining feature.

I saw Amma La, numb with shock, sitting beside a shrouded shape, and my heart clenched.

I fled to the hills.

The rain of rocks stirred the ashes that were now falling in black petals. If that wasn't a funeral setting, I didn't know what was.

If the info they put in my head was correct, we lost all of our kas'shams, as well as over half of our aerial forces, and an untold number of people on the ground. But my thoughts kept circling back to Laik Var. I was right by him when that happened. I could have...

What?

I wrested my thoughts away from my vessár. But the second subject my mind came up with was not much better.

My father.

He was a rough, almost callous man, but I knew that in his own way, he had loved me. Sometimes he seemed more interested in his animals than the people around him, and in that regard, I was just like him. He died shortly before I joined Mespana, and, however dirty that made me feel, I wouldn't be able to do so if he lived. Bah, I wouldn't even dare to express such a wish! I would probably do as he said, marry a girl he chose for me, build a house, try to have children.

His death put an end to such plans. I was free. I was... relieved.

Did that make me a bad son? A bad person? I loved my father and had great respect for his words and deeds, even if they weren't always pleasant. I tried my best to mourn when he died, and I failed to understand why I couldn't...

Why couldn't I feel back then what I felt right now?

And there was Amma La. The daughter of Laik Var. How could I not notice? She had the same grass-blue eyes and prominent nose. But what gave him an aspect of almost regal authority only made her look like a witch from old tales.

I recalled the moment I first saw the two together. She didn't call him father. Wasn't that ironic? It made me wonder… if there was someone, somewhere, for whom Haneaith Tearshan was what Laik Var was for me.

How strange it all was!

I wondered if talking to someone, like Myar Mal suggested—although regarding a different issue—could help me clarify things. But I couldn't do that. It was too shameful, too… wrong. I wasn't in the mood for company, anyway.

Sadly, not everyone understood that.

"Got tchalka?" I asked, too tired and resigned to protest.

Without a word, Tayrel Kan procured two pieces of reed, lit them with a flicker of his fingers, then handed one to me. It seemed less unpleasant than the first time, and the relief came faster. I knew it wasn't real and when it passed, it would leave me more disturbed than before, but I didn't care at that point.

We smoked in silence for a moment.

"Laik Var was the only person who stood up for me," I said finally, not able to keep my feelings bottled any longer. Was. Not is, not anymore. It sounded surreal. The words left my mouth, but my brain refused to process them.

"I'll stand for you," Tayrel Kan replied, and I couldn't hold back a chuckle. He sent me a puzzled look. "What?"

"I think everyone in the camp has heard Myar Mal yelling at you."

He made his Dahlsian wave-shrug. "Yeah, he likes drama."

The ease with which he took it—everything, Myar Mal's wrath, and that fiasco—grated me. How could he be so calm? Did those deaths mean nothing to him?

"He blames you for what happened," I said, wishing to break through his indifference.

"He'll get over it."

He seemed completely unaffected, the dark circles under his eyes the only mark of this morning's events. The bastard didn't even have a bruise from where I hit him with the brazier. His scars, though… they were red now, not pink, and deep, with skin taut around them, as if something was digging into them, threatening to cut through.

Although, if the unfocused gaze was anything to go by, I'd say it wasn't his first tchalka. Perhaps he was lulling his nerves, too.

"You seem confident," I remarked.

He chuckled mirthlessly and asked, "What is your score?"

It took me a while to figure out what he meant. Kevar scale, used to measure one's magic potential.

"Zero point eighty-nine," I said, somehow reluctantly. I'd heard some sorcerers were closer to two, and I suspected he'd be one of them. But he only smiled bitterly.

"Three point two," he said.

What?

"Most humans have around one," he continued. "Kassams vary, from one point five to two point two. Tsavikii are pretty consistent with two point six. Even fucking vhariars rarely reach two point nine. I have more than three. It's a record, you know? In terms of sheer power,

I'm officially the most powerful human sorcerer who ever lived."

It made sense. If Kanven wanted to make him a better sorcerer, increasing his magical potential was a good start.

"How is that possible?" I asked, my mouth suddenly dry.

Somehow, he understood I wasn't talking about his potential—or maybe he was reading my mind again, I wasn't sure. He scoffed. "It isn't. Not anymore. Few cycles ago there was a big shit-show with one of the companies offering prenatal upgrades and the Directory finally prohibited experiments on humans. But when I was born... it was before that. Before we even discovered Meon. We had limited space in Dahls and already too many people, so the government imposed regulations: one child per couple. And I guess my parents really wanted a daughter."

Somehow, he managed to relate his story completely flatly, without a trace of emotion. Perhaps having to live with it, he got so used to it, it didn't affect him anymore. Or it affected him, but there was nothing he could do, so he pushed it away, pretending everything was all right and seeking relief in inebriation.

"You guess?" I repeated dully. "You never tried to find them?"

He waved his hand. "What for? They dumped me like a used condom. It's pretty clear they wanted nothing to do with me. Besides, their names weren't registered."

"What about your middle name?"

His surname meant 'The Other' and was traditionally given to boys whose fathers were unknown. Argan Am was also Trever.

"Kanven."

I wished I hadn't asked.

Still, there was one thing that I wasn't getting. He seemed young, his hair dark, and skin smooth around the scars. His eyelids were droopy, but that could be due to his drug usage.

But Meon Cluster was discovered over twenty cycles ago. That was two generations, and almost as long as a life expectancy for Dahlsi.

"Magic keeps me young," he said, leaving no room for doubt about his intrusion into my thoughts. "My appearance hasn't changed since I was ten."

He looked older than ten cycles, maybe fifteen. The stubble aged him.

"And those scars?" I asked before I could think better.

His gaze drifted away and he lifted his hand, almost absentmindedly, to touch the offending lines.

"They're on the soul, rather than body. They will not heal."

This time, I had enough sense not to ask. From his tone, I could tell it had nothing to do with his upbringing. Besides, even Laik Var said the scars were a later development. I wondered if it wasn't something all Dahlsi knew, and only us outsiders had to guess.

Then I looked at him again and realized he must've been handsome before. With high cheekbones, perfectly straight nose, dimpled chin, and those strikingly bright eyes under dark, heavy brows. I could imagine the women of Dahls flocking around him. Or the men.

Another part of Laik Var's warning echoed through my mind and I scrambled to shield myself before he could read it. Nevertheless, I felt heat creeping up my cheeks and peeked aside at Tayrel Kan. He never did anything that would make me think…

But he was smirking, and I realized my attempts were in vain. I tried to cover it by conjuring the worst insults I knew, in all five languages, before sidetracking to wonder how many of them made sense without the cultural context.

Mercifully, he refrained from commenting. It struck me that despite everything, most of the time, his company made me feel… at ease.

Sure, he knew more than other people, which was unsettling at times. But he didn't judge me and, as far as I was aware, didn't use any of his knowledge against me. He mocked me sometimes, but he did that to everyone. He even made it easy to forget that he wasn't completely honest with me.

Besides, we'd known each other for a day. I felt like, if we were to get a chance to continue our conversations, maybe he'd finally open up.

His smirk faded again.

"Magic does things to people," he said, seemingly unrelated to anything. "Maybe your nation had a point in restricting it. Humans did not evolve to use it. We're not like vhariars who see the damn thing with their own eyes. Shit, even kassam can sniff it. But we—we have no natural predisposition to magic, and we should have stayed that way."

"Strange words for a sorcerer."

He snapped, "I didn't ask to be a sorcerer." He took a deep breath, steadying himself. "But there's not much else someone like me could do for a living."

I wasn't sure what to say. "It can't be that bad," I stammered lamely.

He gave me a tired look. "Have you forgotten how a few hours ago you had to stop me from getting us all killed? Too late to save poor Laik Var…"

"It's not your fault," I said. I desperately wanted to believe it.

He smiled joylessly. "I think the fault can be split equally between me, Myar Mal, and that bastard on the other side of the wall. And only one of us is gonna pay. But my point still stands. We weren't made to deal with magic."

I wasn't sure about that. For me, magic was pretty handy, but what I used was child's play compared to what he practiced. I couldn't even imagine the toll it was taking on him. Though I had a feeling there was more to it than guilt—certainly more than the guilt for Laik Var's death—but I didn't know what it was. So, I did what I did best.

Spun the conversation in a direction that only made sense to me.

"So, you believe in this theory? That we're not from here?"

At first, he blinked in confusion. But then he scoffed and sent me a pitying look.

"What, from another universe? There's no proof that there's anything other than Darkness beyond the Great Sphere. It's just a story conjured by some old farts with too much time on their hands. Or other species who want to think themselves better than us."

"And yet you say we're the only species with no natural predisposition for magic."

"We're also the only known species with functioning tits. It doesn't mean anything."

"It could mean we evolved elsewhere."

He sighed and reached for another tchalka, but his lips curled up again. My tension eased up a bit. Even if it was a pity, not his usual snark, it beat his previous mood.

Pity I could deal with.

"Kid, the recorded history of humans in this universe dates back many great grosses of cycles. We'd had to have arrived here long before we'd discovered how to use magic. Fuck, before we even learned to make metal tools."

"Yeah, but legends say there were ancient civilizations with magic and technology we can't dream of today."

"And it's bullshit. Knowledge tends to advance, not reverse with time."

"Apparently, there was a catastrophe."

"Yeah, and it's called bullshit. Come on, Aldiaif Han, you speak four languages, so you're definitely smarter than you seem at first. Too smart to believe in that crap. You should put your brain to better use. Get into the Academy instead of dabbling in myths."

But I like myths, I wanted to say. They were simple, easy, and… different. They allowed me to get away from the shit I had to deal with in life; forget about the problems I couldn't solve. I doubted academic research would have the same merit. If anything, it was more likely to just fuel my anxiety.

"Well, I'm not the one with three point two on the Kevar scale," I chuckled awkwardly, but deep inside, warmth spread through my chest. No one had ever called me smart. I didn't even care that he misremembered the number of languages I spoke.

"I'm not interested in studying," he replied. "Look, I hate magic; Kanven made sure of that. If I could, I would run away to grow some fucking coclaxi fruit. Except I wouldn't be able to eat the damn things; I'd probably die of dehydration via runny nose. So I stay here, figuring that way I'll do less harm. But you," he looked me in the eye, and not for the first time, I was struck by how bright his irises were, "You still have a chance."

Chapter 14

"VESSÁR-AI." MYAR Mal swept his tired gaze over the gathered leaders. "There's an empty seat among us today. If you know anyone who could fill it, speak up."

The silence that followed was almost physical; it dragged like a slime, tainting everything it touched.

"Aldait Han should take this place," Tyano Har-Vahir, the oldest man among the vessár-ai, said finally.

Myar Mal felt even more tired than before. It took all of his self-control not to sag.

"I won't make that decision alone."

"What about Arda Nahs?" asked Vareya Lyg-Havet, the only person older than Tyano Har, referring to Laik Var's original nami.

"There's no time to bring her from Sfal," replied Tyano Har.

"How about my nami?" asked Sanam Il-Asa, rubbing his chin. "Adyar Lah-Nasseye. He's good. Loyal. Stepped out during the pursuit of the Llodran mage with the unpronounceable name, half a cycle ago."

Seconds passed. No one answered, but also no one proposed another candidate. Myar Mal waited a moment longer, but realizing the futility, he procured a large, flat box.

"All right then," he announced, setting it on the table. "Let us vote. Blue for Aldait Han, green for Adyar Lah."

All vessár-ai reached for small glass balls and gripped them tight, sending their thoughts forward to their twins inside the box. Those who finished put their balls on the table. When the last of them were down, kar-vessár lifted the lid.

Five balls were blue. Six were green.

Myar Mal allowed himself a sigh.

"Thank you, vessár-ai."

Chapter 15

THE SKYDOME BARELY resisted. Amma La watched as her father's body disappeared Outside, disintegrating into the same pre-matter everything came from.

Long ago, she witnessed Chaarite colonists performing funerary rites. Dancing and wailing as they carried the garishly dressed corpse through the town in a sedan chair decorated with paper flowers. Dahlsi were too practical for such things, and yet she wished there was something else for her to do. Her father deserved better.

But she didn't know what she could do.

She tried to recall the last time they spoke. Really spoke—without arguing, screaming, or blaming each other. It was merely a few cycles ago, but it felt like an eternity. Since then... Nothing passed between them but bitter words and reproach. And the heavy silence that fell when the words ran out.

What had happened to them?

Moments passed. Her eyes were fixed on the dome as she searched her mind for answers, and while she didn't find them, there was something. The moment where it all started. The person at the center of their strife.

Amma La clenched her fists and turned back.

Chapter 16

HE WAS A SIGHT to behold. Tall, for a Dahlsi, although still shorter than me. And heavy—not from muscles or fat, but a combination of the two, merging to create an image of sheer, unstoppable mass. How it was possible to grow to such size on Dahlsian food rations?

And yet, no one was looking at him. They were looking at me. The blue sash burned my chest like a fresh wound. I wasn't sure if I should keep it or tear it down in some dramatic gesture. But that would probably only draw more attention.

"I wanted to assure you," said Adyar Lah with a low and powerful voice. "That despite our loss today, our Cohort will prevail. We will stand strong. We will continue fighting as if nothing has changed. We will show them we cannot be broken and then…" he paused dramatically. "We will avenge Laik Var." My comrades roared in approval.

The new vessár nodded, satisfied, and when the applause died down, he turned to me. "Aldait Han." I lifted my head to meet his eyes. They were small, mere slits in his wide face. "I want you to uphold your duty as nami vessár."

"Yes, Adyar Lah," I said dutifully. What else could I say?

He motioned at me and I approached. Then, quietly, so only we could hear, he ordered, "Prepare the report about the Cohort's status."

I studied him for a moment. Of course. He was from another Cohort. He knew no one here, had no one to rely on. And that meant I was going to have to do the job I was given. Should I inform him my promotion only happened so Laik Var could make a point? That I had absolutely no idea about the responsibilities of nami vessár? That, despite my own feelings about this whole situation, he would probably be a better vessár than I could ever hope to be?

His face scrunched, and all the words died in my throat.

"I didn't ask for this," he murmured.

Not sure what to say, I only nodded. Much later, I realized it was meant to be an apology.

I was actually doing pretty well. Chiefly because I decided to start with something easy—the equipment. I went swiftly through all of our bikes (luckily, none were destroyed; a few were damaged, but our mechanics assured me they could fix them in around an hour), then the special weapons that also remained undamaged.

But that left the hardest part—going through our personnel. I needed to go to the field hospital for the list of the deceased, but before I could do that, the tingling of magic ran down my back.

"Aldait Han, please come with us."

My body stood and turned around without any conscious input from my side. Adyar Lah was waiting a couple of steps behind me, along with some other man I didn't recognize. Both sported almost identical grim expressions.

"What happened?" I asked. At least I could still use my mouth.

But my question was ignored, and the two led me inside one of the tents. A perfectly impersonal place that could be anything. I wondered which of them was casting the spell controlling my body. Whoever was doing that, made me sit in the center, making both men tower above me.

Psychological dominance, I realized, and paradoxically felt a bit better. As they say, seeing through someone's trick was half-way to defeating them.

Well, if you ignore the fact that I was fucking arrested.

"What happened?" I asked again.

"Myar Mal suffered an anaphylactic shock," explained Adyar Lah. It came at me like a bucket of cold water.

"How?" I stammered, but at some level I knew, I just didn't want to—couldn't—admit that…

The world around us was burned to the ground. The only possible allergens had to be brought from the outside.

"That's what I'd like to know." Adyar Lah's words barely broke through the jumble of my thoughts. "There was a carai-nut in his water."

At this point, my jaw dropped. I gasped for air. Carai-nut. Carai-nut!

"And yesterday, you were seen threatening all vessár-ai with one of them."

My head was spinning, so I lowered my gaze to the floor, desperately grasping for any semblance of stability.

His shadow fell on me as he leaned over and whispered menacingly: "So let me ask instead: how did that happen?"

"I didn't do it," I rasped, breathing heavily, screwing my eyes shut. I didn't do it. That's one thing I knew for sure. My muscles ached and I realized I was trying to rock against the magical restrains. "Look, I'm… I'm an idiot who never knows when to shut up, but I'm not… I'm not a murderer."

"Aren't you?" He arched his eyebrow, leaned back, and crossed his arms, and I wanted to scream, shout in his face, or just punch him. Then I felt all the emotions draining from me and realized that whoever was controlling my body, was also reading my mind. The things he must have seen there would haunt me for a long time after that.

"Why would I even do that?" I asked, sounding unnaturally calm, even to myself.

They couldn't charge me without a motive. And maybe I had a reason to wave that nut around—although I was the first to admit I often overreacted and did stupid things when I was angry— killing someone was another matter.

"Everyone knows you had a row with Myar Mal."

I closed my eyes. "Did I?" I asked weakly.

"You threatened him—"

"I didn't."

"And he left you out while nominating a new vessár."

"From what I understand, there was voting."

"Which he initiated. Against protocol."

I didn't know that, but it didn't matter. This was outside of my scope of authority, and I was ready to accept it, like every other decision ever made by my commanders. Shit, I didn't even want that position, I didn't want to be nami either, but it had all happened too quickly for me to refuse.

"Even if I wanted to get rid of him, why would I do that in the most conspicuous way possible?" I asked, not willing to give up. "Someone's trying to frame me, don't you see that? You keep pumping me, when the real killer is out there, getting rid of both of us with one strike!"

"Calm yourself, Aldait Han."

I hadn't realized I was screaming. I exhaled, struggling to stop my body from shaking. Another idea popped in my mind.

"It's because I'm Tarvissi, right? You all still think I'm only waiting for an opportunity to betray you?"

"That's a possibility we're considering, yes." His tone was frigid and my stomach dropped. I'd ben hoping to catch him off guard.

"You fail to consider one thing," I said. "Other Tarvissi were ready to torture and kill me; why would I ally myself with them?"

"I don't know, Aldait Han. Maybe they changed their minds."

"But why would I change my mind?"

"From a misplaced sense of superiority?"

I froze.

"What?" I managed to stammer.

Where did that come from? I studied his face, hoping to find some hint that all of this was some fucking joke.

He wasn't laughing.

"From what I've heard, you tend to keep to yourself," he said. "Not mingling, not talking to anybody. Why's that?"

"I'm not a sociable person."

"Why not?"

"I don't know, I'm just not good with people. It's not a crime."

"Or you think yourself better than us?"

"No!" If I refrained from social activities, it was because of anxiety. I knew I was gonna screw something up and it was... it was just safer this way. "I didn't have friends among the Tarvissi, either."

"Huh. It's convenient everyone who could dispute that is out of Dahls."

"So is everyone who could confirm that."

This was ridiculous. The worst thing was, I had no idea how to rebuff his charges. And there was no one who'd stand for me, this much I knew, even without considering the alleged murder attempt.

"Where did you even get that idea?" I asked, resigned.

For the first time, Adyar Lah hesitated. He then looked at the other guy, as if searching for affirmation, before speaking, "You were heard uttering a racial slur."

Oh, fuck. I pressed my eyes shut, trying to banish the memory, but that only seemed to make it spring to life: the big tent lit by the magical diagram on the floor, the pelting of the falling rocks, Tayrel Kan's eyes glassy, unseeing as I tried desperately to grab his attention...

But as much as I wanted to blame it on my fucking brain picking up the worst possible things—from those bastards on the other side of the wall for sure, since they were the only ones I'd ever heard uttering this word—I had to face the truth that... perhaps I wasn't different from my compatriots. Perhaps the bigotry my race was known for was still running in my veins, waiting for the opportunity to rear its head.

"I spoke in anger," I stammered. Shitty excuse, if I ever heard one, but I had nothing better. I knew I wouldn't be able to put to words everything I thought. "It was an emergency, I wanted… I wanted to get Tayrel Kan's attention. I could just as well have called him an asshole."

A sense of betrayal set heavily in my stomach. Not so long ago, we spoke freely, joked, laughed—shit, he wasn't always kind to me either! But then, as the tides turned, he was the first to rat on me.

"But you didn't."

I exhaled. A part of me wished to remain angry, but as much as I loathed to admit it, he was right.

What was wrong with me? Why did I always have to say the worst things? Quarreling with supervisors was bad enough, but threatening them in front of the entire camp? And then running around screaming the only word I absolutely shouldn't have? It's not hard, Aldeaith! One fucking word!

I didn't know if I want to laugh or cry. I had joined Mespana to steer clear of this shit, hoping the rigid structure would keep my tongue in check. All in vain. It was not the structure I needed; it was a fucking muzzle.

"Look," I said, panting heavily. "It was… a lapse of judgment. I'm prone to them."

"Yeah, I noticed."

"You really think I would join Mespana, spend most of my life among Dahlsi, if I thought myself better?"

"Sentiments change. Especially in times like this."

What could I say to that? I closed my eyes, the defeat bitter in my mouth.

"I guess your friend is busy scanning my mind," I said. That was my last line of defense. I was innocent—of attempted murder, at least—but that word itself was enough to get me kicked out of Dahls. The Peridion family was probably waiting for me on the other side. I only hoped Mespana would let me keep my wand. "How about you ask him if he found anything discriminating?"

Adyar Lah didn't answer straight away. I raised my eyes to him, but he averted his face, pressing his lips into an embarrassed grimace.

"She's your friend, actually," he explained.

"What?"

For the first time since we came into the tent, I looked at the other person. Adyar Lah was right. It was a woman, though with one of those nondescript faces that could belong to anyone, and a body that was all skin and bones, crossed arms hiding whatever feminine attributes she possessed. But also, I knew her. We'd worked together a couple of times in the past, and I was pretty sure we were introduced at some point. I just couldn't, for the life of me, remember her name.

"Dalyn Kia-Havek," she said, and I didn't know if it was to put me out of my misery or to humiliate me more.

"Sorry," I murmured, then turned back to Adyar Lah. "See, that's what I mean. It's hard to make friends when you can't remember fucking names."

"You seemed to recall those Tarvissi leaders just fine."

I licked my lips nervously, though my tongue was almost as dry as them. That wasn't a pleasant recollection, definitely not one I wanted to share, but... Ah, fuck it, Dalyn Kia probably read it in my mind anyway.

"When I was younger, they liked to gang up and beat the shit out of me. I was always alone, easy to pick on. Kinda hard to forget."

"Even then—" he stopped abruptly and snapped his head up, listening.

At first, I wasn't sure what for, but it didn't take me long: from the edge of the camp, came an unmistakable whistle.

Adyar Lah frowned. "Stay here," he ordered and turned toward the exit.

Before he could take a step, another whistle tore through the air, followed by a pop as the tent wall gave up, then a painful grunt. Adyar Lah sucked in a breath and collapsed, a tail of a bolt sticking out of his chest. The spell binding me loosened and I dropped to the floor. The next bolt flew over my head. I murmured a quick blurring spell, hoping it would at least make it harder to aim at us. Nothing better came to my mind.

Across the tent, Dalyn Kia was also crouching, seemingly unharmed. Vessár laid on the ground. I crawled toward him. The wheezing breath suggested he was alive, and wide opened eyes—that he was conscious, but most likely in shock. Pink foam formed on his lips.

Dalyn Kia joined me as I was reaching for a pack of healing clay. I glanced up.

"You're gonna stop me?" I asked, bitterness tainting my words.

"Nah, I was trying to tell them it's bullshit. You don't have it in you to be a traitor."

155

Adyar Lah's words echoed through my mind, She's actually your friend. Heat rose to my cheeks.

"Thanks, I guess," I murmured.

"One needs to be good at communication and cooperation to be a part of a conspiracy, and you're incapable of either."

I flinched, but her words were hard to argue. Plus, we had more pressing matters to deal with.

I pointed to a bolt sticking out of Adyar Lah's chest. "You gonna help me out with this?"

She grabbed it without a word and looked at me with expectation.

"On three," I said, preparing the clay. "One, two, three."

Dalyn Kia yanked the bolt out, wringing a painful groan out of vessár's mouth, and almost at the same moment I crammed a handful of clay into the wound. I hovered my palm above it as I whispered the healing spell. Doing it always made me uneasy. I had an instinctive fear of magic, so I never really got good at it. Most of the spells we performed on duty were simple and unobtrusive, but healing was a different matter. Especially healing someone else.

I should probably ask Dalyn Kia to do this, I realized too late.

Despite my concerns, when I removed my hand, there was no trace of the wound. The clay melted and fused seamlessly with the surrounding tissue.

Maybe I wasn't so bad after all. Or maybe I had screwed up, and in a few cycles, Adyar Lah would grow a malignant tumor. One of the two. After all, it's much easier to kill a man than patch him up.

For now, he stopped wheezing, his breathing became regular, and it seemed like he lost consciousness. There was nothing else I could do for him. I turned toward the exit. The flap was open and Dalyn Kia was already peeking outside with a wand in her hand. I followed her gaze. Mespanians were running around and, if I squinted, I could make out tall, dark silhouettes standing in the distance, releasing series after series of crossbow bolts.

"Tarvissi," hissed Dalyn Kia.

I rolled my eyes. Who else could it be?

Yet I hesitated. Healing a fallen colleague was an automatic response, acquired after cycles of training. But now that I had time to think… What should I do? Go out and fight? For what? A country that considered me a pariah? People for whom I was a traitor?

I should just stay here. With all the shit going on outside, no one would blame me. Well, they blamed me for everything anyway, so what difference did it make?

Worst case, Tarvissi would come first and see me cowering…

Ah, fuck it.

I took out my wand, but it was an empty gesture: the enemies were too far away for spells. I needed to get closer. Preferably without getting myself killed. I considered putting up a magical shield, but then I looked at the bolt we removed from Adyar Lah. The head was made of iron; no magic would stop it.

Someone grabbed my arm, and I yanked it automatically. My eyes met Dalyn Kia's.

"Look, I'm not such a bitch to keep you stranded in the middle of the fight. But getting yourself killed is a shitty way of clearing your name."

I had no intention of getting myself killed. Without a word, I cloaked myself with another blurring spell and crawled out of the tent.

"Yeah, sure, keep acting like an asshole," she grumbled after me. "I'll stay behind and make sure our vessár stays alive."

By now most Dahlsi had managed to find cover. All I had to do was move from one piece of machinery to the next, from one fallen body to another. Some I recognized, but I didn't stop.

Soon, ash filled my mouth and nose, making me regret shunning the breathing masks the true Dahlsi carried at all times. I could scavenge one from one of the bodies. But when I thought of it, I was already at the edge of the camp, crouching behind a hitched bike. I paused to catch my breath, but had to jerk away as another bolt pierced the machine inches from my head. I cursed. Damn nubithium was as good as paper. Well, at least it was shielding me from the Tarvissi's view.

Carefully, I peeked over the seat and tried to estimate the distance. The bastards were just outside my wand's range. Chewing on another curse, I squatted back and weighed my options. I could charge and get myself killed. Or sit there and wait for them to come and kill me. Choices, choices…

Before I made my decision, the familiar tingling ran down my neck. A moment later, a surge of air threw ash into my face. I coughed and spurted, screwing my eyes shut in a vain effort to protect them… Then it was gone and I opened my eyes to see again.

It was Tayrel Kan. He walked right past me, surrounded by whirls of ash and flames. A few bolts were sticking out of his body, but he didn't seem to care. Apparently, aging wasn't the only thing he was immune to.

Stopping at the edge of the camp, he waved his hand dismissively and the crossbowmen fell like toys swatted by an unruly child. He raised both arms and the tent on his left flew from the ground, fell into bits, and erupted into flames. The cloud of fire shot at the enemy like a pack of hungry dryaks.

But one whirl tore from the pack and rushed toward me. It snapped its flaming jaw, exploding in the last moment on a hastily conjured shield. Tarvissi had no such means and their shrieks filled the air. I doubted any of them survived.

I waited till the screams died out before daring to peek out again. Tayrel Kan stood a few paces away, still spurting the fiery demons, as if unaware the battle was over. One of his pupils spotted me, but I banished it before it could get near.

"Tayrel Kan, stop!" I screamed.

He ignored me. Haven't we done that before?

Another demon jumped at me and I barely managed to expel it, its breath burning my face. The screams started again, this time closer.

Cursing, I looked around, searching for something to throw at him—I didn't dare to use my wand against a rampaging sorcerer. But I saw nothing. All nearby objects were too heavy to lift, and even if I managed, I would probably kill him in the process.

Without other ideas, I stood up from my hiding spot. Dispersing another demon, I approached Tayrel Kan and somehow managed to grab his shoulder and yank him toward me.

The view almost took all my courage. His face was pale, crossed with lines so red they were more like fresh wounds than scars. And I could swear, every single one of them spread in its own mocking grin, the flesh between the stitch marks akin to teeth. His eyes shone like lanterns, and at this moment, I felt there was nothing human left in him. He was just a force of nature, wild, untamed, and completely indifferent.

"Tayrel Kan, that's enough," I shouted, fighting the tremble in my voice. "You're gonna get us all killed."

He only laughed, a high-pitched, inhuman sound that made the hair on my neck stand on end.

"No one will mourn you here," he replied, pushing me away with a blast of magical wind. But his words were more daunting than any spell; mostly because I knew them to be true.

And he probably wasn't even aware, I realized, unable to tear my gaze from his crazed face.

"I'm sorry," I said just like before, this time without the faintest hint of remorse. My fingers closed around a tiny object on the bottom of my pouch. I took it out and shoved it in his mouth.

Tayrel Kan's eyes widened, and he spat; my last carai-nut, red against the bare ground.

But it did its job. Within seconds, the inhuman grin gave way to confusion, light all but disappearing from his eyes. Tayrel Kan gave out a weak huff, then another. He tried to walk away but stumbled to his knees. His left hand shot up to clutch uselessly at his neck, as his right scrabbled to recover the syringe from his belt. I rushed forward just in time to catch him before he collapsed. His face was red and swollen, eyes glassy.

He was dying.

With growing dread, I attempted to wrest the syringe from him. But then a spasm shook his body, his hand cramped and a disgusting crunch tore the air. I froze. When I looked down, I saw broken glass, glimmering like stars against quickly darkening ground that greedily drank the last drops of the medicine.

Tayrel Kan didn't have any more shots. My meds had expired, and I hadn't bother to pick up new ones. He was gonna die and it was all my fault. I killed him. I killed him...

Someone pushed me aside and pressed something into Tayrel Kan's thigh. The sorcerer stopped struggling, and slowly, his breathing normalized. When I looked up, my eyes met Adyar Lah's.

Chapter 17

THE SMELL OF burnt meat lingered in the air long after the last screams died down.

It's all wrong, Taneem thought. Karlan was full of shit: two battles, and the Dahlsi didn't seem ready to run. No, they were regrouping, preparing for the counterstrike. And with the gate of the mansion wrecked, there was very little to stop them.

"We're all gonna die here." The words fled Taneem's mouth before he could think of them.

"Not all hope is lost," retorted Kiraes, his tone as even as if he was talking about the weather.

Taneem couldn't hold back a burst of hysterical laughter. "Have you seen what has just happened?" He swept his hand toward the window; needlessly, as Kiraes's eyes were locked on the outside, not sparing his friend a glimpse. "They didn't even need to mobilize. All it took was one lonely sorcerer to dispatch our entire team. Can you imagine what will happen when this bastard comes here?"

"There must be a reason why he hasn't already!" Kiraes huffed, and it became clear that despite the calm facade he was as shocked as Taneem. "There's a limit to how much ae one can process in a day. He's probably all spent."

Kiraes was always fascinated by magic and had even tried his luck at the Academy in Sfal—a chance he'd never have gotten if their families remained in Tarviss. The irony was not lost on Taneem.

"There may be others like him."

"Hopefully not."

The silence descended, heavy and precarious.

"Why are we even here?" asked Taneem. He never wanted any of this. His life in Sfal was better than he deserved; he didn't even care about having revenge on the Tearshan family. He only bullied the kid because others did it, and he wanted to fit in. He wondered if Tearshan knew this.

He wondered if it mattered.

"We're here to undo what was done." Kiraes's tone was solemn, a citation more than an expression.

Taneem's lips twitched. "So that's it. You just follow Karlan's words, believing that we can fix one evil with another..."

"There's no fixing it!"

The outburst was so sudden, Taneem reeled back.

Kiraes took a deep breath before picking up. "Nothing will bring our parents back. Nothing will undo cycles of pain and humiliation we had to endure. All we can do is make sure our children won't suffer the same fate as us."

"If you cared about your children, you would take them and Kayda and fuck off to Tarviss," hissed Taneem, feeling

164

his blood rushing. "They were already sent there, deported due to your own actions. Do you care about that?"

"Damn you, Taneem, what do you care about? Is there even anything? Or you just do what you're told. No wonder you don't mind the life of a peon, you already have the soul of one!"

The words struck him like a physical punch, and Taneem stepped back, looking at the man he considered his friend. Kiraes's cheeks were red and sweat glued his hair to his forehead. His eyes were wide open, frenzied, almost like Karlan's.

He made a mistake, Taneem realized. Not just now, but all throughout his life. His attempts to fit in with those people were futile; and probably not even worth it.

He leaned forward, narrowing his eyes, and spat, "I lived in Sfal with the man I loved, knowing full-well that if we were ever to return to Tarviss, we would be gelded or killed. If there's one thing I care for, it's that I didn't have the balls to tell you and Karlan to go fuck yourself when you knocked on our door. Make of it what you want."

He whirled on his heel and strode off, leaving Kiraes too stumped to reply.

Chapter 18

THEY DIDN'T PUT me back in the hole. Instead, after Adyar Lah and I took Tayrel Kan to the field hospital, I was told to go to my tent and await further orders. Kalikka brought me from the initial shock, but as I stretched on my cot, terror and guilt still churned in my stomach.

I wondered if I should leave. Just pack my stuff and slip away in the night. There was nothing—and no one—keeping me here. I was alone, surrounded by enemies. Dahlsi, Tarvissi—what the fuck was the difference? The Tarvissi would torture and kill me, while the Dahlsi would sentence me to exile or death—provided they didn't shoot me in the back. And maybe after what I'd done to Tayrel Kan, I deserved it…

The only problem was there was nowhere to go. The merge was closed, the only sorcerer I knew was out cold. I could hide in the country and wait for the war to end, then try to return to Kooine. Probably get arrested on the spot. But the surrounding area was burned to the ground with no shelter in sight, so they'd have no problem catching me. So,

I stayed—not because of conviction, but out of simple resignation.

With nothing to do, I reached for the only thing that ever brought me solace: food. Led by compulsion more than hunger, I gorged on nuts and sunberries until my stomach was bloated and my mouth filled with sticky sweetness, thinking if I ate all the nuts, no one else would get hurt…

In this whole mess, I hadn't even asked if Myar Mal was alive. Not that it mattered; he wasn't a friend of mine. And after that nut incident, I doubted Tayrel Kan would be. I was on my own.

A rustle ground my musing to a halt. I strained my ears, wondering if I'd imagined it. But the sound repeated, and I was now certain: someone was behind my tent. Why not the front? Were they trying to sneak in? Didn't they realize there was only one way in?

Was there?

Carefully, I turned my head toward the direction it came from. There was a shadow creeping near the ground, barely visible against the white sheet. I cast a quick blurring spell and as quietly as I could—which I admit wasn't very quiet—I darted outside, wand in hand, hoping to catch the intruder before they fled.

When I saw them, I froze.

"Ellare," I groaned. "What are you doing here?"

The girl raised her teary eyes to me. "Help me," she whispered.

I quickly scanned the area. We were at the very edge of the camp, and there was no one in sight. I grabbed Ellare's arm and dragged her into my tent. She was dirty, covered in ash and grime, almost blending in with the environment—

that's probably how she got this far without drawing attention.

When we were inside, I placed the seal on the entrance, and she slumped down on the ground, scattering flakes of dirt all over my pristine floor. I cast a quick cleaning spell; Ellare didn't even notice.

"I made a mistake," she sputtered between sobs.

Yeah, no shit.

Like me, Ellare was from Nes Peridion. A couple of cycles younger, but already notorious for her beauty—especially since she wasn't above taking advantage of it. Rumor said she had the hots for Karlan, but of course, her parents wouldn't have it. They even arranged for her to marry an honest peon boy. I guess she did follow her heart after all. Right to the fucking Montak Mansion.

I ran my hand through my hair and slumped to my cot.

"What were you thinking?" I asked.

"It wasn't supposed to be like this," she whimpered.

I felt a stab of anger. What was it supposed to be like?

"Karlan said..." she sobbed again, "He said that we'd just get in, make our demands, and they'd do as we say. He said no one would die."

To that, not a stab, but a wave of hatred washed over me. Was he really so dumb? Did he think so little of Dahlsi?

Did all of them?

As if sensing my anger, Ellare shrank. "Karlan is mad," she whispered unsteadily. "Look, I— he..." She paused, then sighed, then picked up her speech. "He made it sound easy. Plausible. It was hard not to trust him. But I see now, he is delirious, Aldeaith. He wants to undo what our parents have done."

I scoffed. That much was clear from the beginning, but when I opened my mouth to say it, she raised her hand in protest.

"No, you don't understand. He treats it like some kind of ritual. He wants to do everything that happened in Nes Peridion, but in reverse. And he won't rest until he hangs your head above the gate to the mansion."

"He's in the wrong fucking world," I remarked. And there was no siege in Nes Peridion, as far as I was told. No Dahlsian presence. Plus, if he wanted to do everything like it happened back then, shouldn't he need my father's skull?

"I know." Ellare shook her head, making a few strands of hair loosen from her braid. I noticed she wore a few beads of olivine in her hair. As if to make her allegiance clear. "And he knows that, too. He knows his ritual is not working, and that makes him desperate. That's why he sent us in this stupid-ass charge."

The images flashed through my mind. The bodies of Mespanians sprawled in the dirt. Tarvissian fighters, consumed by fiery demons, contorted in agony. It wasn't stupid; it was tragic.

"And there's more," her voice quietened as she leaned toward me, raising her eyes to look into mine. "The people he brought with him... they are Tarvissi."

My confusion must have been obvious because she shook her head slightly.

"No, Aldeaith. Not colonists like us; people born and raised in old Tarviss."

A cold shiver ran down my spine. So, our worst suspicions were true. It wasn't just a bunch of dumb kids with a plan that sounded better on paper, but an alien power trying to destroy us from the inside.

"Before we came here, Karlan spent some time in Tarviss with his family," continued Ellare. "But he didn't tell me what happened there, what their plans were. I started to think… they were just using us. They never cared about our liberation."

'Liberation'?

"Were you really so unhappy in Dahls?" I asked, the bitterness seeping into my voice.

New tears shone in her eyes. "I don't know."

We went silent. I thought about what she said, and I couldn't help wondering about Karlan's role. Was he a part of the Tarvissian plan to gain more worlds and influence for themselves? Or was he just a pawn, used like the poor fools who followed him? And what exactly did the Tarvissi expect? Did they want us to surrender? Or they were looking for an excuse to declare war and invade the Dahls itself? Was this provocation approved by the government, or was it a rogue action of the Peridion family?

So many questions. And the biggest of them: what was I supposed to do? Reporting what I learned would require me to admit to Ellare's presence, and that could mean her death. Despite everything, I didn't want to be responsible for it. She was like me, younger and dumber, but Nes Peridionian, one of the last in the colonies. How could I bring her doom? But keeping it to myself would be betraying Dahls. And yes, my position at the moment wasn't the best, but if I were to choose, I'd prefer Dahlsi to win rather than Tarvissi.

But would revealing what I knew change anything?

Her hand on my knee snapped me back to reality.

"Can you help me?" she whispered again, looking into my eye.

Could I? I was in pretty deep shit myself. A murder attempt, grand insubordination—twice, if we count refusal to submit my foods and disregarding the arrest—and reckless endangerment that almost resulted in death. My future in Mespana looked bleak at least. The last thing I needed was an allegation of harboring an enemy.

"I don't know what I can do," I said. "I'm in trouble myself. If they find you here..."

"Then let's leave."

Ellare's palm slid up my knee, sending an uncomfortable shudder up my leg. I quickly grabbed her hand and pushed it away, drawing my legs closer.

She continued, unperturbed, "Just you and me. We have no place here, anyway."

For a second I was tempted to agree.

"There's nowhere to go," I replied, thinking of all the options I discarded earlier. "The only merge is in the mansion and I doubt Karlan would let me use it."

"But... you guys got here somehow."

"Yeah, our sorcerers opened a temporary path, but it's closed now."

She was watching me wordlessly with wide, pleading eyes, but I could almost hear the alarm bell ringing in my head. Ellare never looked at me before. I'd no doubt she wouldn't be doing this now if she had any choice. She was merely seeking the strongest male to latch onto, and decided I was slightly above Karlan at the moment. But her "you and me" would only last until literally anyone else showed up.

I was so glad I was immune to such sentiments.

A tingling of a doorspell ran down the back of my neck and I froze. Who was that? Did they see Ellare? They certainly would if I were to open.

The tingling intensified, verging on a headache. If I didn't let them in, they could force their way in. If not by themselves, then after calling for reinforcements. But if that happened, I wouldn't be able to explain myself. And if I tried to use the moment to flee…

But there was nowhere to go!

The tingling vanished and I felt control seeping back to my limbs. I snapped from my cot and ran to the entrance, Ellare's fingers brushing my knee as she attempted to stop me. I broke the seal and almost stumbled outside.

Saral Tal was already a few paces away. Alone. He turned back, opening his mouth to speak, but then his gaze reached past me, and it was his turn to freeze.

"It's not what you think," I stammered, my mind completely blank. I should at least try to come up with an explanation. But what could I say? What could make my situation better?

Saral Tal's gaze slowly drifted toward me, his hand resting on his wand.

"She's not a rebel," I shouted desperately, not sure when I decided to go with this line of defense. "She lived here. In Maurir. When the rebels came, she hid in the mansion and only now managed to sneak out. When the gate was broken. And the rebels were busy."

I realized I was babbling, so I snapped my mouth shut.

173

For a long moment, he was looking at me without a word, before shifting his gaze back to Ellare, and I couldn't help following it. She still sat on the floor, her hands splayed wide, lips parted and trembling slightly, eyes full of tears.

Saral Tal wasn't exactly imposing, but he had the means to kill us both. He would be doing his duty, disposing of an enemy and a supposed traitor. No one would hold it against him. On the other hand, executing someone in cold blood was different from killing in the heat of a battle. I prayed Saral Tal wouldn't find the strength to do it.

After an excruciating eternity, he finally nodded, but didn't take his hand off his wand. He was still tense, his jaw clenched, but at least he didn't look like ready to kill us.

"Kar-vessár wants to see you," he said to me, though his eyes were on Ellare.

My stomach sunk. So Myar Mal was alive? Or had they just announced his successor?

"Let him decide what to do with her," he finished.

I nodded, my throat tight. I gestured Ellare off the floor and we went out, with Saral Tal closing the procession. Was it because he didn't trust me enough to turn his back on me?

In any case, his presence faded into the background as more and more people stopped whatever they were doing to stare at me. My guts were churning like a bag of worms. Traitor, they seemed to scream. I wanted to sink into the ground.

Two healers awaited in front of the vessár-ai tent, demanding to see my bags. The joke was on them: I ate my last nut before coming here. In anycase, they barely looked at my stuff, so transfixed were they on Ellare. Even if I had some nuts, they would probably miss them.

When they finally handed them back and parted before us, I breathed a sigh of relief at the thought that we would soon be out of sight of most of the camp. It was quickly snuffed out, though, when I realized who was waiting on the other side.

Cool air hit me as I entered. I tried my best to brace myself, but my knees were like jelly, and my insides twisted into a knot so tight, there was no room for them to turn anymore. And yet, as I crossed the threshold, my eyes fell on a figure even more grotesque than Tayrel Kan at his worst. I froze.

His skin was red and so swollen, it resembled raw dough more than a human flesh. Lips took up almost half the face, while eyes were reduced to mere slits. In sausage-like fingers, he held the breathing mask, but he refused to fasten it, only lifting it every once in a while.

"You should rest," berated the elder vessár—Tyano Har-Vahir—but the figure brushed him off.

"I'll rest when I'm dead," he said with a raw, raspy voice, waving his hand dismissively. Light glimmered on a dallite ring and only then did I realize who it was.

Myar Mal.

He finally noticed me and for a moment his violet eyes met mine. Then they shifted toward Ellare and my heart stopped.

Two days ago, I claimed to never have given anyone reason to doubt my loyalty. But there it was, plain and simple.

Traitor, screamed kar-vessár's voice in my head.

"Aldait Han claims this woman is a local who hid from the rebels and only now managed to escape the mansion," reported Saral Tal before I collected myself enough to speak.

Myar Mal was studying us. I wished I knew what he thought. Did he believe Saral Tal? Believe me?

After a few seconds, without a word, he twisted his wrist and Ellare collapsed like a sack of vye. I tried to grab her, but she slipped from my hands and hit the floor.

"Kiarn At, make sure our princess stays asleep until this mess is over," said kar-vessár. Then he turned to me. "Aldait Han"

He threw something at me and this time I managed to catch it. I looked down: a silver sash. My stomach churned.

"Put it on and sit down, we don't have the whole day. You take over your Cohort, Adyar Lah replaces Sanam Il in Second."

I looked around, spotting the man sitting next to Innam Ar, eyes fixed on the tabletop, seemingly determined to avoid my gaze. His head was slumped and shoulders hunched. There was also another person, a woman I'd never seen before and had no artificially implanted knowledge about.

"We lost two more vessár-ai," explained Myar Mal, the first notes of impatience seeping into his voice.

I hurriedly put on the sash and took the last available seat.

"All right, first things first," started the kar-vessár. "Aldait Han, you received an order to submit all of your food products."

I dropped my head, heat rushing to my face. My insides were twisting again, as if ready to burst from my body and skitter away.

"Yes, kar-vessár," I murmured.

"You didn't."

I could feel his eyes boring into me. Everyone's eyes boring into me. I tried to imagine myself melting into the chair.

"There was no… opportunity," I stammered.

"What were you so busy with?" sounded a mocking voice from the side. Raison Dal-Aramek, whispered Tayrel Kan's voice in my head. Vessár of the Eleventh Cohort, and unofficially, the leader of the medical team.

I clenched my fists, trying to calm myself. I was just hoping the fight would be over and we'd be back in Sfal. And then Laik Var died and I…

"You're juggling nuts, Aldait Han," said Myar Mal. It was a Dahlsian expression, meaning playing with dangerous things. Juggling swords, I guess. "Laik Var vouched for you, and that's why I'm willing to let your insubordination slip. But this is the last time. One more act like this, and you will be disciplinarily discharged. Do you understand?"

I swallowed heavily. "Yes, kar-vessár."

"Good. Raison Dal, you're going to organize sanitation teams to confiscate all possible allergens in the camp. From everyone, not only our little rebel here."

I flinched. Did he have to drag this out?

"I don't give a shit about your delicate palate." He looked at me pointedly and I did my best to escape his gaze. "This is a safety hazard and it has to be removed. From now on, the only food permitted within the camp are rations. If everything goes well, we'll be home in a day and you'll be able to indulge to your heart's content without putting anyone at risk. Is that understood?"

"Yes, kar-vessár," we answered in unison, though of everyone present, I'd be the only one affected by this decision. With two anaphylaxes happening within the last day, I didn't blame them for extra caution. But no matter how hard I tried to convince myself of that, I couldn't help a pang of anger. It was my food about to go up in flames.

Contrariness, I told myself. A childish obstinacy of someone who can't have their way. I should be above that...

"Aldait Han." I flinched again, wondering what new accusations he had against me. "As soon as we return to Sfal, you will retake your first aid course. I know operating a syringe may seem folly to you, but it affects more lives than yours, and I won't tolerate any ignorance in that matter."

"Yes, kar-vessár," I murmured. That phrase seemed to be the only thing I was capable of saying. My cheeks heated as I wondered what he—and all the others—must have thought about my intelligence.

"Did you at least collect the fresh adrenaline shots?"

I gritted my teeth. How did the bastard know? I guess it was his job to oversee everything happening in Mespana. Still, didn't he have more pressing matters than caring about my medicine stash? Who was I to deserve his attention anyway?

Vessár of the Seventh Cohort. A chill ran down my spine as the realization dawned upon me, as if only now did I understand what his words meant, the silver sash on my chest, the necessity of replacing Laik Var. Tears prickled my eyes, and I did my best to push the last thought away.

"Yes, kar-vessár," I replied, mentally thanking the gods that the medics pushed the new meds into my hands when I delivered Tayrel Kan into their care. Then I cursed myself, realizing I used that damn phrase again. Had he anything else to flay me for, or could we move on?

"Finally, we'll attack tonight."

I almost wished he kept flaying me. A cacophony of voices exploded around me, with every vessár set on expressing their displeasure.

Myar Mal silenced them all by banging his fist on the table. "We've been stalling long enough!" he said sternly.

"We were just attacked, Myar Mal," protested the new woman. Marks on her arm identified her as the vessár of the Sixth Cohort. "Many people died or were wounded."

"That's why Tarvissi won't expect us to move now."

"And we still don't have any way of protecting ourselves from their bolts," added Tyano Har.

"Kiarn At and his men are working on an advanced version of a blurring spell. The Tarvissi can pierce our shields, but they can't hit something they don't see clearly."

"If we try to storm their mansion, all they have to do is shoot at the incoming mass," noted Ayrela Va-Roma, vessár of the Tenth Cohort. "Your spell won't make any difference. More people will die."

"And if we keep on debating, they will have more time to prepare the next attack," said Adyar Lah in unexpected support for Myar Mal. "They made it pretty clear they're not interested in a peaceful resolution. By stalling, we're only giving them an opening."

"And even if we do get to the mansion, then what?" asked Raison Dal, vessár of Eleventh Cohort. "They still have the numbers. The training. The magical weapons. They can swat us away like annoying flies."

"We have our training, too," replied Myar Mal. "And our magic. And ssothians."

"We used to have kas'shams too," added Raison Dal, and the kar-vessár paled.

"We have to devise a tactic that will allow us to maximize the effectiveness and minimize the losses," he said, perfectly collected despite the adversity.

"The losses you speak of are human lives," remarked Ayrela Va.

"They are inevitable. We didn't start this fight, but we have to finish it."

"One way or another?" asked Raison Dal.

Myar Mal looked him in the eye. "If you have any objections to my leadership, you can take them to the Directory."

"I object to your recklessness and arrogance," he snapped, and I barely held back a gasp at his insolence. "Is it true it was you who devised that disastrous spell?"

Kar-vessár paled even more. "Yes."

Raison Dal scoffed. "You got drunk on the power Tayrel Kan gave you; so much so that you never stopped to consider if it was worth taking."

I was stumped. How dare he speak like this to Myar Mal? Was he immune to our leader's strength?

Or was I the only one susceptible? I tried to discretely look around, for the first time wondering how other people acted in his presence, but the continuing argument made it hard to focus. I'd have to go back to it later.

"I took a chance, I failed. It won't happen again."

"I bet you were saying the same while leaving the Academy."

"At least I graduated."

Now Raison Dal's face turned red. I recalled he studied both medicine and psychology but finished neither. What about the kar-vessár? The hole in the knowledge implanted by Tayrel Kan jarred me again, but a second later thinking about the sorcerer sent a wave of guilt down to my very core.

"Are you going to try to veto me?" asked Myar Mal after a moment of silence. Both men were staring at each other, neither willing to give up and despite not being the object of the scrutiny for once, I felt uneasy.

"I would if I had any chance," replied Raison Dal without hesitation. "But you put in three new vessár-ai in this room, they're not going to stand against you."

"Those of us who know what we're doing won't either," said Vareya Lyg coldly.

"Myar Mal is right, we need to finish this rebellion. The sooner we do that, the better," added Innam Ar.

"What would you propose, Raison Dal?" asked Tyano Har. "Stepping back and letting them do as they please? Trying to wait them out? Should I remind you about the potential involvement of Tarviss that we still aren't sure of? Every moment we waste here is another moment they have to gather their army and lead it on Dahls."

My heart jumped to my throat at the mention of Tarviss, but before I gathered courage—and words—to speak, Innam Ar was already talking.

"Besides, the rebellion here may serve as inspiration for others. It's no secret that some settlers are not happy with

Dahlsian domination. If they see they can just fight us without facing retribution, they won't hesitate."

"The rebels must die," stated Myar Mal, the weight in his voice crushing. "All of them. They must die, their mansion must be blasted to pieces and covered with salt so that nothing grows here, and everyone can witness what happens to those who oppose Dahls."

"I'm not denying that, I just can't support the mindless charging," said Raison Dal. "Especially from you, Innam Ar. You trained every single soldier you're now sending to die."

The vessár of the First Cohort looked him in the eye. "I sent them to die when they left my Cohort," he replied calmly. "I gave them the best training I could; what they do with it is their responsibility."

"Is that what Iria In taught?"

Innam Ar leaned back in his chair. "I already saw leaders who spent their lives contemplating every single death, wondering if there was anything they could have done to prevent it. It consumed them."

"Ah. It's good to hear our leadership is holding human life in such high esteem."

"We're wasting time," said Myar Mal. His tone made it clear he was not interested in further objections. "The losses are inevitable. If you have a problem with that, I suggest changing your line of work." He drew his gaze over all of the vessár-ai. "I want you to survey and regroup your Cohorts. Engage your haip if you must."

Haip-vessár-ai were first in every dozen. It was a semi-official position at most times, but it had its uses. If only I had any idea who the fuck my haip-ai were…

"I expect to see your reports in an hour. Keep them short. Also, tell your people to start preparing. Those with medical training stay with the wounded. All sorcerers with a score of one point three and above are to report immediately to Kiarn At in Cohort Four to prepare the blurring spell. Now come on, move it!" He made a shooing motion and the vessár-ai scrambled from their chairs. "Aldait Han, you stay."

Fuck.

Myar Mal waited until everyone else had left, so I had a few seconds to figure out what to say. But every option that came to my mind seemed worse than the previous one. When the tent flap fell behind the last vessár we sat in silence for an uncomfortably long moment.

"Is that girl a friend of yours?" asked Myar Mal finally.

I shuddered. Not the question I expected, but no less terrifying.

"We grew up together."

Too late, I remembered I was supposed to pretend she lived here.

"And I guess you'd be terribly sad if something bad happened to her."

I clenched my teeth. She was my compatriot, if nothing else, and I didn't wish her harm. On the other hand, she made her choice—she was a rebel, and according to Myar Mal's own words, they all had to die. I didn't want to die with her. I didn't want to die for her.

But then I already decided to lie. Should I change my story now? Admit to my lies? I couldn't bring myself to do it. So, I kept my mouth shut and waited for the kar-vessár to elaborate.

He didn't.

"All right," he said instead. "Let's get back to more pressing matters."

Maybe it was because of his macabre look, but there was only one other pressing matter on my mind. I exhaled nervously and started speaking,"Myar Mal, I assure you, I had nothing to do—"

"If I had any doubts, you wouldn't be here," he cut me short, stern and to-the-point, and I felt a pang of annoyance. "Sit back."

I obliged automatically, slumping into my chair and clasping my hands together.

"If there's one thing that incident taught me, it's you would never be able to plot," he said, despite his half-closed eyes managing to look at me as piercingly as before.

Another stab of annoyance broke through my anxiety. "You think I'm too stupid?"

"More like… too straightforward. But someone heard you threatening me and decided to take advantage of that."

Annoyance melted into embarrassment. I started wringing my hands under the table. "I'm sorry, kar-vessár. It was inappropriate of me. I want to assure you—"

"That you don't know when to shut up. Yeah, I noticed. But I need you to do it now. Yesterday in the hangar. Do you remember who was there?"

I paused my wringing, taking a moment to consider. "Vessár-ai, me, the kas'sham… but I doubt it's them."

At moment like this I was glad that Dahlsi-é had no grammatical genders, because I had no idea how to tell kas'sham genders apart.

"Why not?"

I scoffed. "Everyone knows Tarvissi are speciesists. I can't imagine non-humans working with us."

"Who said Tarvissi had anything to do with that?"

I snapped my head up, my hands frozen in place. "I beg your pardon?"

He put his mask on and inhaled deeply before his next words. "Do you know what happens when kar-vessár dies?"

I hesitated, not sure what answer he expected. I had some ideas. We would be left without leadership, without direction. No attack could be planned, and we would become open for an enemy charge.

But his reply came before I could say any of this.

"Another one gets appointed. It's even better when the whole thing can be blamed on someone they already hate. I mean, he's Tarvissi, he has been seen arguing with current kar-vessár, he has the means. It's all too perfect, don't you think?"

I tensed. Previously, I reached a similar conclusion, but I still assumed all of this led back to the Tarvissi. Was I wrong? Did the conspiracy originate within our own ranks?

"No offense, kar-vessár," I asked weakly. "But could any Dahlsi handle carai-nut?"

"Some of us are more resilient than others. Some of us have good relations with non-humans."

I remembered the other person that was in the hangar. "You mean the kas'sham—"

I stopped abruptly. I realized I didn't even know his name.

"Dria'ri Na." He waved his hand dismissively. "They died in yesterday's charge. But it doesn't matter, really. At best they were just a pawn. It's the head I want to get to."

Understandable. But…

"What do I have to do with it?"

"Well, I always thought you quiet types know more than you let out."

At first, I was surprised, but that quickly passed. I couldn't help a bitter smile. "That's a nice sentiment, Myar Mal, but I'm afraid in this case, you're wrong. I'm just a shy guy with no social skills. People only think I'm interesting because of the times we live in."

He gave me an inquiring look, and I knew he was wondering if I told the truth. But I was. For Vhalfr's sake, without magic aid, I couldn't even remember the names of the vessár-ai. How could I know which of them would be most likely to wish the kar-vessár dead?

"So, you don't sit in shadows, watching everybody and gathering information to use later on?" He sounded almost disappointed.

I chuckled self-depreciatingly. "I can't imagine why anyone would want to displace you."

But before I even finished speaking, memories came back.

"Raison Dal…" I started.

Kar-vessár nodded. "Opposing me doesn't mean he'd like to kill me. Frankly, I doubt he has it in him… but he would have no problem obtaining the nut. I'll keep him in mind. My top pick was Sanam Il, it's a shame rebels got him. Wouldn't it be a wonderful irony if he died along with me, leaving the position he craved so much up for grabs?"

The only answer I could offer was a blank stare. I knew Sanam Il—a Tarvissio-phile who recently shaved his

186

beard—but for the life of me, I could not remember having any type of interaction with him.

"He was the one who suggested Adyar Lah for vessár of Seventh Cohort," Myar Mal offered.

"Perhaps he confided in Adyar Lah?" I hazarded a guess.

Kar-vessár shook his head. "I doubt that. You should see his face when I commissioned him to lead Seventh Cohort. No, he wouldn't be able to keep the secret. He's a decent guy, all things considered. Just needs a little shaking up now and then."

I remembered Adyar Lah's beaten-down appearance at the meeting. It made me almost feel sorry for him.

"He reminds me of you a bit, you know. Quiet, withdrawn. I bet if you met under different circumstances, you'd get along pretty well."

Yeah, I could imagine that: two quiet guys, sitting in awkward silence, trying to figure out what to say.

"I'm going to grill him later on," kar-vessár continued. "But I think there's no point. If it was Sanam Il, the conspiracy died with him. If not, I suppose they will try again."

I felt as if someone punched me in the gut. I should have known. All this talk about respecting Laik Var's wishes was just a ruse. Myar Mal had to have a better reason to keep me here, to promote me. Something personal.

"And you think next time they will go for me," I guessed. "That's why you put me in this position."

Myar Mal rolled his lips in a dark parody of a grin, then reached out to pat my shoulder. "See? You're not as dumb as you seem."

Chapter 19

FOR THE SECOND time that day, I stood before my Cohort. Now officially, with the silver sash burning against my chest. It didn't feel any less uncomfortable.

I tried to recall all the grand motivating speeches I'd ever heard, be it from Innam Ar, Laik Var, or even Adyar Lah, and come up with my own. My mind was blank.

"Kar-vessár gave new orders," I stated lamely, shame and self-loathing churning in my guts. "We'll be storming the mansion tonight. I want you to suit up and be ready in an hour. All sorcerers with a score of one point three and above are to report to Kiarn At in Cohort Four for a special assignment."

"Yes, vessár!"

The answer came without hesitation, and the tightness in my shoulders loosened a bit.

I looked around. The Seventh Cohort consisted mostly of Dahlsi. There were three Xzsim, one human woman whose origin I couldn't place, plus a handful of nonhumans.

There used to be a few kas'shams... I tried not to think about them.

I cleared my throat before continuing: "Also, due to the recent increase in the number of life-threatening allergic reactions, we are to hand over all of our natural food products. The decontamination team will be making rounds around the camp and I ask for your full cooperation."

"Yes, vessár!"

This time the answer was less enthusiastic. The Xzsim were glaring at me with murder—although that could be their default state. They had those round, yellow eyes that seemed evil, and lining them with kohl didn't help. Nonhumans were unreadable. I'd heard chavikii could go for days—and that's Dahlsian days—without food, so I wasn't expecting too much resistance from them. Ssothians on the other hand, could be unpredictable, and given their size and aggression, I couldn't imagine anyone bullying them into submission.

Well, the decontamination team would deal with them.

There was still one more thing. I scanned the crowd, looking for familiar faces. But most people I knew were either dead or wounded.

"Saral Tal," I called finally

He stepped out, not smiling, but the corners of his mouth were twitching.

"I want you to be my nami."

He wasn't able to hold it any longer: his face brightened with a smile. Apparently, he already got over Ellare. Maybe Myar Mal's acceptance of my lie banished all traces of distrust.

"Yes, vessár!" he exclaimed happily.

He was the last person I knew—save for Dalyn Kia, but her opinion of me was pretty low, and I had no intention of decreasing it even further. At least Saral Tal seemed incapable of meanness, so I could pretend that he liked me. Anyway, there was no one else I trusted. Argan Am would probably be a better pick, with the experience he amassed leading our dozen, but I wasn't going to drag him out of the hospital.

I waved at Saral Tal to come closer. "In half an hour, I need a full report about the status of our Cohort. Dead, wounded, equipment loss, everything. I made a start before… well, it's probably rubbish now, but you can have a look at that."

"Can I get the original list of our personnel?" he asked. My brain blanked out. He quickly clarified, "It should be among the documents left by Laik Var."

I felt heat rising to my face. "I didn't think about that," I mumbled. Just showed how little I was suited for this job. The blasted sash grew heavier against my body.

Truth be told, I avoided thinking about anything related to Laik Var. Now, my eyes darted to his tent, clearly distinguishable thanks to the insignia of Seventh Cohort.

My tent.

A wave of nausea rolled over me.

Saral Tal grabbed my shoulder. "Are you all right, vessár?"

"Yes." I let out a shaky breath. "Yeah, I'm fine. Let's go." At the last moment, I caught myself, and turned back to my Cohort. "Dismissed."

I shook off Saral Tal's hand and headed toward the tent. But it felt as if someone cast a repelling spell: I had to fight for each step, my knees threatening to buckle any time. Saral Tal was walking beside me, and even without looking I knew he was watching me, ready to offer his hand if I was about to fall. He made no comment, but my guts coiled in shame.

Sooner than I wanted to, we stood at the entrance. The flap was in front of me; all I had to do was reach out and...

But I couldn't do it. I was standing, taut as a bowstring, waiting for an all-too-familiar voice to call me in.

Saral Tal pulled the flap.

The tent was empty. There was no one there.

I let out a shaky breath. What did I expect?

The heavy desk occupied the center of the tent, topped with a little honeycomb shelf filled with scrolls. I was tempted to unfold the second chair and fall into it, waiting for orders, but I knew if I did that, I would never stand up.

I circled the desk. There, my eyes fell to the miniature portrait glued to the back of the cabinet, visible only to the person sitting in the vessár's chair.

Amma La.

I wondered if she was back.

Slowly, I slumped down. It felt wrong. I wanted to jump out, run around the desk, and stand on the other side. But my limbs were as heavy as stone. My hands gripped the armrests so strongly it hurt. The pain sobered me. I started limply going through the papers cluttering the counter, looking for the list that was supposed to be there, but my mind was so addled, I couldn't make sense of the words on the paper.

"Got it," I heard from beside me. I turned my head to Saral Tal. He was holding a particularly thick scroll he took from one of the shelves. He rolled and sheathed it, then hung it from his belt. "I should go to the medical bay and compare it with the list of the deceased. Are you all right?"

No.

"Yes."

He opened his mouth, but the tent flap flew open and Adyar Lah entered with an awkward mix of barging and creeping. My chest clenched, and I sunk deeper into the chair.

"I'm sorry, I left something here," he murmured, slouching his shoulders. Without waiting for a response, he scurried to the desk, and scooped the papers into his arms. That's why I couldn't make heads and tails out of them.

Until then, his eyes were on the ground, but now he lifted them at me and his brows knitted slightly.

"It's hard, isn't it?" he asked.

I didn't know what to say. My throat was so tight I wasn't sure if I could even make a sound. I dropped my gaze to the desk and clenched my hands on the armrests.

"You think they'll be here forever... until they're not."

Still, I didn't speak. It didn't seem like he was expecting an answer anyway. With the corner of my eye, I saw him turning his head and biting his lip. What was he thinking of? Did his thoughts mirror mine? But what were my thoughts? Who was Laik Var to me? Commander, nothing more. Almost a stranger.

And at the same time, he was the only thing I took for granted, the only reminder that as long as I did as I was told, everything was going to be all right...

Until it wasn't.

"Sanam Il was a good vessár," said Adyar Lah finally, ripping me from my thoughts.

"So was Laik Var," I replied hollowly.

He looked at me and his lips spread in something between a smile and a grimace. "For what it's worth, I'm glad it's you here."

I nodded.

"And…" he hesitated. "Thanks for healing me before. With all that happened, I wouldn't have been surprised if you left me to bleed out."

And have everyone in Mespana blame your death on me, I thought, but there was no bite in it. On the contrary, I felt the tightness in my chest easing off a bit and even managed to lift my head to look in the vague direction of Adyar Lah.

"I was doing my job," I said lamely, then added quickly, "You should get that checked, though. I'm not very good at this, as you probably realized." A nervous chuckle escaped my lips but died as I remembered my failure with helping Tayrel Kan. "I should have let Dalyn Kia do it. She's a sorcerer, isn't she?"

Adyar Lah smiled, and I got an impression of it being a little condescending. "Yes, she is. And don't worry, I had it checked. It's procedure, remember?"

I cursed myself mentally. Of course it was. My gaze dropped to the desk. I wished he would leave, but he stayed, hesitating.

"Also," he added finally, "I'm sorry for… before."

He didn't have to specify.

I shook my head. "You were doing your job," I said before realizing I was basically parroting my previous statement. I wanted to add something, anything that wouldn't make me look like an utter idiot, but before I figured out what, he spoke again.

"My job was to find the traitor. But I let the others sway me. I was so convinced of your guilt, I didn't even want to listen to you. I'm sorry. I shouldn't…" He licked his lips and added, lowering his voice, so I barely heard him, "I shouldn't have judged you without knowing you."

His words made something in my chest stir. Why, though? Everyone judged me, usually unfavorably and almost always without knowing jack shit about me.

I turned my head to avoid looking at him and shook it slightly. "I'm used to it."

"It doesn't make it right."

Life is not right. I waved my hand, wishing for nothing but to end this line of conversation. "All is forgiven." Something he'd said earlier struck me, and I couldn't help myself asking, "Who exactly declared my guilt?"

His gaze hardened, and I got a feeling he understood the real reason behind my questioning.

"Myar Mal already asked me all about it," he admitted quietly, then paused. For a moment he was studying me, as if expecting something, but I kept my mouth shut. I wasn't sure how much he knew, how much I could let out. So, I preferred to stay silent.

Finally, his lips twisted into a sour grimace. "He has this way of looking at people… he doesn't need to say anything to make you know you screwed up."

I recalled Adyar Lah's downcast appearance during the vessár-ai session. It seemed my suspicion was right. I felt a pang of satisfaction, but it vanished as quickly as it showed, replaced by pity. I wouldn't wish anyone to get on Myar Mal's bad side.

"I thought that was his default look," I tried joking.

Adyar Lah's eyebrows shot up, but then his features relaxed and… he smiled.

"Yeah, I guess," he chuckled, and I realized my hands weren't clutching the armrests anymore. For the first time since I was appointed, I felt almost… relaxed.

Maybe Myar Mal was right. Maybe we could get along.

"Well." He sighed. Then his smile receded into a scowl. "Whoever it was behind that attempt, let's hope they'll be found soon."

"Yeah." I nodded. "Let's hope."

The good mood brought by reconciling with Adyar Lah didn't last long. A few moments after he left, the tent flap opened again. I glanced up to check and almost immediately lowered my head. Innam Ar-Leig. He took a seat across the desk and stared at me wordlessly.

"Can I help you, vessár?" I asked, wanting nothing but for him to leave me alone. The forty days I spent training under his command were some of the worst in my life.

"What the fuck have you done, Tirsan?" he asked, and I felt a stab of anger.

"I haven't done anything—" I started, but he didn't let me finish.

"You pissed off a lot of people. Surprising; since from what I remember, you were always rather unassuming."

"Ah." I leaned back in my chair. Unlike other furniture, it had armrests and a proper backrest. Sadly, it was too tight for my size, making it even more uncomfortable than normal stools. "I'm afraid my main offense is being born to the wrong parents."

"Yes," he sighed. "I'm afraid you're right. Wouldn't it be beautiful, if all of our problems had simple, rational causes?"

He retrieved a small silver box of vaka pills and offered me one. "Come on, take it. It's a mood stabilizer too. You shouldn't let anyone see you like you were before entering this tent."

I took it but didn't unpack it. I wondered if it was poisoned.

"Why do you care?" I asked. "Sorry, Innam Ar, but you never struck me as considerate."

He chuckled. "Kid, my job is to make soldiers, not friends. I can't afford leniency, because our enemies won't. Be glad you didn't train under Tyano Har. I swear, the bastard relished in our misery."

The accusation would probably carry more weight if I wasn't able to say the same about him.

"I was only trying to make you a man," he continued, meeting my gaze without blinking. "And looking at you now, I wonder where the fuck I went wrong."

I seethed. "What the fuck do you know—"

"Oh, I do, believe me. You enlisted at that precious age when you still confused your leader with your daddy. You want him to hold your hand and lead you to victory. Well, guess what, Tirsan? It's time to grow up."

197

For a moment I looked at him, stupefied. How did he know? How can some people figure out your deepest, most guarded secret, then drag it out like that, hit you where it hurts the most, without even seeming to try? Then I remembered what Tayrel Kan put into my head: he was a psychologist, it was literally his job.

Except maybe the hurting. That was just him.

I was not sure if it was my anger, my tiredness, or his casual behavior, but before I could think better of it, I snapped. "If you only came here to insult me, you can get the fuck out."

My insolence shocked me. A part of me half-expected him to take over my body, walk it outside and leave me standing, paralyzed, in the middle of the camp for a day or two. It was a standard disciplinary action in Mespana, one I experienced once and dedicated my life to never experiencing again. It took me a while to realize that, at least for now, he was not my vessár. He was my equal.

The bastard smiled. "That's better. I have something for you."

He reached into his pouch again and handed me an amulet: a small tertium disk with a perfectly transparent crystal in the center, dangling from a silver chain. A protective charm.

"It won't make you invincible," he warned. "But it should deflect any deadly spell aimed at your back. That's a singular 'spell' by the way. Don't play a hero; as soon as you feel it sting, get the fuck down."

I put the amulet on and hid it under my uniform.

"Now, take your pill. Don't worry, it's not poisoned. I'm not one of them. Get your shit together, get your report done—"

"I had my nami do it."

"Good. That's what they're for. Now you have more time to get ready. Don't waste it on brooding, Tirsan. The battle's ahead!"

Some people considered rough treatment to be motivational, and Innam Ar was no exception. But for me, it did the opposite. I couldn't bear staying in the tent; its walls seemed to press in on me, suffocate me. I ran outside and stood for a while, breathing deeply.

No way I could get anything done in there.

For better or worse, I spotted Raison Dal's decontamination team and remembered the other part of kar-vessár's orders. Cursing, I darted to my tent. I didn't have much food left, having eaten all the snacks; just a few dry ingredients. In the last few days, I had been in no mood for cooking, but then, as I was packing them away, I thought of all the dishes I could have made. Even the driest, least seasoned porridge beat Dahlsian rations. And having the food I wasn't eating beat seeing said food go up in flames.

Silly, I knew. But thinking about provisions helped me not to think about other things, so I cut myself some slack.

My fingers wrapped around a bag of naya spice and I froze. My mother made it in Nes Peridion, using traditional Tarvissian ingredients as well as local herbs. Probably the last batch she prepared…

Technically, it was not food. And since I only used it for cooking, it had no chance of leaving my tent. It was no threat to anyone. Just to be on the safe side, I made a little cut in my pillow and slipped the spice bag in, then fixed the hole with a spell. There. Unless someone slept in my bed, it should be fine.

I felt a bit better about handing the rest of my stash to the decontamination team.

When they left, I spotted Saral Tal heading toward the field hospital and realized I still had some time to kill. It crossed my mind that I should probably prepare for the upcoming battle. Not myself, necessarily, that would take minutes, but my Cohort. I quickly discarded that idea. Myar Mal's words still echoed in my head. I was here only as bait; I didn't owe him a job well done.

Besides, what could I do? We didn't even have a plan yet!

So it was all right, I told myself, as I approached the hospital. I wasn't sure when exactly I decided to visit Tayrel Kan, but it seemed proper. I owed him an apology, after all.

But as soon as I reached the hospital, it was as if cold fingers wrapped around my heart. The area was crowded; even outside the main tents, people were sitting or lying on the ground, some bandaged, others just pressing cloths to their untended wounds. A couple of sorcerers bustled about, casting minor healing spells, but neither of them wore the yellow coat of a true healer. The air resonated with moans of pain and cracks of magic.

I rushed toward the tent, hoping to leave the scene behind, but what greeted me there was even worse. It was quiet. There was a hum of magic, but no sobs, words or screams. Dozens of cots stood squeezed next to each other, all of them taken. People crushed by rocks, pierced by bolts, a few burned—by Tayrel Kan's spell? I didn't want to think about that. Mercifully, most of them were unconscious. Gods, I hoped they were unconscious.

Earlier, I considered suffering life-threatening anaphylaxis qualified someone to be here. Now I wasn't so sure.

Wishing to be out of here as soon as possible, I grabbed the nearest healer, earning a look of pure exasperation, and asked about Tayrel Kan. Apparently, he was already discharged. The healer pointed me to where his tent was, then fled before I could ask further questions.

No matter. I was ready to leave, the mixed smells of blood, antiseptic, burned flesh and nyarai extract making me nauseous. But a familiar voice sounded behind me, stopping me. "Vessár?"

I turned around, the sash burning my chest. Argan Am was lying on one of the cots, with a generous amount of nyarai paste applied to his face and head. I only recognized him by his eyes. He held his hands on the blanket, but while the right one was merely bandaged, the left one ended in a stump, just below his elbow.

"Yeah," he said, and I realized I must have been staring for a while. "I liked my hand, you know. It was a useless lump, but it was… mine."

"What happened?" I stammered, my mouth completely dry. I struggled to remember if he was right- or left-handed, until I realized the futility. He was a sorcerer; of course he was left-handed.

"I asked to be part of Kiarn At's strike force. I got hit—not directly, but my suit caught fire. Those spells they were throwing must have been made to counter our protections. I managed to get down, but just barely."

Bile rose in my throat. "I'm sorry."

He shook his head. "Not your fault."

Wasn't it? I'd been sent to the mansion with the specific task of investigating enemy weapons. If I'd foreseen the crystals could serve as projectiles, our fliers could prepare.

"It didn't hurt," he added quietly after a while. "It does now, but at the time... I saw my hand burning, saw the plastic melting into my flesh. And felt nothing. My brain just refused to process the pain. But I remember the smell. It smelled... like one of those things you cook, you know?"

A wave of nausea rolled over me. I remembered the odor well from when Tayrel Kan was casting his spell—it made me want to give up meat for a while.

I wanted to say something, but no words came to my mind. I just stared at him, sick and horrified.

He lifted his gaze. It was hard to tell with his dark eyes, but I thought he must've been high on painkillers. He seemed conscious enough to keep the conversation going, though.

"What about you?" He nodded toward my sash. "I see you had more luck."

Luck was the last word I would use, but I didn't know how to explain everything, so I just said, "Laik Var is dead."

"Shit."

"I was thinking about making you my nami," I added after a moment of uncomfortable silence, feeling a strong need to fill the air with something.

The sorcerer scoffed. "Forget it, man. I'm not good at such things."

"You were doing pretty well in Sorox."

"And got enough leadership for a lifetime."

"I had to settle for Saral Tal."

Argan Am looked at me inquisitively and I shifted, uneasy.

"You think he'll be fine?" he asked.

"No idea. I don't know anyone else I could trust." Then, not able to keep it inside any longer, I let my frustration out. "I'm not the best person for this position. Someone else should have it."

"Sorry, man. Can't help you."

"I know," I murmured. I was hoping to hear one of those pointless platitudes you don't care about until you miss them. I guess, like all Dahlsi, he was too practical for bullshit.

"Did you know Laik Var had a daughter?" I asked after a moment of silence.

"Amma La? Yeah, I studied with her."

"Did you?"

"Yeah." He paused. "So, are you gonna ask?"

"What?"

He let out a small chuckle. "I studied with Myar Mal too."

That was a surprise. I couldn't imagine our kar-vessár working as a sorcerer. He was too... dominating. In ancient times, he could have become a warlock commanding an army of golems to conquer some half-forgotten world, but those days were long gone. Now, advanced magic was mostly used in construction or life support. Or in Mespana.

"So… is he any good?" I asked, then realized how ridiculous I sounded.

It was Myar Mal we were talking about. And yet Argan Am hesitated before replying. "His theory is flawless."

"And his practice?"

"His practice is the reason he's in Mespana and not at the Academy," he said in a tone even I understood was meant to end the topic. I recalled Malyn Tol mentioning Argan Am having some conflict with Myar Mal, and I wondered if it stemmed from their time in the Academy. But it was too late to ask.

I didn't know what to say, and he didn't seem interested in continuing the conversation either, so for a moment, we sat in awkward silence.

"I have to go," I blurted finally. "Get some rest."

"Yeah," he nodded. "Good luck, vessár."

I couldn't tell if he was mocking me.

Chapter 20

TAYREL KAN'S TENT was at the edge of the camp, away from everyone, but too close to the vessár-ai premises for my comfort.

I found the sorcerer sprawled on his cot with empty syringes, bottles, and plastic wraps scattered all over the floor.

"In Tarviss, when we visit the sick, we bring them something good to eat, but I didn't know what to get you," I said from the entrance.

He tried to rise but fell back, wincing in pain. He finally settled on turning on his side with a bent hand under his head. He sent me a lazy, hazy smile with no trace of his usual sarcasm.

I realized he was high as a kite.

"It's all right, Aldait Han; I'm glad you're here. And before you ask, it's all painkillers."

I wasn't going to ask, but now that he brought it up, I felt ridiculous. I wasn't sure if he read my mind, or if I was just so predictable.

Tayrel Kan gestured to the mark on the floor, and I helped myself to a chair. Only then did I give him a closer look. His scars had changed again: though pale, they were strangely swollen, like they were ready to burst open. Deep shadows surrounded his reddened eyes. He was only wearing pants, his chest wrapped in bandages, and the sight made a wave of guilt roll over me.

"I'm sorry," I said, waving my hand, "for all of this."

He made an uncoordinated gesture. "It's mostly the arrows."

"Bolts," I corrected automatically. He arched an eyebrow, and I took it as a cue to explain. "Arrows are for bows, crossbows shoot bolts."

I wasn't an expert, but the bolts I saw hit him during the battle seemed deep enough to puncture more than a uniform. Wait, why was I even thinking about it? He got injured and almost died. Who gave a shit about what the weapons that hurt him were called?

"Whatever." He waved his hand dismissively. "The anaphylaxis was nothing in comparison."

I winced, as the memories of my fiasco resurfaced. "How did you even survive?" I asked, striving for a positive note and obviously choosing the worst viable option.

But Tayrel Kan grinned, even though it was a shadow of his usual smile. "Magic keeps me alive. It was nothing compared to some shit I've been through. Wounds, spells, lack of air, lack of food, you name it. I'm not even sure I can die…"

There was something strange in his voice, and before I could bite my tongue, I asked, "Do you want to?"

He didn't answer, and I cursed myself.

Change the subject.

I realized I still hadn't said what I came to say. "Also," I cleared my throat, more nervous than ever before, "I'm sorry for calling you an imp. I didn't mean for it to sound like that."

Tayrel Kan frowned. "You called me an imp?" he asked, sounding as confused as I felt.

Didn't Adyar Lah bring it up during my interrogation?

"This morning, when you were in the ritual tent," I explained. "Myar Mal told me to stop you, and you weren't listening."

"I didn't hear you. I wasn't really aware of anything at the time."

"Well, I'm sorry."

"Don't worry, I've been called worse. Besides, I'm half your size, so you weren't exactly wrong."

"It's not about the size," I stammered, then paused, not sure how to explain what I meant. Adyar Lah's words were echoing through my brain, chasing away all rational thought.

He scoffed. "People these days care so much about words that they never stop to think about what they actually mean. I don't have to read your thoughts to know you're not racist. If anyone thinks otherwise, they're a fucking moron. And yeah, I'm talking about Adyar Lah. The guy has a stick so high up his ass you can see it poking out every time he opens his mouth."

"He's not that bad," I protested, even though I was unable to contain a grin. "He saved your life."

Tayrel Kan closed his eyes and let out a sigh, his face twisted in pain. "He wasn't doing anyone a favor."

My mirth vanished as fast as it appeared, and a cold shiver ran down my spine. "Don't say that."

He chuckled—a strange, self-deprecating sound I never expected to hear from him.

"Come on, has no one ever told you about me? How I'm more trouble than I'm worth? How they can't understand why Myar Mal even keeps me?"

I hesitated. I didn't want to fuel his apparent self-loathing, but I was a terrible liar. He would likely read the truth in my mind, anyway.

"Laik Var told me to stay away from you."

"Did he tell you why?"

"You know," I murmured, looking away.

"Come on, I want to hear it. You look cute when you blush."

Without thinking, I lifted my hand to my cheek. It was burning.

Ah, fuck it.

I took a deep breath. "He told me..." I noticed I was rocking in my chair and forced myself to still. "You may try to hit on me."

He chuckled again, and I felt my blush deepening.

"That's a nice explanation," he admitted finally. "Elegant. One that worked without him telling you anything important and still technically not lying; and placed all the blame on you."

"Why is that?" I asked sullenly. I didn't like being mocked, even though I came to realize it was just the way he talked.

"Well, you're the bigot who can't be trusted around a man who might try to get into your pants."

"That's a bit unfair, I think."

I lived among the Dahlsi for cycles, doing my damnedest to treat everyone equally—man or woman, human or otherwise. I didn't care what species they were or who they were sleeping with, as long as they left me out of it. Apparently, that wasn't enough. "Ever since the rebellion started, people who don't know me assume I'm a bigot, only because my parents came from the wrong world."

"To be fair, you called me an imp, so I think we're even."

My mood soured even more. "Besides, I don't think Laik Var—"

He cut me short, staring me pointedly in the eye, "He was Dahlsi. You shouldn't forget that. If the choice was between being fair to you and preserving his own way of life, which one do you expect he'd chose? I mean, come on, look around. Every other man in Dahls has at least experimented. I bet Laik Var didn't warn you about Saral Tal, hm?"

Once again, I got an impression some things were clear for everyone except me.

"Maybe we'd tell if you asked," he said, and I mentally cursed all the sorcerers in Dahls. Tayrel Kan only smirked. "Seriously, didn't they teach you how to shield your mind, or did you just flunk those classes?"

I gritted my teeth. I passed all of my classes, but that was cycles ago. No one had to do it all the time. Reading other people's thoughts was rude. Get the fuck out of my head, pest!

He laughed. With the mood completely sullen, I put up my shields. I would have to learn to do it every time we were in the same room.

"So?" he prodded after a moment of silence. "Are you gonna ask?"

I huffed, too annoyed to care. "It's not really my business."

"Aw, come on, don't act like you're not curious. Don't worry, we Dahlsi are a gossipy bunch." He paused, then added with a conspiratorial whisper, "Laik Var wouldn't mind."

"All right," I relented. I leaned back in the chair, crossing my arms. "Tell me."

"What?" he asked. Was he messing with me?

"Well," I stammered, at a loss for words, but then took a guess and finished quickly. "You had something specific you wanted to tell me, right?"

He gave an exasperated huff. "Fair enough. I guess you want to know about your favorite ex-vessár."

I was more interested in him, but as soon as I opened my mouth, he raised his hand in protest.

"No, you lost your chance to ask. I'm choosing a topic now. Laik Var then!"

Not exactly what I was hoping for. It seemed to be a habit of Tayrel Kan, to change the subject or come up with a new one every time I thought about asking him a personal question. I wondered if he did that on purpose, perhaps even using his mind-reading capabilities to avoid questioning.

"Where do I start?" he continued. "Maybe with the fact that he hated Myar Mal with a burning passion?"

Just like that, my disappointment gave way to curiosity. If Tayrel Kan was deflecting, he was doing it masterfully.

"Why?" I asked, my mood lightening a bit. After all, any information was better than none.

Tayrel Kan's smile widened and took on his usual predatory sneer.

"Laik Var had a beautiful daughter he loved very much," he started in clear mockery of narrative tone. "He wished all the best for her. He wanted her to be a sorceress. She had talent. One point three, not bad for an unmodified person. And the brains. Everything went well until she met a charming soldier with a stellar record and a bright future. A bit imperious, but that's understandable. And that face, oh, by Vhalfr! Pardon my language, but even knowing what kind of bastard he is, if he told me to suck, I would only ask how hard. Anyway, before you know it, Laik Var's precious daughter abandoned her promising career to follow the pretty soldier."

Tayrel Kan's eyes drifted as he got lost in thoughts.

"Is that it?" I prodded after a moment of silence.

He sighed. "I don't know, Aldait Han. Some people like to explain everything by what happens between the sheets, but maybe there was more to it. Academic life is not for everyone. Neither is being told what to do. Perhaps Amma La just wanted an adventure, and the pretty soldier was an excuse. What I know is, she and Laik Var didn't talk for a long time. Pah, she even refused to be in the same room with him! And he blamed Myar Mal. Ha! People are still talking about the day Myar Mal was commissioned with the rank of kar-vessár and Laik Var had to swear an oath to him."

"But why is Myar Mal..." I wasn't sure how to put my thoughts into words. No, I shouldn't say anything. It was none of my business. Still, it was hard not to notice that Amma La was perfectly average while Myar Mal was, well…

"Maybe she's his little protest too," Tayrel Kan mused.

"Against what?"

"The cult of absolute perfection he follows?"

I frowned. "Does he?"

"That was a joke. I don't know. And I'm not a connoisseur of female beauty, but even I see she's not the best he can get. So either he's really in love… or he has other reasons to be with her."

"Maybe she has other qualities."

"Yeah, I bet she sucks like a siplah."

I frowned. Siplahs were small animals feeding on waste.

"That's gross." I wasn't talking about the creatures. "I meant, maybe she's clever or caring or something."

I had very little idea of how romance worked. Marriages in Tarviss were arranged, and the sheer concept of choosing your partner seemed preposterous when our Dahlsian teacher first told us about it. And even living away from other Tarvissi, I had absolutely no inclination to pursue such things.

"What do you want me to say?" asked Tayrel Kan. "I don't know her, I don't know what's in his head. Or hers, for that matter. Most people shield themselves as soon as I show up."

He paused for a moment. "If anything, I think he feels obligated for dragging her to Mespana and fucking things up with her dad. It's no secret she's not happy here. She probably realized she wasn't escaping, but swapping one man's dream for another's. I wouldn't be surprised if the whole relationship blew up in their faces. But hey, her loss is my gain."

I frowned, not sure what to say. Tarvissian marriages were unbreakable, and personal feelings didn't factor. It was different for Dahlsi, who put personal happiness above everything. Those differences aside, I still wasn't qualified to offer advice. I wanted to say that I wished Tayrel Kan the best of luck, but I couldn't bring myself to wish for Myar Mal and Amma La to split up—even though I didn't know or particularly care about either of them.

"Can't you dream of someone who's not, you know… in a relationship?" I asked.

"You can't choose who you dream of, silly. It just happens. You can't fight it. All you can do is follow the flow."

"Does he even like guys?"

"I don't care about him liking guys; I want him to like me."

I sighed. What could I say to that?

There was still one thing that I felt was unanswered. "So, what does that have to do with me?" Then, remembering how this whole conversation started, I added hastily, "Or you?"

"You didn't get it yet? Laik Var put you as his nami because he knew it would piss off a lot of people. And who would take the heat?"

A sense of betrayal flooded over me, though I wasn't sure if it was because of Laik Var or Tayrel Kan. "But he said—"

"Yeah, I know. But whatever tear-jerking speech he gave you, the only thing he cared about was rubbing it in on Myar Mal."

"You think Laik Var was one of the traitors?"

I realized too late that only Myar Mal and me—and perhaps Adyar Lah—were supposed to be aware of the conspiracy. But, knowing Tayrel Kan's propensity to telepathy, he'd probably already read all about it in my mind.

"Nah, he was too honest for that. But he wouldn't be terribly saddened if something happened. Even if he knew, I'm not sure he'd do anything to stop it."

"Myar Mal didn't suspect him," I noted. "He had other picks."

"Well, Laik Var wasn't here to partake in that little assassination attempt. That probably cleared his name, at least partially. And I'm not surprised Myar Mal doesn't want to touch that particular can of worms. Say what you want, but he cares about Amma La."

I took a moment to digest his words. As much as I wanted to remember Laik Var as a good man and great vessár, I knew very little about him outside of work. Tayrel Kan obviously had more information and perhaps... perhaps his version of events was closer to the truth than mine, however I loathed to admit it.

"Look, maybe it's not all bad," Tayrel Kan said. He was unusually earnest, and I wondered if he regretted telling me all this. "Maybe Laik Var was casting two spells with one wand. He seemed to genuinely like you."

"But not enough to refrain from using me," I replied gloomily. "Or at least tell me about his intentions."

"To be fair, his family drama is none of your business."

Silence descended for a few long moments. Finally, he sighed. "You must be so disappointed. We're the most advanced civilization... but all the magic in the universe cannot shield us from ourselves. We're still humans. We still feel: love, hate, resentment. We still make mistakes." He lifted his hand, seemingly inadvertently, to touch his scars. "It's all terribly petty sometimes."

"What about these?" I nodded to his face, and he caught himself, quickly lowering his hands.

He smiled mysteriously. "Ah, I can't tell you."

"Why not?"

"Because right now, despite everything, you're intrigued. If I told you, you'd feel nothing but pity."

"I won't pity you. Even if it's… petty."

"Then there's no point talking about it, is there?"

I wanted to press, but then the flap of the tent moved aside. I turned around to face Myar Mal. He frowned.

"Don't you have a Cohort to prepare?" he asked, and I almost jumped from my chair.

"Yes, kar-vessár," I murmured, fled.

Chapter 21

"YOU GOT A new friend?"

Myar Mal might have sounded innocent, but Tayrel Kan didn't need telepathy to smell bullshit.

"Are you jealous?" he asked.

"Just surprised. He doesn't seem like your usual fling."

"He's not."

"Oh?" Myar Mal sat in the place vacated a while ago. "Do tell."

"Go fuck a siplah."

The kar-vessár hummed, his lips twitching into a smile. "I wonder why he puts up with you." He leaned forward and added, almost whispering, "Does he even know…?"

"Do you?" snapped the sorcerer.

Myar Mal chuckled. "I think I have an idea."

Suddenly, he straightened up, all traces of cordiality gone. Once again, he assumed his usual pose of impeccable, impersonal authority, and Tayrel Kan relaxed. Assholes he could deal with.

"Anyway," said the commander, in a voice that left no room for arguing. "We're attacking soon. I want you to be ready."

Tayrel Kan scoffed, then turned onto his back. "No chance. I was injured, vessár. Have you no mercy?"

"Don't get all teary on me. With all the shit you took, you probably can't even feel pain."

"Maybe, but I still need rest. I'm depleted."

"That can be remedied."

A shiver run down the sorcerer's spine. "No, I can't—"

"You can," cut in Myar Mal. "And you will." He leaned forward again, reaching to his pouch and retrieving a bulky syringe of metal and glass, filled with gleaming blue liquid. Tayrel Kan wanted to protest, but the kar-vessár didn't give him a chance. "A few hours ago you fought me for the right to get that magic-wielder. Now you're bailing out?"

"I know my limits," barked the sorcerer. "You should try to learn yours, too. I've heard people who suffered a heart attack before their fifteenth cycle are not likely to make it to their twentieth."

"My life expectancy is none of your business."

He liked being unreadable, but the slight flaring of his nostrils and tightening of the jaw betrayed him.

Tayrel Kan smirked. "Oh, I'm just worried about you," he purred, lips stretching in a venomous smile. "I bet you don't get a lot of this at home. Did your sweetheart sit at your side when you suffered? Did she even give you a shot?"

Before he knew it, Myar Mal was on his feet, with one hand wrapped around the sorcerer's neck and the other raised, clenched into a fist, ready to strike.

"Shut the fuck up," he hissed, lips twisted into an ugly snarl.

Tayrel Kan's smile widened. That evidently sobered the kar-vessár, who let go and stepped away, slicking back his hair.

"I don't have time to quarrel." Myar Mal picked up the syringe he dropped during his outburst. "You either take it yourself or I'll give it to you."

Tayrel Kan clenched his teeth. Usually, he could fight the kar-vessár all day, but not like this, not wounded, depleted.

Not with the ghost of Myar Mal's hand searing his neck.

"What's that?" he asked, resigned. "Revenge? You're mad I opposed you, and now you're trying to punish me?"

"I believe that's called an order."

Tayrel Kan hated taking orders. He made no move toward the syringe.

So, swifter than an attacking dryak, kar-vessár grabbed his wrist and rammed the needle in, pressing the piston much faster than recommended.

Tayrel Kan felt the fire filling his veins, creeping up his arm. He tried to muster enough focus to cast a silencing spell, but before he managed, pain flooded his mind in a white-hot wave.

He screamed.

Chapter 22

I KNEW I shouldn't have, but I couldn't help lingering around the tent. I grew to regret it, though, when the air was pierced by an inhuman shriek. My eyes darted around. There was no doubt, the shriek was coming from Tayrel Kan's tent. A few people around paused what they were doing, casting nervous glances toward it, but none of them moved. A part of me wanted to rush in and see what was happening, but remembering Myar Mal's stony gaze, I couldn't bring myself to move.

After all, there was only Tayrel Kan and Myar Mal inside, neither of whom I wanted to cross if they were doing… something they shouldn't. And there were plenty of people around, if someone was in danger, one of them would surely react. Right?

The shriek ended abruptly. After what felt like an eternity, the flap opened. Myar Mal stepped out, followed by a man I've never seen before. Dahlsi, with high cheekbones, a perfectly straight nose, dimpled chin, and dull gray eyes in an eerie expressionless face.

"Poor sap."

I jerked in surprise and spun around. Saral Tal was standing beside me.

"Who is it?" I asked, trying to match the picture to anyone I knew—anyone that could be in the tent with Myar Mal and…

"Tayrel Kan." Saral Tal sent me a weird look.

I turned back to catch another glance of the man before he disappeared. I tried to correlate what I saw with the sorcerer I knew, but in my mind, Tayrel Kan's face was a mass of scars, shining blue eyes, and sardonic smiles. However embarrassing it might have sounded, I didn't even remember how it looked beneath them. This… thing… was not him.

"What's wrong with him?" I asked.

"Katarda." Saral Tal said, as if this word was supposed to explain everything. He must have been used to my ignorance, because he quickly proceeded to elaborate. "It's a drug some sorcerers shoot when they need to recharge rapidly. They say it's like pouring pure acid into your veins, and it only gets worse the more you use it, to the point recovering from the shot may take longer than just recharging naturally. I think Myar Mal had to give him something else to get him on his feet so soon. Those two have, ah, a special relationship."

"Relationship?" I repeated mindlessly, my thoughts immediately shooting to the conversation we held a moment ago. "You mean they're together?"

Tayrel Kan seemed more than interested in our kar-vessár, but I thought it was only wishful thinking. Or was he messing with me again? I knew he wasn't telling me everything…

Saral Tal tilted his head quizzically. "I meant a professional relationship."

Or I was just an idiot over-analyzing everything. I was so transfixed on Tayrel Kan's story—and his personality—that all I could think of concerning him were romantic relationships.

"What do you mean?" I asked, desperate to shift the attention away from my gaffe.

Luckily, Saral Tal was too polite to comment on it. "Tayrel Kan doesn't take orders very well," he explained. "And Myar Mal doesn't like being disobeyed. So the two are constantly at each other's throats."

"But Myar Mal is kar-vessár. How can Tayrel Kan disobey him?"

Saral Tal wave-shrugged. "Have you seen him when he's angry? Or, you know, annoyed? No sane person would stand in his way. Even now, though he technically works for Mespana, he does what he wants. No vessár would put up with him, so Myar Mal created this position just to keep him in. I've heard he wanted to save him for special assignments, you know, the ones you wouldn't send anyone else on, but Tayrel Kan doesn't really like doing anything. For better or worse, he's often in a state in which he can't object. And Myar Mal takes advantage of that."

I thought about Tayrel Kan's hazy eyes and how I never saw him without tchalka. "You're talking about his drug addiction?"

Saral Tal hesitated for a moment before replying, "Well, I've heard people swearing they've seen Myar Mal handing him drugs."

"And no one does anything about it?"

"Would you like to stand between those two? Good luck, Aldait Han. And goodbye. I hope that the next vessár will be with us a while longer."

I sent a last look after the men, but they were gone. Probably preparing for a battle.

Speaking of which...

"How is our Cohort?" I asked.

Saral Tal straightened his back and raised his hand in a mock salute. "Ready when you are, vessár."

I nodded my head toward Laik Var's tent, and he spun around and started walking toward it. I, however, froze as my eyes fell at a figure standing nearby.

Amma La. She faced the same spot I was watching a moment ago, her hair obscuring her face, arms wrapped around her torso.

Did she know? A shiver ran down my spine. I thought I should walk to her, talk to her, offer my condolences or... something; but I couldn't bring myself to make a step.

Saral Tal waited a few paces ahead, his head tilted. "Are you coming?"

I swallowed, nodded, and rushed after him.

As I sat back in the vessár's chair, my eyes turned toward the cupboard filled with scrolls. With a slight pang of guilt, I realized I should probably go through Laik Var's papers and learn as much as possible about the Seventh Cohort.

My Cohort.

But what was the point, if some of its members were already dead and more were about to die? It would be easier if they remained anonymous.

I wondered how Laik Var lived with it. How anyone could live with it? Although, it was the first time we'd lost so many people at once. Did that make it harder? Or easier, turning real people into a slew of numbers?

"A report, vessár." I looked at Saral Tal before my eyes drifted to the scroll he had handed me.

It was a simple list, one gross of names divided neatly into twelve dozens. Occasional green rings with numbers inside denoted sorcerers and their magic potential. Some names were crossed out; others were merely darkened to signify injuries.

Malyn Tol-Syne.

Argan Am-Trever.

I wrested my eyes from the scroll. "We need to disband the last two dozen." The words came from my mouth, but it felt like it was someone else talking. "Distribute their members across the others, fill in the blanks."

We didn't get any official word from Myar Mal about what to do with empty spaces in our ranks. I guess we all were too afraid to ask—as if the act somehow made it more real.

"Yes, vessár."

I exhaled heavily. My eyes fell on the scroll again. "You probably knew them all."

I wasn't sure where it came from. They say a hundred people was the perfect size for one's social group, but I couldn't remember if they meant decimal hundred or a gross. Well, my social group consisted of one, so it didn't make any difference.

Saral Tal hesitated. "I was familiar with most, yes, but I can't say I really knew them."

"Some?"

Another moment of hesitation. "Yes."

"I'm sorry," I murmured.

"It's all right, vessár. It's… in the job description."

"That doesn't make it right."

He didn't answer, and for a moment we sat in silence.

"How are you holding up?" he asked unexpectedly.

My mind went blank. It took a few painfully long seconds before I collected myself, and even then, I only managed to stammer, "Could be better."

"Yeah. You could be kar-vessár."

I flinched back and stared at him, stumped.

He grinned, though it was paler than his usual smile. "Just kidding." He knew me well enough to clarify. "I know we're in a pretty deep shit, but at least you're vessár now. That must be nice."

I opened my mouth to protest, but snapped it shut. Truth is, until then, I didn't even stop to think about that. It all happened too quickly. One Dahlsian day ago I was in the middle of Sorox, with my greatest dream being a full bath. Since then, I was promoted, passed on, arrested for attempted murder, cleared, and promoted again.

And the man I trusted with my life had died.

But amid all that chaos… I was promoted. I earned enough trust to be put in this position, even though both of my superiors had other motives.

"Weird," I admitted finally. "I mean, I think we all know I'm the worst possible person for that job."

A nervous chuckle escaped my lips, and I raised my hand to stop it.

"You're not that bad." He leaned forward to give my arm a friendly punch. "You just need a bit of confidence."

The dark veil clouding my thoughts lifted a bit and despite everything, I smiled. A bit of confidence. Like it wasn't the hardest thing in the world!

Chapter 23

WE SUBMITTED OUR reports and a plan was drawn. The only thing left to do was suit up.

Mespanian uniforms weren't unlike everyday Dahlsian clothing—a single-piece, skin-tight costume covering the whole body. The only difference was plates of tertium inserted over vital areas. Tertium was too brittle to offer physical protection, but unlike steel, it could be saturated with protective spells. Enough to stop malignant magic and change the trajectory of physical weapons—just a couple of inches, but that was usually enough to pass by vital organs.

The boots were the only things resembling proper armor. Knee high and reinforced with steel, they were made to ensure we survived stepping on camouflaged predators. Those things were surprisingly common for the cluster with limited merging and little to no animal life.

Then there was a utility belt, or, more accurately, a medicine belt. Adrenaline shots, painkillers, vaka, healing clay, everything we needed to keep a soldier going. Below it, a wand holster sat on the left thigh, and on the right was a scabbard with a telescopic sword.

On top of it all was the helmet; its visor made of reinforced glass, with a thought-controlled display capable of switching to night-vision, infra-vision, and spell detection. A telepathic link connected me to all the other members of the Cohort. And, of course, it had a built-in air filter.

All in all, it was the perfect suit for a Mespanian. It kept away toxins and allergens, protected from extreme temperatures, pressure changes, wild magic, acid rains, and alkali lakes. It prevented animals from getting enough purchase to do real damage. If I fell off the mountain, it would make sure I wouldn't scrape my knee.

I had no idea how it would do against swords and crossbows.

But, what I realized, not without certain amusement, was that at this moment I probably had more spells on me than most warlocks. With zero point eighty-nine on the Kevar scale. Suck on that, natural talent!

"Line up!" I shouted, and watched as my Cohort formed rows of twelve people each. Except for the last one; that only had eleven. And a hole.

A big, human-sized hole.

"Count to twelve."

We put so much work into organizing dozens just to ignore them. But we couldn't fight in groups; we weren't trained for that. We fought as individuals. And for such we planned.

"Remember your number; there's a chance we'll have to split. In that case, I will command you as numbers—ones, twos, threes, and so on. Understood?"

"Yes, vessár!"

"Good. Now mount."

The Seventh Cohort was meant to be a part of the first wave. Our job was to breach the walls and neutralize or otherwise engage the crossbowmen, clearing the way for the main forces. The Fourth Cohort, or what was left of it, provided aerial support, while the Second stayed behind to guard the camp with the sorcerers doing their best to keep us all alive. Some vessár-ai opted to stay as well. Not me.

I could feel the curious gazes of my colleagues—my subordinates—wondering what I was going to do. But there was only one thing to do, right?

I mounted my bike. I leaned forward, almost resting my chest on the seat, and the magic shield automatically unfolded around me. No spell could stop iron bolts, but the tingling of magic all over my skin gave me a sense of security.

I picked up the telepathic signal from Myar Mal and passed it to my soldiers.

With a predatory growl, my bike came to life. We set out.

Very quickly, I spotted bright orange shapes taking the lead. Ssothians were too heavy for bikes, but fast on their feet. I sent a telepathic order; we had to hold the line.

The Tarvissi had probably noticed us bustling around the camp, so now a group of crossbowmen took up position right in the middle of the way. They must have been ready to die, because there was no way they would make it back to the mansion. I whispered a magnifying spell and saw them up close, cocking their weapons. Arbalests, I realized, not regular crossbows. Enough power to shatter rocks, but not great speed. They raised them in unison, prepared…

And shot.

For a moment, it was like a wall of darkness rushing at us. And then it fell… right on the illusion proceeding our forces. The images dispelled, and the bolts hit the ground a few paces before the first bikes. With the magnifying spell, I saw shock and fear painted on our enemies' faces. No chance they would be able to draw their weapons again. I smirked, then dispelled the magnification.

"Evens dismount, odds carry on."

Ignoring my own words, I pushed on, straight into the line of crossbowmen, twisting my bike sideways seconds before impact and jumping off. I rolled and sprung to my feet in no time, reaching for my weapons.

"Fours, eights, and twelves at defense, the rest on the attack."

The dozenal system had its advantages. While half of my Cohort dismounted to take care of the crossbowmen, I could further divide it into pairs, making one person responsible for defense—in this case, summoning a wall of fire—while another attacked. Simple and efficient.

The first strike came from above. I parried the opponent's ax and kicked him in the chest before my brain caught up with my muscles, and I raised my wand. A flash of light, and he was dead. Another enemy ran toward me. I killed him before he got close. A third one was kneeling, his eyes wide in shock, bloodied hands still clutched the hilt of the sword protruding from a Mespanian's chest. Anger rushed through me, and I cast the killing spell.

Only instinct saved me from the next one. I jerked to the left, and the sword brushed my ribs, clinking on the tertium plates. I twisted and lifted my own weapon, just in time to block her next charge. She was good; fast and clever, coming at me with quick, sharp thrusts that left me no time to even think about using my wand. She feigned an attack to my right, and when I focused on blocking it, pain exploded in my knee. My leg buckled, I hit the ground. Instinctively, I rolled aside, barely avoiding being pinned like a bug. But the movement gave me the seconds I needed. On my back again, I shot.

I jumped to my feet, but the fight was over. I should probably feel bad about killing my own. The girl I'd just slain was tall and lanky, with dark hair with the slightest hint of red, and large, green eyes staring lifelessly at the sky. She could be my sister.

But I felt nothing. They were enemies. They would slaughter me without remorse, so why should I hesitate?

"Evens, back on your bikes."

I didn't turn to see if my orders were followed. I didn't turn to see how many of my evens were no longer able to follow. All I cared about was pushing on.

I climbed back on my bike.

Once again, ssothians were trying to overtake the rest of us and this time, I didn't stop them. Tarvissi dragged heavy furniture from upper floors to form a provisional barricade where the gate used to be, but the ssothians barged through it like battering rams. The enemy pelted them with bolts, but I doubted that they dug deep through the fur. A shame I didn't have more of them in my Cohort.

The first of our bikers also approached, but they needed a moment to dismount. The enemy took this opportunity to rain bolts and crystal balls at their heads. Some Mespanians tried to aim at the invisible shooters, but most of their spells bounced off the walls.

I got an idea.

Just before reaching the battle, I jerked my bike upright and jumped off of it. The momentum carried it forward, straight into one of the windows. It exploded—not enough to break through the wall, but if the screams coming from the other side were anything to go by, just enough to burn a few assholes.

"Odds to defense; evens attack," I commanded.

A wall of flames rose before our troops. Saral Tal appeared beside me, wand raised in conjuring. I switched my helmet to magic vision—and that was the last thing I remember clearly. From that moment on, the muscle memory took over and the battle became a blur. Just like I was trained: walk, kill, move on.

That's why I joined Mespana. It was easy. Mechanical. Walk, kill, move on. No drama. No nuances. No making a fool of myself. Just me versus them. Kill or be killed. Simple.

Walk, kill, move on.

I lost track of time. My universe shrank to contain only the nearest enemy, until they fell and another took their place. My sword snapped at some point, stuck in one guy's ribcage, but I just grabbed the one he dropped—shorter and heavier than a Dahlsian blade, but I could work with that—and moved on.

Walk, kill, move on.

Until my visor exploded, and a myriad of glass shards bit into my face. Vaka made everything more intense, even pain. But before I could so much as grunt, a kick in the chest sent me tumbling. I fell on my back, the stolen sword slipping away. I opened my eyes—miraculously, none of the shards got to them—to at least see the one to kill me.

Well, fuck.

Karlan Peridion towered over me, grinning like a maniac. He clutched a weapon I'd never seen—a spiky ball connected via a long chain to a wooden handle. That's what he must've hit me with. Or rather brushed—a proper blow would most likely turn my head inside out.

He took a swing, and the spiked ball rushed at me, but I rolled out of its way. I tried to send a distress signal. No answer.

Saral Tal, I thought. Where was he? He was supposed to be my defense. But the only person I could see standing was Karlan. The ground around us was littered with corpses and clangor of weapons seemed distant, like the battle had moved to different part of the mansion.

Another swing, another roll. I tried to kick his shin, but he evaded and swung at me with the sword he held in his left hand. I felt it brush my suit, but didn't have time to stop and check the damage. The spiked ball flew toward me. I pulled back, then raised my wand. Before I used it, a perfect stroke of the sword cut it in half.

"You really should stick to farming, Tearshan," rasped Karlan.

At least I wasn't the only one struggling for breath, I thought irrationally.

"A pitchfork is a right tool for you, not a sword." His grin got wider.

I crawled back, feeling around for something to use. We were in the side yard, though I didn't remember how we got there. I tried to grab a weapon from any of the bodies, but before I could get any of them, Karlan attacked, forcing me to back off.

"It's a shame your old man died," he said, taking another swing. "I'd love to kill him, too, avenge my father. Alas, you'll do."

Another swing, another roll.

My ribs caught on something, sending a flash of pain through my body. With a striking clarity, I realized I was going to die.

And despite everything, calmness descended over me. It was over. Nothing more I could do.

Peridion stood over me, grinning. He lifted his spiked ball, ready to crush my skull. "I'll cut your head off and hang it over the gate for all to see. That's how peons who don't know their place end up."

My hand, which apparently didn't get the memo from my brain, grasped something.

Without thinking, I grabbed it and thrust it forward. Peridion's face widened in shock. His mouth hung open, sputtering blood.

Only then did I look at the object I held.

I burst into laughter.

A pitchfork. Somehow we had made our way to the stables, unused for some time but still cluttered with old tools.

And so it came that Karlan Peridion, facing the most advanced human civilization in the universe, was killed with a fucking pitchfork.

I wasn't able to stop myself, I laughed and laughed, the pain gone, the battle around us all but forgotten.

Finally, though, I exhausted my mirth, and the pain in my side came back. Peridion collapsed beside me. His eyes were glassy, but he was still wheezing. My hit wasn't clean; I probably only pierced his lungs. He had some time to reconcile with his gods.

I grabbed the shaft of the pitchfork and used it to lift myself. My head spun and I barely managed to keep myself upright. Something cold and wet dripped down my side. When I looked down, I saw blood.

So Karlan had hit me after all. And judging from the amount of gore, it was more than a graze. My brain must have blocked the pain at the time, a typical reaction during high-stress situations. Argan Am didn't even feel his hands burning until long after they were gone…

I snapped awake. What was I doing? I was bleeding out, and I stood there like an idiot, ruminating. I had to heal myself. Fast.

Red spots danced before my eyes as I reached into my pouch. I should probably sit down. But then I might never get up again.

Finding what I needed was difficult with rapidly numbing fingers, but when I tried looking down, blood dripped into my eyes, reminding me of my shattered helmet. I took a moment to take it off; it was useless anyway.

Finally, my fingers closed around a familiar shape and I felt relief. I took the package out and started unwrapping, but as soon as I did, the clay slid from the foil and fell to the ground.

Fuck!

Deep breath. I can't give up. It's just a graze; it's not lethal. But if I lose consciousness here, I may never regain it. I have to focus.

I clenched my fists so much it hurt. There. They were working fine. This time I didn't have to look, having already located my medicine pouch. All I had to do was be careful. Use the other hand for support.

That's it. Then roll it. All right, that's enough. Press it into the cut—

A surge of pain blinded me for a moment, but it was good—it meant I was alive.

I put my left hand over the wound and started an incantation. My mouth was numb, my tongue felt like lead, and the words came out all wrong. Panic prickled my mind as I realized I might not be able to cast the spell.

But then a wave of heat ran through my body and my head cleared. I tore my hand away and looked down. The wound was sealed. A piece of suit fused into my skin, but at least I wasn't bleeding out. Nothing I could do for my face; the wounds were too shallow for clay, and the complex healing spells were beyond my scope. I only tried again to wipe the gore from my eyes, but the sharp pain made me realize what I took for blood was actually a strip of skin.

I took a deep breath, readying myself for what was to come. When I pushed away from the wall, the world spun, almost sending me back to the ground. I took a moment to steady myself.

Behind me, Karlan Peridion was still wheezing. I could end his misery. Or heal him and take him as a hostage.

I walked away.

The battle was still ongoing, but I had no intention of joining it. I was only hoping I wouldn't encounter any more Tarvissi. My wand was broken, and I was too weak to wield a sword. I had to find my way out.

A tingle ran down my neck.

Innam Ar's warning ringing in my ears, I tried to get down, but my body refused to listen. It was all for nothing, I realized with dread. They weren't going to kill me with a spell; that would be too obvious.

My legs buckled, and I fell on my face with a groan, sand biting into my wounds. A second later, someone stepped into my view, and I glimpsed the edge of a silver sash.

Myar Mal was right. The traitors were among us.

The guy bent to pick up Peridion's sword, and I caught the sight of his face. I didn't recognize him. I wished he would speak; perhaps then I could identify him. But he was silent. No gloating, no super-villain speech, not even a grunt. I guess I wasn't worth the effort.

He walked back to me. He was going to kill me—no, murder me. And the only thought in my mind was, who the fuck is this guy?

His feet filled my view now. He didn't show any inclination toward turning me around. I was gonna die from a sword to my back. In old legends, that was the death of a coward; I wondered if he knew that?

A surprised yelp sounded above me and the threads of the spell loosened. I jerked back and pulled myself to a sitting position, to see my would-be-killer suspended in the air, stretched with magic. When I looked around, I spotted Myar Mal, hands raised and surrounded by a white gleam.

Of course, he was a sorcerer.

"Raison Dal-Aramek," he stated coldly. "I have to say I didn't fancy you to be power hungry. Or you're just campaigning for someone else?"

"Fuck you," rasped the captive.

Myar Mal smiled joylessly and twisted his hand in a studied movement. The prisoner shrieked in pain.

"Don't worry, we'll get your friends in time. I guess you were the one who got the nut. Was that the one Aldait Han dropped?"

The vessár didn't speak, but Myar Mal didn't seem like he expected an answer, anyway.

"One thing bothers me, though." He cocked his head. "How did you get it to me? I don't remember picking up new meds before the battle, and no one had access to my food or drink."

Raison Dal made a rasped sound. It took me a while to realize it was laughter.

"You think I did that?" he asked. "Try someone closer."

Myar Mal's face remained blank, but his arms slumped. "What do you mean?"

"I wasn't the only one who wanted you dead. You have a lot of enemies, Myar Mal. Entire families, I'd say…"

Myar Mal paled. "No," he rasped.

Raison Dal chuckled. "Oh, yes. You saw the hatred in her eyes. You know she blames you. And you know she's right."

"No!" Myar Mal yelled and pushed his hands forward, sending his prisoner hurling into the wall. He let out another yell, haunted and full of anguish, then fell to his knees. His head slumped, fingers digging into his scalp. Despite being surrounded by dead enemies and having uncovered the conspiracy to end his life, he looked utterly defeated.

There was only one person Raison Dal could be talking about.

I was at a loss. Should I go to him? Try to comfort him? But what could I say? I barely knew him; I certainly didn't know Amma La. That traitorous asshole could be lying about her involvement, but even if he was alive, he was in no state to tell. And Myar Mal must've at least suspected something, given how easily he accepted her betrayal.

What the fuck could I say to that?

"Myar Mal," I stumbled forward, fighting legs that still tried to buckle under me.

"Leave me," he rasped.

I fled.

Too late, I realized Myar Mal might not have left the mansion alive. I read somewhere men tried to take their lives less frequently than women, but were more often successful. He certainly had the means. And more than enough reason. But was he capable of such a thing?

Tayrel Kan was wrong. Myar Mal's love for Amma La was real. Nothing less could justify such suffering.

I realized if the kar-vessár took his own life, I would be the only one who knew about her involvement in the conspiracy. Shit, I could be the only one who even knew about the conspiracy! How much would my word mean against hers?

I was so lost in my thoughts, I didn't even look where I was going. My body was weak, my movements erratic, and when I stumbled, I had no strength to arrest my fall.

When my vision cleared, Saral Tal's face was next to mine. The enemy sword had cut through his helmet, shattering the visor before getting stuck in his jaw. Splotches of dark red marked the pale blue sash of nami vessár.

I reached out and closed his eyes. I heaved myself to my feet and moved on.

Walk, … , move on.

All I wanted to do was crash on my bed and sleep. Maybe cry a little.

"Vessár!"

No…

I was in the main yard. I wasn't sure how I got there. A Dahlsi soldier stopped me almost immediately. I squinted, trying to remember his name, but to no avail.

"The enemy has surrendered," he said, gesturing to some two-dozen people gathered at the center of the yard. It took my fogged brain a while to realize why they seemed so out of place among Dahlsi soldiers.

"Tearshan! By Vhalfr!" One of the captives ran to me, then grabbed my hand.

"The merge is not far from here," whispered Taneem Kiovar. "Let us go. No one needs to know. Come on, Tearshan," he pleaded. "We're from the same nation."

Were we? I studied his face: it was covered in soot, eyebrows burned off, and eyes wide in fear. I searched for any sign of affinity. But all I could see was the face of Saral Tal, cut in half, pale blue sash tainted with dark red in a perverse inversion of the Dahlsian flag.

I wrested my hand from his grip.

"The merge is blocked from the other side," I said wearily, and watched hope drain from his face.

I turned to my troops. "Myar Mal's orders were clear. No survivors."

"Vessár?" A Dahlsi soldier was watching me, rolling his wand between his fingers uncertainly.

But what could I do? It was an order. I was as bound by it as him.

I turned my back on Taneem.

"No survivors," I repeated, feeling hollow.

Chapter 24

THE LAST SPELL cracked. Using Tayrel Kan's body, Myar Mal pushed one more time and the colorful lines, invisible to everyone but him, flickered and vanished. He started walking. He was on the top floor of the mansion, far away from the yard where the real Myar Mal watched Aldait Han struggle with Peridion. The true enemy, the magic-wielder who turned their spell against them, was ahead. Hidden in his lab and surrounded by ephemeral barriers, he still radiated more power than any human sorcerer.

Except Tayrel Kan.

Controlling two bodies was difficult, and it didn't leave enough brainpower to process sensory input from both. That's why it took him a while to smell the smoke—and another to determine where it was coming from. He frowned. Then he sped up.

Too late.

The workshop was filled with flames. He extinguished them with a flick of the hand, then waved to clear the air.

The only thing revealed was scorched remains of furniture and a small pile of strangely misshapen bones.

On the other side of the mansion, Aldait Han collapsed to the ground and Myar Mal slipped his consciousness back to his body. Tayrel Kan swayed and slid along the wall, too tired to scream.

Chapter 25

AMMA LA LET out a long puff of smoke.

"So, you know," she said.

"I don't believe it."

She chuckled. The air inside her tent was heavy with smoke and regret. Yet, she seemed comfortable, sprawled in the chair with her legs stretched out before and crossed at the ankles, her back turned to Myar Mal, who stood at the entrance, not daring to step in.

"I'm sorry." There was not even a hint of remorse in her voice.

He flinched. "Why, Amma?" he pleaded. He never did, but now he couldn't help it; he needed to know, to understand. He knew things were not going well—he knew it for a while—but he still hoped they would work things out as soon as the rebellion was over. Was he really so wrong?

Amma La drew in a lungful of smoke before she replied. "Maybe I just wanted to take something from you for a change."

He sighed in defeat, the weight settling in his chest. "So that's it. It wasn't enough that Laik Var blamed me for your falling out…"

"We quarreled over you, there's no way around that. And now we can't even do that, because you ignored the danger and got him killed."

Her tone was flat, and yet her words felt like nails driven to his heart.

"Amma—" Myar Mal sucked in air before continuing, "I made mistakes. Big ones. And you are right, Laik Var's death is on me—"

"Oh, don't feign remorse," she spun around to face him. "Everyone knows he was in your way."

"I never wanted him dead. By Vhalfr, Amma! I urged you to reconcile with him! I said I would step back—"

"And you really thought you could just do that? Step back?" She laughed, a shrill, manic laugh. "You beautiful, innocent thing! How could I ever live without you?"

"You tried to kill me!"

For a moment there was no answer as the woman hid behind another whiff of smoke. Only now Myar Mal noticed dozens of tsalka butts littering the floor, and his heart clenched.

"I just thought…" she started, but trailed off.

Myar Mal kept silent, giving her a chance to collect herself. Wishing, against everything, there was a logical explanation.

"If you died, I would be free."

She looked away, but Myar Mal caught the light reflected in the tear rolling down her cheek.

He gritted his teeth. "I hope it was worth it."

Chapter 26

WHAT HAPPENED LATER was a blur. Someone dragged me to the medical tent; someone took care of my wounds. I knew we had to secure the area and wrap things up in Maurir, but I didn't remember any of it. Then we were discharged—I guess? Because at some point, I found myself in my quarters in Sfal.

Then I crashed. Vaka could only keep me going for so long, and my body wasn't used to it. Even when I finally woke up, it took me a while to realize where I was.

Automatically I reached toward the mail-drawer. There was only a brief note from kar-vessár, wishing me good health, saying that Ellare had already been sent to Tarviss, and Arda Nahs would take care of the Seventh Cohort until I recovered. The memories of the previous days flooded my mind in a tangled mess, and it took me a while to organize them and push them away.

My stomach rumbled. What was the point in contemplating? We were all going to die—it was in the job description. Or rather, a part of being mortal. Sooner or later, what the fuck did it matter?

My chest felt heavy. I had to get out.

I kept some Tarvissian clothes here—loose dark trousers, a purple shirt, and a gray jyat with carnelian beading. But as soon as my eyes fell on the familiar pattern, stitched with black and white thread, I froze, my hands clutching the edge of the drawer to the verge of pain.

It was ridiculous. I'd worn such garb for most of my life. As did my parents, my peers, everyone around me. And yet, looking down, all I could think of was people wearing the same garb running at me with raised swords. Karlan Peridion bringing a knife to my eye. Saral Tal with his face cut in half…

I slammed the drawer shut. My Dahlsian uniform would have to do for now. I would buy more dignified clothes when I went out. Later, I thought, as my stomach rumbled again.

Marka-na-Sfal consisted of two parts, and the difference between them couldn't be more striking. When I finally left the maze of narrow, artificially-lit corridors, suffocating despite the constant flow of cool, filtered air, I felt like I stepped into another world. The area opened around me, and the tiled floor gave way to an unpaved road. The walls receded and transformed into a tall house of yellow brick on the left and sprawling concrete barrack on the right. The air became thick, redolent with the smells of bodies, food, waste, and bushland. Two suns flooded the world with sweltering heat, and the pervasive mist quickly settled on my clothing in fat droplets.

But in one regard, the cities were very much alike. The emptiness. I could expect that from the Inner City, because Dahlsi were recluses who did their best to avoid each other. But seeing the Outer City, usually bustling with activity, now traversed only by singular individuals, hunched and casting around nervous glances, felt like a punch.

On wobbly legs, I headed toward what was called The Tarvissian Street. It started near the dome and led almost to the Great Ribbon, the commercial center of the Outer City. On both of its sides sat squat buildings with whitewashed walls and roofs of red tiles.

There was not a soul in sight.

I caught a dash of green and spun around, my hand on the wand.

A green ribbon flapped in the window. Leftover from the Edira festival. It should have been replaced by red by now.

With heart in my throat, I resumed the walk. But when I reached my destination, I froze. My favorite restaurant was closed, its windows and doors boarded up, stupid green ribbons still flapping in some of the upper windows.

I should have known. It was too late, I realized, choking on a sudden surge of despair. We fought in vain; Meon had already changed, and nothing we did could stop it.

The owner had been such a great guy. Nice, but not intrusive. He always let me enjoy my meals in solitude.

So why did thinking about him make me reach for the wand?

I closed my eyes, squeezing out tears, and rested my forehead on a window. I took a deep breath. One, two. My heartbeat slowed.

What was wrong with me?

Slowly, I raised my head and looked around. Not far away was a Chaarite restaurant, The Mirange Blossom. It was something out of this world: a tall tower made entirely of imported redwood, its strangely curved roof supported by pillars shaped like Mirange trees, decorated with big, garishly painted flowers. Blue, pink, orange, red and purple. No sign of green. It was open, the scent of spices and roasted meats wafting from the door.

I approached it on wobbly legs. The wave of heat hit me from the entrance. The place, though exotic, felt cozy—walls covered in dark wood panelling with warped masks beneath the ceiling, little tables separated by painted screens and potted trees with red leaves and pale flowers. Invisible musicians filled the air with the soft chiming of steel tongue drums. For the briefest moment, I was relieved.

But then I realized that all the people inside were looking at me.

My shoulders slumped, and I hurried to my favorite place in the corner. It was shielded from other patrons while still providing a good view of the entrance, and luckily, it was rarely occupied. But as I walked through the room, my legs shook, and heart hammered in my chest. My Dahlsian uniform seemed ridiculously exposing, and I fought the urge to drag the tablecloth from one of the tables and hide behind it. The only thing that stopped me was that it would draw more attention.

After what felt like an eternity, I reached my place and slid onto the seat. Only then did I muster the courage to look around. People were returning to their meals. I briefly considered leaving, but that would mean going through the hall again. Plus, I was famished. I tried to remember the last proper meal I had. It was before sleep, before battle... probably even before I became vessár.

One of the waitresses approached—a small humanoid who never spoke and only communicated by gestures—clad in a loose white dress, and a paper mask. The first time I came here, the staff creeped me out, but now I was used to them. I still wasn't sure if they were servants, slaves or automats, but that was none of my business.

I ordered a whole bowl of their famous red stew, with steamed fish and sweet dumplings on the side. What I really craved was Tarvissian sausage stew with nutloaf and sauteed mushrooms, but that was out of my reach.

When the waitress left, I dropped my head, determined not to raise my gaze for the rest of my meal. My table was a beautiful piece of furniture, intricately inlaid, but the strangely contorted figures reminded me of the battlefield, and my stomach turned.

Maybe it wasn't such a good object to contemplate after all.

I lifted my head just in time to see another patron entering the restaurant and, for a moment, was too surprised to avert my gaze.

Adyar Lah.

He spotted me too, and after a momentary hesitation, walked my way. I dropped my head immediately, my heart racing. Maybe he didn't notice. Maybe he was meeting someone else. Maybe—

"Aldait Han."

Shit.

"May I join you?"

I nodded and gestured toward an empty seat. "Of course."

He sat hesitantly and didn't speak for a moment.

"Look," he started awkwardly. I probably should have found some comfort in the fact that I wasn't the only person in the whole Mespana with communicative difficulties, but I didn't. "I still feel a bit shitty about that... arrest. Can I buy you dinner? You know, as compensation?"

"You don't have to," I murmured, daring a peek at his face.

He was looking away and his brows were slightly furrowed. "Well, I'd feel better if I did. Or something else, if you'd prefer. I'm not trying to hit on you," he assured me hastily, and a slight blush crept into his cheeks. "I have a girlfriend. It's just..."

"Dinner's fine," I said with equal haste, wanting only to finish that line of conversation before we both died of embarrassment.

He smiled with relief. "Thanks."

Shouldn't I be the one thanking him?

The waitress came again, bringing the koocha set: a kettle inlaid with firestones and two drinking bowls of natural glass. She took Adyar Lah's order—almost identical to mine, except he preferred his stew sweet and savory, while I liked it a bit spicy. And he ordered extra dumplings. But frankly, what else can you eat in a Chaarite restaurant?

The waitress left, and I hid behind the drink. The first sip spread a wave of warmth through my body, too much to come from temperature alone. Koocha was a brew similar to Tarvissian tea, but more refreshing with a more complex flavor. I never learned if it was a drug, medication, or just a damn good drink. But Chaarites enjoyed it on every occasion with no adverse effects, so I wasn't worried.

And it did provide a nice shield.

"So, how are you holding up?" asked Adyar Lah.

The question surprised me so much that for a moment I didn't know how to reply.

"All right, I guess." I caught myself shrugging, then did my best imitation of the Dahlsian hand wave. Then, I figured that Adyar Lah's presence here meant he was at least familiar with the outworlders's ways. Only I wasn't sure what type of gesturing Chaarites used—probably none, as, apart from servants, they were very non-expressive people.

I realized that my hand was hanging uselessly in the air and dropped it, embarrassed. "Frankly, I came here right after waking up," I blurted. "I didn't have time to think. About anything."

"Yeah." He nodded, absentmindedly. "I was just walking down the Outer City. It looks grim."

My throat tightened. Too late, sang the voice in my head, and fresh tears stung my eyes. I somehow managed to collect myself and answered with a noncommittal grunt.

For a moment, we both looked around, trying to avoid each other's eyes, and searching desperately for something to say.

Just as I had imagined.

I caught myself rocking slightly and did my best to stop, scrambling for something else to occupy my mind.

"What are you even doing here?" I asked, too late realizing how that may sound. I added hastily, "You were stationed in Tydus, right?"

He grimaced. "Yeah, well, there's this… investigation. Regarding Sanam Il's actions."

My stomach clenched.

"I'm sorry," I murmured, dropping my gaze back to the table. The inlaid figures seemed to mock me.

"It's not your fault." He paused, then added, with audible effort, "Turned out that Tarvissi did send a response to our queries earlier. They demanded their citizens be returned to Tarviss unharmed and promised to deliver their own justice. Except that message never got to Myar Mal."

"Did you know about that?" I asked before I could bite my tongue.

"No!" His jerked back, as in shock. I felt like an asshole. "I knew as much as everyone else; that Tarviss had denounced its citizens and didn't bother responding. If I knew…" He faltered and fell silent.

What would he do, I wondered? Confront his vessár, and risk being killed or involved in treason? Or run straight to Myar Mal, betraying his leader?

"Did you tell them that?" I asked, wanting desperately to fix the impression left by my previous question.

Adyar Lah sighed. "Yes, I did. They said they don't really suspect me; it's just a formality. But I needed to come here, let them scan my mind, and stay until they let me leave."

"I'm sorry."

"Yeah." He sighed again. "You know, I was thinking… Maybe it's better Sanam Il died by a Tarvissi's hand…"

Rather than live to be tried for treason.

I wasn't sure what relationship Adyar Lah had with his ex-vessár, but it was clear his legacy troubled the young leader. In a way, I understood.

That's why I didn't ask if the investigation brought up anything against Laik Var.

"Now Tarviss wants to hold us accountable for the death of its citizens," he continued grimly. "And it doesn't look great. It's not official yet, but I've heard that we may have an actual war ahead."

The only answer that came to my mind was a nondescript hum. I didn't expect anything less. Still, it was a sad state of things. And if we were to fight again... I wasn't sure if I could do it.

"It's not all bad," he switched unexpectedly and somehow apprehensively. Was he trying to convince me or himself? "Since that rebellion, so many people want to enlist that in one cycle we'll be able to double the number of Cohorts. That means a lot of advancements."

"Well, it's too late for us," I joked.

He chuckled and raised his bowl. "I'll drink to that."

I did the same. We drained our koocha in no time and poured ourselves another round. Neither of us said anything about the holes in existing Cohorts. What was there to say, anyway?

The waitress arrived again bringing appetizers. Chaarites believed that anything freely given would return to you twice, so even ordering at a restaurant it was customary to receive more than was put on the bill. Milkseed, ruby beans cooked with spices and Mirange peel, steamed buns, seaweed, vegetables fresh, fried and pickled, and paper-thin slices of steamed meat and fish were laid out before us. For a moment the lavishness made me feel that everything was all right. I was just back from another mission, killing time before the next.

If only I could believe it…

We attacked the food with the enthusiasm of people who hadn't eaten in ages. I couldn't help stealing a peek at Adyar Lah every once in a while, half-expecting him to drop into anaphylaxis. He must've noticed me staring because his lips twitched in a crooked smile and he asked innocently,

"Have you passed your first aid course yet?"

A pickled plum stuck in my throat.

"Not yet," I admitted after coughing it out. My face was burning. "I crashed after the battle."

"Hm. A shame." Despite the words, he was smirking. "Looks like if something bad happens, I'm on my own."

A twinge of annoyance broke through my embarrassment. I looked around ostentatiously. "With so many people, there's bound to be someone who knows how to give an injection."

"I don't know, Aldait Han. If they all have your attitude…"

I couldn't find an answer to that. I clenched my teeth and dropped my head in defeat.

"But don't worry." His tone was light, and I finally realized he was messing with me. "I'll be fine."

"I guess you wouldn't come here if you expected something different," I said, unwittingly making it sound like an accusation.

"When I was a kid, my family lived in a Chaarite colony." To my surprise, he managed to pronounce the name impeccably. My reaction must have been visible, since he quickly confirmed, "Yes, I can say Chaar... Tirshan."

It was actually Tearshan, but his version was still better than what most Dahlsi used.

"There was a restaurant," he continued, "The owners liked me and couldn't stand the thought of me growing up eating only tubed food. So, they started feeding me."

"No adverse reaction?" I asked, curiosity sweeping away my annoyance. Adyar Lah seemed like a nice guy; it wasn't his fault I couldn't take a joke. "No allergies?"

"Surprisingly, no. At least, nothing serious. Don't ask me why. Maybe there's something in Chaarite food that makes it easy on the stomach. Or it's just because I have foreign blood."

"Do you?"

He wave-shrugged. "Like every other Dahlsi, our women are crazy for foreigners. There's a myth that mixed babies are stronger and healthier."

My thoughts immediately shot to Argan Am. Probably because his half-foreignness was so obvious. He suffered such horrible injuries in Maurir... But by taking him off the final battle, perhaps they saved his life.

I squeezed my eyes shut to banish the image of Saral Tal's face creeping up.

"Are they?" I asked, desperate for something else to occupy my mind. It sounded weak.

Unaware of my sudden gloom, or just ignoring it out of politeness, Adyar Lah waved his hand. "No, not really. Not when we keep living in sheltered cities and eat processed shit. Still, for a nation known for its rationality, we can be pretty stubborn sometimes."

"I don't think much can be done," I said, remembering Tayrel Kan's reluctance when we talked about natural food. "Your people are too far gone."

"Well, I'm here. And if I can tolerate natural food, so could others. If they really wanted to. Can you honestly say that what we eat does not affect us? I mean, I bet you've never eaten the processed shit we live on. Have you ever had an allergic reaction?"

"Never even had a cold in my life," I admitted, not without a hint of pride.

There was more to it, of course. Tarvissian medicine, at least what I had access to, was pretty primitive. If someone was sickly—or simply unlucky—they usually didn't make it to adulthood.

"See?" He pointed his drinking bowl at me. "That's what I'm talking about. Life outside, real food, and you don't need a single pill. Or an injection."

The main meals arrived, and for a moment, we cherished it in silence. Red stew was a signature Chaarite dish, packing such a punch of savory flavor that you could feel your muscles swell even before it hit the stomach.

"If you don't mind me asking," he said at some point. I tore my gaze from my bowl to see him fidgeting with his spoon. "Why did you leave your world? I always thought you colonists were pretty happy with your lives."

I took a moment, considering my reasons.

"When I was a kid, a Dahlsi woman, Girana Da-Vai, came to our world and opened a school. Obviously, she could only teach us Dahlsian things—Dahlsian language, Dahlsian math, some general knowledge, and basic spells."

I chuckled. "You know, I didn't even learn to write in Tarvissi-é until I was an adult."

"Well, to be fair, all you really need is Dahlsi-é," he joked.

"Fuck you. That's my mother tongue you're talking about. Anyway, I think she awakened some deeper yearning in me. I wasn't happy being a farmer anymore. I wanted more… though I had no idea what. Until one time, a tax collector came with a Xzsim guard, and I learned that you accepted foreigners in Mespana. So, I decided to join."

I decided to keep the part about hiding my ambitions from my father and waiting for him to die to myself.

"I'm certainly glad you did," said Adyar Lah, raising his glass again, and we drank.

"What's your story?" I asked, emboldened by the drink.

"What, why I'm Dahlsi?" He smirked.

"Why you're in Mespana?"

"Oh, it was a no-brainer. I always fantasized about seeing other places. As a child, I aimed at Chaar, but later decided I wanted to explore new worlds. So, it was either Mespana or the Cosmographic Society, and I had no talent for math."

"And you don't want to go outside anymore? Visit one of the old worlds?"

"I do. I was actually planning a journey to Chaar." He grimaced. "I feel like it's going to be harder now."

Harder. I wished my job was merely as hard. We had defeated the rebels, but I still had to bring my family back. From Tarviss.

If they were still alive.

I pushed that thought away.

Given how easy our conversation was, I thought maybe I could use it to get some answers.

"Can I ask you a question?" I chanced.

He arched his eyebrow. "A personal one?"

"Well, not really. It's about someone else."

His smile faltered. "I don't know," he said slowly, considering. "I don't like gossiping."

I felt a twinge of disappointment, but decided to press on. "Someone described Dahlsi as a gossipy bunch to me."

"That's a bit of a stereotype, isn't it?"

His gaze became harder and my cheeks heated. I scrambled, trying to think of anything that would prove I'm not... the person he initially took me for.

"He was Dahlsi," I blurted.

Adyar Lah didn't seem impressed. "One can be racist against his own race. What do you want to know, anyway?"

I hesitated. I wasn't so sure anymore if I wanted to ask. But the curiosity still gnawed at me, and I didn't have many other ways to satisfy it.

"What's the deal with Tayrel Kan?"

Adyar Lah gave me a weird look. "If you're asking if he sleeps with Myar Mal, I know as much as you."

I was glad I was done eating, otherwise, I would certainly choke. "Is he?"

Adyar Lah's eyes widened almost comically before he lowered his head sheepishly. "I don't know. That's what some people say."

I quickly rectified, "That's not what I wanted to ask."

I took small comfort in Adyar Lah seeming to regret taking the conversation in that direction.

"What then?"

"Why does everyone seem to hate him? Laik Var warned me to stay away from him," I explained, seeing his doubtful gaze. "Giving the reason that Tayrel Kan later told me was bullshit. And Tayrel Kan said if he died, no one would mourn. So, why is that?"

Adyar Lah didn't answer immediately. He looked away, biting his lip as if considering. Finally, he turned back to me. "Did you ask him?"

"Yeah, and he told me to ask someone else. He said gossiping only makes sense when you talk about others."

Adyar Lay smirked, but it seemed pale. His arms were hunched and his fingers drummed on the table. "I don't know, Aldait Han. It's not my story to tell."

But I felt I was getting close, so I reached for my ultimate argument. "He said he didn't mind."

"And you think he really didn't, or he was just resigned to the fact that everyone already knew?"

I couldn't answer that. If the latter was true, I guessed that made me an asshole for prodding. On the other hand, if he hadn't meant that, why did he even say it? If you say something you don't mean, you can't blame people for misunderstanding you.

But after a while, Adyar Lah sighed and started talking. "I guess, there's no harm in that. If I don't tell you, someone else will. It happened... five cycles ago? I was just starting my duty, and we were both in the Second Cohort. He had a partner—"

"You mean a work partner or a lover?" I asked, once again failing to bite my tongue.

"Both." He shrugged awkwardly—mimicking me? "But it was a turbulent relationship. They fought as much as they fucked, pardon my expression. Anyway, one time they went on a mission to explore a new world." He paused. I realized I was leaning over the table with anticipation. "Tayrel Kan came back alone, scarred and so spell-shocked he didn't speak coherently for days. And I mean proper, Dahlsian days."

He stopped.

My mouth was suddenly very dry.

"What about the other guy?"

Adyar Lah shook his head. "No one knows. But he—his body or whatever was left of it—was never found. There was another expedition to that world, and they didn't find anything; nothing that could kill one of our best men."

He paused and it took me a while to understand what he was implying. "You think Tayrel Kan killed him," I said, surprised how calm my voice sounded.

I remembered a few things about Tayrel Kan that struck me as odd. How he insisted that humans shouldn't wield magic, and how he never worked with a partner. It made sense now.

Surprisingly though, I couldn't bring myself to think about him as a murderer. I spoke with Tayrel Kan; I knew he wasn't a bad man, and having witnessed the power he wielded, it was not hard to imagine it getting out of control. So even if his partner died, I couldn't think of it as anything other than an accident. Especially when one looked at the effect it had on him.

So no, knowing didn't make me think less of Tayrel Kan. The only thing I felt was deep sorrow.

Moreover, the warnings given by Laik Var and Malyn Tol made much more sense now. I just wished one of them had bothered to tell me the truth. But that was a very Dahlsi thing to do—not to lie, but just not tell you things.

"I don't know." Adyar Lah turned his head away. "Look, I learned my lesson about not judging people from what others say, but… everyone thinks so. Tayrel Kan doesn't talk about it. There was an investigation, but he wouldn't say a word, and without a body, there was no evidence, so…"

"So, he was acquitted. But still, everyone believes he's a murderer."

"Yeah." He waved, but it lacked conviction. "You want to know the creepiest part?"

I gave him an encouraging nod.

"This guy's first name… was Myar."

He looked at me expectantly.

Again, I wasn't sure what he was implying, but then remembered his first reaction to my question about Tayrel Kan. Was the name another thing that made the sorcerer gravitate toward our kar-vessár? I wondered how popular it was. Come to think of it, I had never met another Myar.

"Next you're gonna tell me that he looked like our kar-vessár," I tried joking, but it came out flat.

"I honestly don't remember. I only saw him once or twice and always at a distance. But many people noticed Tayrel Kan displays an unhealthy obsession with our current leader. More than a simple infatuation. Crazy theories are circling, about how he sees him as a sort of reincarnation of this other guy."

I couldn't help raising my eyebrow. "That… does sound a bit crazy."

"Everyone knows he's not exactly stable. Wouldn't that be something though? Tayrel Kan devoting himself to Myar Mal because he reminds him of the lover he killed?"

"I'm not sure if 'devoting' is the right word. I've heard they're fighting all the time."

Only when I finished thesentence, Adyar Lah'ssummary of Tayrel Kan's previous relationship popped in my mind. Fought as much as they fucked. I blushed.

"Yeah, but it's all for show. Tayrel Kan may moan and bicker, but as soon as Myar Mal raises his voice, he shuts up and does as he's told. I think some people exaggerate his defiance because no one else dares speaking up to kar-vessár."

"I've heard Myar Mal was feeding Tayrel Kan drugs to make him easier to control."

Adyar Lah sent me a lopsided grin. "You think someone like Tayrel Kan needs an incentive to get high? Not that he doesn't have a reason, but still…" He paused for a moment, before picking up. "Look, there are a lot of rumors—really nasty ones about Tayrel Kan. I don't want to repeat them, or even wonder if they're true. But anyway, there was a time when he was close to getting kicked out of Mespana. He pissed off all the vessár-ai; no one wanted to work with him. But then Myar Mal took him in and basically created a new position just for him."

"Tayrel Kan is a powerful sorcerer."

With over three points on Kevar scale, he was probably more valuable than all the other sorcerers in Mespana combined.

"Yeah, but how often does he use his skills?"

"He was pretty useful last time."

"And it was his first job since Myar Mal became commissioned. Some people go so far as to call him Myar Mal's pet."

I couldn't think of anything to say to that. I leaned back, struggling to reconcile what I'd just heard with everything I'd learned before, wondering what was true and what was hearsay. I didn't suspect Adyar Lah—or Saral Tal, for that matter—of trying to bash our leader or Tayrel Kan or anyone else. And yet, they couldn't both be right. And both of them only based their knowledge on hearsay. It was impossible to discern what was fact, what was misheard, and what was just slander. In the end, the truth either lay somewhere in the middle or was completely different, and to figure out which, I would have to speak with one of the interested parties.

I couldn't imagine it going well.

Besides, what I realized—and not without regret—was that I didn't even know how to find Tayrel Kan now that we were back in Sfal.

My mood for company died after that. The waitress came to clear the dishes and asked if we needed anything else, but I wasn't hungry. Adyar Lah paid the bill, and we both got ready to leave.

A man approached our table. A Chaarite, with skin like copper and dark, almond-shaped eyes. His head was completely hairless, with a line of white tattoos running through the middle, and he wore intricate clothing with more layers than I could count. I dimly recalled him standing in the opposite corner every time I was here, watching over the establishment. Was he the owner? I was hoping he would talk to Adyar Lah, but he addressed me.

"Please forgive my intrusion, good sir. There are not many Tarvissi left in this area."

I nodded, not sure what to say. I was probably the only Tarvissi left in the area.

"Would it be too rude of me to ask if, by chance, you are the member of Mespana who put an end to that abhorrent uprising on Maurir and slew its leader?"

That was an overstatement if I ever heard one. It's true, I killed Peridion—and for a moment felt some irrational guilt about that. But the fight would probably be won even without my input. If I didn't do it, someone else would. Confused, I looked at Adyar Lah.

He cleared his throat, slightly embarrassed. "That's the version presented in media," he explained.

The media. Unwittingly I reached for the mirror hanging at my belt. I didn't think about checking the official reports, not to mention the media. Quite the leader, I was! But I realized there must have been a reason that this version of the story was being spread around. I thought of the late Laik Var and what he wanted me to do. I wondered if that meant…

"I gotta go." I stood and darted off.

Chapter 27

MYAR MAL LOOKED like shit. The post-anaphylaxis swelling had subsided, but his eyes were still red and surrounded by deep shadows, while his face was pale and gaunt. Even his normally iridescent irises settled on a dull, stormy gray.

He pushed the scroll toward me.

"That's all I could manage," he explained. "The permission for your family to return."

"Thank you, Myar Mal."

He leaned back in his chair and assumed his usual emperor pose—right arm bent and propped over an armrest, left stretched out on the desk. He was sizing me up with a gaze that, although tired, was as piercing as always, and I lowered my head automatically.

"I was right about the conspiracy," he started, not waiting for me to ask.

I wouldn't have asked, by the way. Curiosity was eating at me, but I would rather consult my mirror or wait for the newspaper. I still hadn't managed to overcome the nervousness that the kar-vessár filled me with. I had an irrational suspicion that despite him doing all the talking, he was getting more information from me than he was giving.

"The conspiracy started with Sanam Il-Asa. I should have known. He was... a sensitive guy. Very self-conscious. He was fascinated by Tarvissian culture, and when Peridion and the others rebelled, he took it personally. You were his primary target, I presume, but when I allowed your promotion, he decided to get rid of me too. He roped Raison Dal in after the decontamination team took a hold of that nut you dropped. Then, got Ayrela Va-Roma to help. I'm not sure when they recruited Amma La. Anyway, it's over now. The surviving traitors were sent to Xiburk. Except for Raison Dal—he's in house arrest, only because I accidentally broke his back, and no one can be bothered to heal him."

Xiburk was a Dahlsian penal colony: a small world with a barely breathable atmosphere and a rocky, mineral-rich surface. It merged with a tiny island on Tydus, so even if someone managed to escape, there was nowhere to go. Prisoners were set to work extracting noble gases and precious minerals, and all provisions had to be brought from other worlds since Xiburk had no native life or water.

As for the rest of his revelations, I was at a loss for words. Not for the first time, it struck me how little I knew about the world and the people around me. Like Ayrela Va—I never even spoke with her, and she was conspiring to kill me!

If another next attempt at my life was made, would I even know it was coming? Would I stand any chance of protecting myself? But what could I do?

And Myar Mal—I witnessed him at his lowest, yet I thought I barely knew anything about him. It was like there was a glass wall between me and the rest of humanity, one I could look through, but never hope to scale.

I wasn't sure why Myar Mal told me about the investigation, and even less so how to respond. So when he finished, for a moment, we sat in silence.

"And there's this whole mess with Tarviss," he murmured, to me or himself I couldn't tell. His next question dispelled my doubts, though. "Have you heard? Tarviss wants war. Luckily, so many people want to enlist, a cycle from now, we'll be able to double the number of Cohorts."

He sent me a pointed look.

"I thought it was just an exaggeration," I blurted, just to say something.

"It wasn't. We're already talking about opening a second training center."

And all of it happened when I was sleeping the battle off. No wonder he was kar-vessár, and I was… not.

Speaking of which…

"I'm very sorry, Myar Mal," I said, reaching to my sash. "I realize it's not the perfect moment, but I have to resign from my duties."

I was careful putting it down, but as it touched the surface of the desk, I snapped my hand back, as if it was a snake ready to attack, wrap itself around me, and keep me in this stupid position.

"Why?" He didn't seem surprised, more disappointed, and I felt a pang of shame.

Not enough to change my mind, though.

"I'm not suited for the job." I chuckled nervously. "Let's be honest, Laik Var only wanted me as an example and you as a bait. Now, neither of you need me."

"We always need good men."

I lowered my gaze to look at my hands, twisting them on my lap, but my heart actually skipped a beat at the praise.

"I can stay in Mespana," I said uncertainly. In truth, I couldn't imagine myself anywhere else. "Just... not as a vessár."

He didn't answer straight away, but I felt his eyes drilling into me. I got an irrational fear that he would reject my proposal and do—what, really? Insist on keeping me as vessár? Or kick me out completely? Why would he do that? My worry escalated, turned to agitation, and I was scrambling for anything else I could say to convince him, when he put an end to my suffering.

"Laik Var believed in you. He wouldn't promote you if he didn't think you were suited for the job."

"I've heard he only promoted me to spite you."

I regretted the words as soon as the left my mouth. Myar Mal was silent for a moment, and my heartrate spiked. Why did I even open my mouth?

"You believed that?"

I raised my head just to meet his incredulous gaze, then dropped it so fast my neck creaked.

"I don't know," I murmured. It made sense when I'd heard it, but now I wasn't so sure.

"Neither do I," he admitted after a brief pause. "But in the end, he is dead. All we are left with is what we choose to believe."

What did I believe? I remembered Laik Var as a great leader, but maybe it was only because he was the only leader I'd served under. And maybe Innam Ar was right, and I'd grown needlessly attached. It made my duty easier. But, in the end, I knew nothing about who he was outside of the uniform. So perhaps…

Perhaps faith was the only thing I could use to sort through my feelings.

"He was a decent man," picked up Myar Mal. "A bit too stern for his own good. Too set in his own convictions."

I got a feeling he wasn't necessarily talking about my relationship with Laik Var.

"A common trait among older men, I noticed. They assume if they've lived this long, they must know everything and we youngsters have no choice but to obey. I imagine that if he was less stubborn, Amma and I would have had better chances. But maybe that's just wishful thinking." He finally caught himself, and his gaze turned razor sharp again. "I'm sorry, Aldait Han. I shouldn't bother you with my problems."

"It's all right," I answered automatically.

But nothing was right about this. Not Laik Var being dead. Not Amma La trying to kill Myar Mal.

Not our supreme leader being so depressed he couldn't carry a simple conversation without trailing off.

"You know, I think the only thing preventing you from being a good vessár is yourself."

273

Although I appreciated his effort to get back on track, a bitter smile crept over my face.

But Myar Mal leaned toward me, almost conspiratorially, and continued, "Come on, kid. What makes you think you're worse than anyone else? Ten-per-twelve of Dahlsi are medicated for mood disorders."

His words hit a bit too close to home for me, so before I bite my tongue, I snapped back, "Are you?"

"Now, that's a personal question," he scolded.

I automatically slouched in my chair. "Sorry."

"But between you and me, yes I am. For now."

I lifted my gaze, and for the first time, dared to give him a closer look. On the outside he wore the same aspect of strength and confidence as usual—his back ramrod straight, head held high. But up close, I could see his mask cracking. Dark circles around tired eyes, creases that weren't there a few days ago, and lips pressed tighter than before.

Until the corner of his lips lifted in a crooked version of an ironic smile, and I realized that I was staring.

I immediately dropped my eyes again, trying desperately to come up with some apology that would make sense. "I'm not good with people," I blurted. "That's a pretty important skill for a leader."

He gave out another noncommittal hum, but finally reached out to take the silver sash from the desk.

"I will honor your wish. It was a pleasure working with you; as much as it could be under the circumstances. Maybe one day you'll want your sash back. In the meantime, is there anyone you would recommend for that position?"

Saral Tal's face flashed before my eyes. I pressed them shut.

"No," I said weakly.

Myar Mal hummed and turned away, thoughtful. I wondered if I should take it as a cue to leave.

"There's one more thing I have to ask," I spurted. "I need permission to travel to Tarviss and back."

He waved his hand. "That's all sorted."

Of course it was. I wasn't sure if I should be more impressed or annoyed.

He reached to another drawer and handed me a scroll. "And your alibi. You will travel to Tarviss as Tomoi Harrath, last of the colonists. You were working as part of the Taran Hassemel court. When Mespana came, you evaded capture by hiding in the mountains. But we finally got you and are now sending you back.

"After you find your family, you'll have to find your own way to Dahls. We will provide you with a device to locate and identify merges: the one with Dahls will probably be guarded, but you can still get back through M'velt Strabana and Xin Nyeotl. I would suggest getting a guide before you venture there, especially with civilians. Good luck."

"Thank you." I prepared to leave, but he stopped me with a question.

"Will you at least stay for the ceremony?"

"What ceremony?"

He clicked his tongue with reproach. "To honor our best soldiers. There's a ring for you, too."

The rings were given to the most accomplished Dahlsi. I wasn't sure I deserved one.

"I'm not fond of ceremonies," I said, and technically I wasn't lying.

"You deserve to be there."

His response was so close to my thoughts that an unpleasant suspicion crept up on me. I couldn't stop myself from asking, "Were you reading my mind, too?"

He smiled, a small, sardonic smile, strangely familiar, but not suiting him very well.

"Now, if there's nothing else you need, please excuse me, I have work to do. See you at the ceremony."

"Of course." I nodded, then, guided by a strange impulse, I added, "Kiar vashir."

He gave me another pale smile.

"Just don't ask me to repeat that," he joked, then gestured me out.

I didn't tell him that in Tarvissi-é 'vashir', while technically meaning the same as vessár—that is 'the leader', was never used as a title and 'kiar' meant 'exceptional'.

Chapter 28

MYAR MAL'S HAND stopped suddenly. Tayrel Kan kept his eyes closed, but he could almost see the other man frowning, and he was just waiting…

"You think she knew?"

The sorcerer exhaled. "I'm not talking about your ex," he said sternly. He heard the body shifting beside him as his partner lifted himself on his elbow.

"I loved her. I think I still do."

With a sigh, Tayrel Kan sat up and procured a tchalka. He was naked, sweat gluing dark hair to his arms, legs, and chest, but he didn't care. Some could even say he reveled in his filth, not bothering to wipe the sperm off his stomach, displaying it proudly like a badge of conquest. He would display more, but his magic was already in action, making bruises on his neck and wrists pale, and the red handprints all over his body disappear. His penis was half-erect, ready for the next round whenever the other man stopped moping.

"That's why you jumped in as soon as I offered you a blowjob?" asked the sorcerer mockingly, lighting the tchalka with a flicker of his fingers.

Myar Mal pouted. "They gave her five cycles in Xiburk," he said instead of answering. "I tried to speak for her—"

"Of course you did," murmured Tayrel Kan, but the other man ignored him.

"But they treated her actions as a crime against the state."

The sorcerer sighed again. "Are you going to visit her?" he asked, finally giving in.

"Maybe. We haven't really spoken since…" Myar Mal waved his hand in some uncoordinated gesture and paused, the frown on his face deepening. He was also naked, but he'd previously used a spell to clean himself, leaving no trace of their intercourse.

His body, with smooth skin and perfectly sculpted muscles, provided Tayrel Kan with a much more interesting view than his worried profile. The sorcerer wondered if there was some mathematical formula coded in his body— not a far-fetched idea. Myar Mal led a sedentary lifestyle, his looks were the effect of magic, not exercise.

"I think if we talked more—"

"Then you'd break up sooner," cut in Tayrel Kan. "But then again, if you did that, maybe she wouldn't try to kill you."

He didn't let his facade slip, but his stomach clenched, his own words dredging up memories. He drew in his tchalka.

"People destroy what they love. You got out easily," he said against his better judgment. He quickly collected himself, "But if you hate your life so much, go back to her. I don't care. Or find yourself another sweetheart. I didn't come to you looking for love. And I didn't offer mine."

"How gracious."

The sarcasm in Myar Mal's voice made something inside him snap.

"If you want to blame the decay of your relationship on me, I don't care either. But you know it was dead long before I came. If it wasn't me, it would be someone else; a buxom lady or a pretty boy with firm cheeks. Or hey, maybe she would find someone. Someone like Aldeaith: a simple guy her dad would approve of."

Before he was finished, Myar Mal was on him, straddling his hips, with one hand clasped around his neck, the other closed into a fist and ready to strike.

"Shut the fuck up," he growled, looking Tayrel Kan in the eye, but the sorcerer didn't even blink.

"Make me."

Chapter 29

THE CEREMONY TOOK place in the central plaza—the only part of The Inner City big enough to contain everyone from Mespana. Or everyone that was left.

It was located at the crossing of two main market streets. In the center, rose a round platform covered by blue Dahlsian grass and surrounded by an artificial stream. Another, temporary platform was built on top, and our leaders lined up on it.

This time, I did my homework. The Directory had three members. An elder woman with a tanned face and long, silver braid was Lyria La-Nidru, one of the first explorers of the Meon Cluster. A younger woman, pale, with more respectable short hair, was Rinay Kia-Varey, a politician from a family of politicians. The only man was Kiav Rin-Sannos, who used to be sil-kahar—the leader—of some colony, then proceeded to be a governor of Sfal, Chief Governor of Meon, and finally a member of the Directory.

Behind them governors and ministers lined up. On the left side of the podium stood Myar Mal and a bit further other vessár-ai. I noticed Adyar Lah at the head of the Second and Arda Nahs—Laik Var's nami—at Seventh. Why didn't I think about her when Myar Mal asked for a recommendation?

I wished I could stay behind, hide in a corner and watch from there, but as one of the honored, I had to take a position at the base of the platform. As always, the majority of people around me were pure Dahlsi, and I stood out like a sore thumb.

"Mespanians," spoke Lyria La. Despite her age, her voice was loud and clear—probably magically amplified. The murmurs filling the plaza died down. "You defended your country against the greatest threat it faced in centuries. For this, we are all grateful. The sacrifices many of you made were immense, and I cannot imagine there's a way we could ever pay you back. It's a great tragedy that even here, in Dahlsian worlds, there are people who value material goods and land more than human lives. Who would send hundreds to die to satisfy their greed and false claims. Alas, we cannot change who they are. We can only defend ourselves and our way of life."

She flicked her hand and an obelisk of black stone materialized in the middle of the platform. It's tip almost brushed the dome topping the plaza and the light reflected on the twelve mirror-like sides covered in red lettering.

"For their crimes, many of you—our best men and women—paid the ultimate price. This monument will be here to remind us of their sacrifice," continued Lyria La. She procured a piece of writing plastic and started reading their names.

I was flooded with emotions I had no words to describe. Each name she listed was like another stone laid on my conscience. And there were so many of them! I knew about it, I saw it on the news—and with my own eyes in Maurir—but hearing their names, uttered one by one in a loud, somber voice made me realize they were not just numbers in the newspaper or nameless bodies on the battlefield. They were people. Each had two parents and probably extended families: friends, lovers, children.

Thousands of lives ruined by the greed of one man.

But as the list went on, the names started blurring. There were too many... It was impossible to remember them all. Hence the monument, I thought. One piece of rock to commemorate them all.

Lyria La stepped down, and I hoped the dreadful ceremony was over, but no; she passed the paper to Rinay Kia, who proceeded with the dead of the Fifth Cohort.

So many lost, and we were only a third of the way through.

Tears prickled at my eyes as I looked at the memorial, trying to decipher the writing. I guessed each wall stood for one Cohort. But despite the size of the obelisk, discerning the names was impossible from my spot.

Rinay Kia arrived at the Seventh Cohort.

Laik Var-Nessop.

Vareya La-Ketan

Saral Tal-Sannos.

His face flashed before my eyes, blue sash tainted with blood. I shut my eyes and turned away from the obelisk.

I felt hot. Sweat drenched my body as I struggled for breath, my chest tight, heart racing as if trying to break free.

I tried to withdraw, to turn my mind to happier times, but my head was spinning, assaulted by visions. A flurry of bodies, flames, and blades, bloodied corpses, Karlan Peridion standing over me with a manic grin, the paralyzing spell, Saral Tal and Taneem Kiovar.

A wave of calm washed over me. I felt the weight of someone's hand on my shoulder, and as I turned around, I saw a Dahlsi woman with the yellow armband of a healer. She nodded, and I realized she had calmed me with a spell. I returned the nod and turned my attention to the ceremony.

It ended soon after, and I wondered how long my episode had lasted. I had to get a grip. My journey was far from over, and if I zoned out like that in Tarviss…

"But let us remember that after every storm comes the harvest," concluded Kiav Rin, putting the sheet away. "The dead shall not be forgotten, but neither will the living. Many of you who are gathered here today demonstrated an exceptional courage and valor. They also deserve recognition."

The crowd behind me roared with approval, and my insides clenched painfully. The moment I dreaded most was coming.

Kiav Rin returned to his initial spot, and Myar Mal stepped forward to replace him with his own list. I don't know why, but something in him made him stand out, even among the Directory. He seemed bigger, brighter, more concrete. My chest swelled with a mix of pride and jealousy. This was my vessár. I could never be like him.

He commenced reading the names. First, the vessár-ai whom he decorated with dallite-studded rings. Then, he proceeded to the ordinary Mespanian, and those received awards from their leaders.

To my annoyance, he started from the First Cohort. My skin was crawling with anxiety. I was well aware of people's eyes on me, and I wanted to get this over with. Yet the ceremony dragged on. Each name followed a slow ascent of the announced Mespanian, decorating, the ovations, descent. It seemed to last forever.

When he finally called for Seventh Cohort, my stomach lurched. My time was coming.

I twisted my fingers nervously and went over the speech I was given prior to the ceremony. Since it was implanted by magic, there was no way for me to mess it up. Yet, I was nervous.

"Aldait Han-Tirsan."

I shuddered. If the hall was quiet before, now it was dead. I dared to sweep my eyes around, but everyone was looking at me. I dropped my gaze. Tried to swallow, but my mouth was dry.

You can do it, I told myself.

On wobbly legs, I ascended the platform. Arda Nahs held my ring. She was an outworlder—the only outworlder vessár—though I couldn't say where she was from. She was even taller and bulkier than me, dark skinned and sharp-faced, with honey brown hair braided into a crown.

I tried to focus on her, pretending it was only me and her, with no crowd around. She always made me uneasy, but now she was my haven. Only once did I dare peek at the gathered officials, but meeting their eyes, fixed on me, proved too much.

I stopped before Arda Nahs, then extended my left hand, letting her put the ring on. The dallite in it was as big as a human eye, green in the artificial light.

I exhaled. Now to the hard part.

I turned to the crowd and cleared my throat. I felt like I should near the front of the platform, but I didn't trust my legs to carry me.

Why couldn't they find someone else to do it?

The silence dragged. How long was I standing there, too nervous to speak?

I have to push through.

I clenched my fists until my nails dug into my palms.

"Mespanians," I started, then paused, startled by how loud my voice had been. Magical amplification, damn them all. "As you see, I'm the only person of Tarvissian heritage present here. The only one of my race left in Meon Cluster. But I want to assure you, that rebellion was the act of a few. Most of us never wanted to break from Dahlsian dominion. The insurrection brought us nothing but hurt; it ripped us from our homes and threw us back to the world from which we escaped."

I paused, partially because that's what the script said, partially because I needed to calm myself again. "I stood with you in Maurir, and I will stand if Tarviss proceeds with its threats. Most colonists will stand too, if you give them a chance. We may be different, but all of us, Dahlsi or Tarvissi, strive for the same thing—to live our lives in peace, safety, and prosperity."

I turned to walk down the platform, my head down, but the sounds rising above the crowd stopped me. Clapping. Cheering.

"Aldait Han," carried above the other voices and soon the entire crowd was chanting: "Aldait Han! Aldait Han! Aldait Han!"

It took a while for my brain to understand what was happening. Tears prickled my eyes and my throat tightened.

For so long, I wanted people to call me by my Tarvissian name. But in all my life, it never felt as right as the Dahlsian one did then.

I lifted my gaze above the throng to where I knew the Immigration Center and the merge with the Old Worlds was.

Tarviss, I was coming.

Epilogue

IT TOOK A few days before Myar Mal found time to visit the charnel lab. He didn't announce his visit, and yet the house's director was waiting for him. She looked nothing like he expected: a young, athletic woman with slicked hair and fashionable, black-rimmed glasses.

She rose from her desk and stiffened, hands clasped behind her back, eyes fixed on something beyond kar-vessár's left shoulder.

"Myar Mal," she greeted, nodding slightly.

"Lygia No," he replied. He'd never met her, but there was only one female necromancer employed by Mespana. Maybe three in the entire Meon Cluster. "Kiarn At told me you are the person to ask about the progress of the investigation."

"Yes." Her eyes flickered to the sorcerer who decided to accompany Myar Mal, then back at the wall. She cleared her throat. "We just finished analyzing the samples. There were one-great gross-and-ninety-six of rebels. Of them, around three-grosses-and-sixty spent less than a day in Meon cluster."

Myar Mal took a moment to digest that information, making sure his face betrayed none of the emotions the discovery brought. It was hardly a surprise, merely a confirmation of what they extracted from that female rebel's mind before sending her back to Tarviss. Still, he hoped she had been wrong.

"And the sorcerer?" he asked when he was sure his voice wouldn't falter.

Lygia No licked her lips. Apparently, like many of her profession, she couldn't handle authority.

"There, ah, seems to be a problem," she said, avoiding his gaze.

Myar Mal arched his eyebrow. "A problem?"

She exhaled deeply and started explaining, "Every living thing upon death, no matter how violent, leaves a trace of its essence. Detecting those traces and matching them comprises the majority of our work. But these... bones. There's nothing in them."

Myar Mal tensed. "What do you mean?"

"They're empty. Like they were never part of a living being. I tried a dozen different methods, looking at both magical signature and vital energy. To no avail."

"Could magic sever such connection?" asked Kiarn At, frowning slightly.

"I've never heard about anything like that. I did some research when our usual methods failed, spent a lot of time in the library, but... " She waved her hand.

"You found nothing," guessed Kiarn At.

"Did you try reanimation?" asked Myar Mal, looking over her shoulder, at the large steel table cluttered with charred bones.

"I'm a serious researcher, not a folk-tale villain!"

The fire in her voice made him tear his eyes away from the bones. Her lips were pursed and cheeks flushed.

"Sorry," he said automatically. "I don't know much about necromancy."

Lygia No huffed and fixed her glasses. "Such spells, if they're even possible, are exceedingly rare. I've never met anyone capable of casting them successfully."

"What about unsuccessfully?"

"Cautionary tales."

Myar Mal grunted in frustration. This was his main question. Anyone capable of resisting the most powerful sorcerers Dahls had in stock deserved special attention. Particularly if Tarvissian threats were to turn out to be more than words.

"That's not all," added Lygia No after a moment's hesitation. "I tried to rearrange those… bones. No magic, just good old-fashioned anthropology. At first glance, they seem human. But they're not. In fact, they don't match any sentient species."

Myar Mal tensed even more, doing his best to keep the boiling frustration from spilling out. "But these are bones, right?"

"Technically, yes. Though they have no growth rings. It's almost like they were… fabricated."

Myar Mal felt as if the ground broke beneath his feet. Ever since the battle, he had poured all of his hope into those bones. They were his answer, his foe.

They were useless.

"What are you suggesting?" he croaked, wishing she could say anything other than what she was about to.

"You didn't see the sorcerer dying." She looked him in the eye. "You said there was a fire… and this is what we found."

"A false trail to throw us off," added Kiarn At. "While the real culprit went into hiding."

THANK YOU FOR reading my novel. This was a deeply personal project for me and it means a lot that you gave it a chance.

If you enjoyed it, please leave a review on Goodreads (https://www.goodreads.com/book/show/58012174-the-outworlder) and Amazon (https://mybook.to/TheOutworlder) . It really helps me out!

You can also subscribe to my mailing list for a free short story, Prequel to The Outworlder (https://dl.bookfunnel.com/izzrmofulv).

Or check out my other works:

Other Worlds (short story collection) (http://mybook.to/NJHOtherWorlds)

OctopusSong (a novellette with Tayrel Kan as a protagonist) (http://mybook.to/OctopusSong)

Acknowledgments:

Special thanks to Becky for her unyielding support.

Also thanks to my alfa, beta and gamma readers: John, Christopher, Kirk, Karolina, Madeline, Sarah, Janna, Cassia, Gabriel, and everyone I might have missed. It's been a long ride.

About the Author

Natalie J. Holden lives in her head with a bunch of imaginary friends. She would prefer to be born as a cat, though then she wouldn't be able to eat chocolate or drink herbal teas, so maybe not. Probably belongs to a different species than the rest of humanity.

Glossary

Great Sphere – the universe

Vhalfr – the lone star of this universe. All suns and moons are merely holes in the skydomes through which its light reaches worlds.

Cycle – a time in which Great Sphere makes a full spin around the Vhalfr; approximately 2 earthy years.

Merge – a point existing in two worlds simultaneously, allowing a free passage between them

Old Karirian Cluster – a cluster of worlds inhabited for millennia

Dahls – a world in the Old Karirian Cluster, home to the Dahlsian civilization

Dahlsi – native of Dahls

Dahlsi-é – language of Dahls

Tarviss – a world in the Old Karirian Cluster, home to the Tarvissian civilization

Tarvissi – native of Tarviss

Tarvissi-é – language of Tarviss

Tayan – a world in the Old Karirian Cluster, home to the Tayani people

Xzsin Nyeotl – a world in the Old Karirian Cluster, home to the Xzsim people

Meon Cluster – a cluster of previously uninhabited worlds discovered and colonized by the Dahlsi twenty cycles ago

Sfal – the only world in the Meon Cluster to connect with a world outside of it (Dahls).

Junction world – in Meon Cluster most of the worlds only merge once with one of the four junction worlds: Sfal, Kooine, Tydus and Daesi

Ae – magical energy

Ampik – unit of ae

Magical potential – the amount of ampiks a person can process in a second

Keverim scale – used to measure person's magical potential. One point is median for all humans.

Mespana – the closest thing to an army in Dahls. The organization was initially created to ensure safe exploration of new worlds, but was later entrusted with upkeeping peace within the colonies. Mespana is divided into twelve Cohorts, each has approximately 144 members divided into twelve dozens.

Kar-vessár – head commander of Mespana

Vessár (plural vessár-ai) – commander of Mespana

Nami-vessár – adjutant

Vaka – a drug with invigorating properties

Kalikka – a drug with tranquillizing properties

Tchalka (tsalka) – a piece of reed filled with herbs used for smoking; can have various properties.

Ytanga – a heavy drug

Katarda – a drug used by sorcerers to quickly recharge

Humans – arrived in this universe approximately 100 thousand years ago from Earth and since then have evolved into a separate subspecies. Still, they're pretty close to us.

Chavikii – an intelligent species. Small, stocky humanoids with yellow, rubbery skin, eight beady eyes and short trunks. Obligate herbivores with the ability to digest any plant matter and neutralize every plant toxin.

Kas'sham – an intelligent species. Slightly smaller than humans, with slim, fur-covered bodies and expressionless faces. TKnown for their amazing agility. Obligate carnivores and excellent hunters.

Ssothian – an intelligent species. Massive creatures covered in orange fur, with vertical mouths and four beady eyes. Men sport large, hollow horns that grow through their entire lives.

Vhariar – an intelligent species. Tall and lanky humanoids, with grey skin and two bowl-shaped growths on the sides of their heads. Considered (especially by themselves) to be the most intelligent among sentient species. Physically weak. Belong to the same evolutionary tree as besheq.

Besheq – an intelligent species. Humanoids with atrophied arms and ten tentacles growing from their shoulders like a fan. Known for their meek and non-aggressive nature, but watch out for those tentacles, they may be filled with toxins. Belong to the same evolutionary tree as vhariars.

Dryaks – vile beasts that are surprisingly common im Meon cluster and are pain in the ass for everyone in Mespana

Printed in Great Britain
by Amazon

67249649R00180